Canis

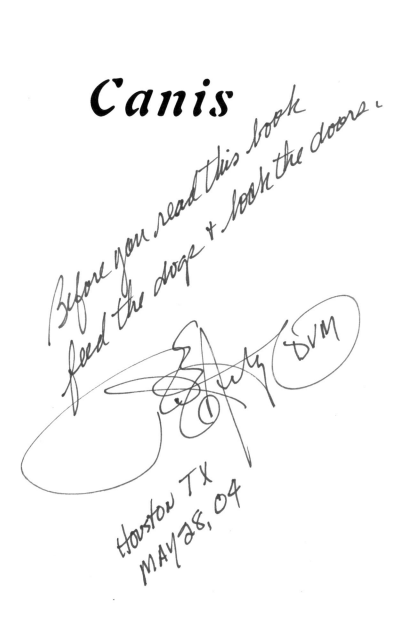

Before you read this book feed the dogs & lock the doors

[signature] DVM

Houston TX
MAY 28, 04

MAY 26 '04

Canis

Robert E. Armstrong

Writer's Showcase
presented by *Writer's Digest*
San Jose New York Lincoln Shanghai

Canis

Writer's Showcase
presented by *Writer's Digest*
an imprint of iUniverse.com, Inc.

For information address:
iUniverse.com, Inc.
5220 S 16th, Ste. 200
Lincoln, NE 68512
www.iuniverse.com

ISBN: 0-595-14703-8

Printed in the United States of America

For Margaret "Maggie" Barnshaw.

Acknowledgements

I would like to extend my sincere appreciation to the members of my reading committee: Anne Sloan, Roxanne Claire, Carole Wiater, Carlie Arntsen and especially to my wife, Nita.

CHAPTER ONE

February, 1965

Happy Hills Farm and Kennel

Burdett, Kansas

PUREBRED PUPPIES FOR SALE!

*F*earsome sounds prowled Bobby's dream and he struggled to identify them. First he recognized the never-ending prairie wind as it drove
crystals of ice and grit against the window next to his bed. He could
hear all the pregnant bitches in the outdoor pens raising their furious
clamor. It rattled the metal gutters on the feed shed. In a moment he
detected new sounds. A truck motor, grinding gears, doors slamming,
then a terrible moan of feral desperation. The bitches fell silent.

Subdued at first, then louder, another sound arose. It started as a dull
but steady tapping. Tap, tap, tap. In the perpetual Kansas gale Bobby
imagined a loose shutter or an unlatched gate. No, this sound he knew,
but he couldn't identify in his drowsy half-sleep. He drifted. A hammer
maybe…? No…? No, it was an ax!

Rough hands moved under the covers, grabbed him—had him by
the ear. Pain shot through Bobby's neck like maul-struck steel, searing

his face. "Oh! Ow, oww, owww," he cried. Bolting up, he tried to cover his chest with the thin quilt his mother had stitched.

"You hear that? That's your mama out there, choppin' kindling in the snow, you darlin' little shit." It was the foul voice of Darvin, his mother's boyfriend, and her new partner in the business.

Tears started to leak out, but Bobby knew better. He squeezed his eyes tight, as much to check the salty flow as to shut out the bright light.

"Get yer little ass out there 'fore I pull this ear offen yer empty head."

Pain radiated from Bobby's ear and neck to the middle of his back.

"I need my pants!"

"Yuh do huh? She's out there bare-legged." The man lifted him by the ear, making him walk on tiptoes.

Bobby pleaded. "Lemme git my shoes?"

"Outside, now, goddammit!"

The first thing Bobby did when he got back to the kitchen was rub his bare feet with a towel and put on yesterday's socks. The house smelled of cigarette smoke, fried eggs, and beer, and the weirdo from Texas was back again. He was taking fifty pups to Dallas. The men argued prices.

Bobby dressed, ate quietly, and listened to them talk about something called *high-breds*. After a menacing nod from his mother's boyfriend, Bobby put on his coat, pulled down his stocking cap, and went out to the pens. His legs still hurt from the belt buckle and he had blood on his underpants. As cold as it was, it was good to be outside.

After a time the wind relented, turning gritty sleet to slush, and bogging the rusty wheels of Bobby's Radio Flyer. He punched ice out of the water pans with an old railroad spike; fed the Bostons, the Yorkies, and the Pugs. With pin-prickly fingers he collected frozen puppies along the way. He put them in the wagon along with a jar of kerosene. The smelly fluid slopped and leaked as he towed his burden past the hair and dung-encrusted cages and up to the sagging porch. Nearing the oil drum he paused to rub his arms and stamp his feet. Chores would get done, he thought, if he didn't freeze first.

He poured the kerosene and lit the oil-blackened barrel with a kitchen match. He couldn't wait for his tenth birthday. Maybe then things would change. If this was his place, he would fix it up. He knew exactly what he would do. First, he would plant a row of junipers on the north side to protect the pens from the blowing wind. Then, as the pregnant bitches neared their time, he would bring them into the old sheep barn and put shavings in the whelping boxes. In the summer he would dig a trench and bury the water pipes to keep them from freezing in the winter. He had lots of ideas.

Bobby poked the coals with a stick as he prepared what he liked to think was a viking funeral. Silent sparks ascended like last minute prayers, as he fed the fire with the six frozen pups. He rubbed his aching ear through the knit cap and edged closer to the drum. A bitch and seven assorted whelps had not survived the night. Picking up the last frozen body, he held it by a foot, letting it twist and turn above the flaring barrel before he let it fall.

Sissy had come out on the porch. She sat on the top step with a half-dead pup in her lap. She was three years younger than Bobby, and he was certain she didn't understand about life and death, and making money in the dog business. The pup bobbed its blind eyes across her knees searching for warmth.

Bobby stepped toward her. "Gimme the pup."

"No," she pouted. Her voice sounded far away. "Mama said I could keep one."

He could see her lips moving. He rubbed his ear. He knew the pup would die. He knew Sissy would grieve, and there was too much grieving in this business. "Give me the goddamn pup! Its mama's dead."

The girl put a hand across her eyes and peeked into the pale dawn. "I'm telling," she whispered. "You said a bad word."

The boy took another step and grabbed for the animal.

"Nooooo!" she screamed and held the flopping creature high above her head.

The two children struggled and Bobby made a fist.

The door swung in and without warning two men shuffled onto the porch. Looking down, the boyfriend snatched the spent pup from the girl's outstretched arms. He examined it. "Stop being such a little bastard," he snarled. Raising the pup, he swung it in a short arc and cracked its fragile head against the porch rail. He tossed its lifeless body at the boy. "Don't be teasing the girl, you little freak."

"I wasn't gonna hit her."

"Shut up!"

"You ain't my daddy," Bobby said under his breath.

The man faced him square and Bobby knew he'd been heard.

"You ain't got no daddy, you pig-faced little snot." He hesitated, then grinned. "You're a true bastard, no mistake about that."

The girl slipped inside.

The man from Texas shoved his hands in his pockets and started down the sloppy path between the rows of weather-rotted cages. "Come on, man. I wanna show you them two critters I brung down from Montana. Then we gotta load up if I'm gonna make it to Dallas."

The boyfriend turned away and headed down the path.

Bobby raged inside, trying to grasp the meaning of what he had been called. Then, remembering the sounds from his dream, he trailed after the men, keeping a cautious distance. A fresh din rose among the bitches as the men approached. Glancing back, the boyfriend spied Bobby. "I done tol' you to feed them goddamn terriers," he yelled, "an' if they don't quit that racket get a hose and wet 'em down. Now move!" A few steps down the path he pulled a small flask from his pocket, took a quick swallow, then offered it to the Texan. "Little bastard's a retard."

Chapter Two

January 1993

Houston, Texas

*M*orning traffic in the fast lane of the Eastex Freeway was at a standstill. Duncan MacDonell watched as the mini pick-up ahead inched forward. The little truck was dappled with primer and its bumper sticker displayed the flag of the Confederacy. In pinched letters it advised prying a gun from the driver's cold, dead fingers.

As MacDonell stared, a shapeless yellow tuft of fur appeared on the pavement between the two vehicles. He squinted. It moved. A yellow cat, a kitten really, maybe three weeks old, was pressed tight to the asphalt, oblivious to its impossible situation.

On his right, traffic move two car lengths, then stopped. He was in the fast lane, two feet from the concrete barriers erected while US-59 was converted to six lanes. He looked again, set the emergency brake, reached for his Stetson, opened the door. The man in the silver BMW behind him honked. Those damn Beemers! MacDonell dismissed him with a wave of the hand and squeezed to the front of his low-bid city sedan.

A few feet away a blast of compressed air mingled with diesel fumes and the roar of a giant sheep's foot roller. In the northbound lane an eighteen-wheeler oozed forward, blocking the sun. The kitten clutched the surface as if the world was spinning out of orbit.

MacDonell reached down, lifted the kitten by the nape, held it up at eye level. It squirmed, wide-eyed, petrified. MacDonell looked it over. Detecting no sign of physical injury, he stepped back around his wide-open door, opened his rear door, held up the kitten for the Beemer to see, then deposited it on the rear seat. It zipped under the front passenger seat and pulled its tail in after. The Beemer gave a faint smile, shook his head, and flashed a quick thumbs-up signal. MacDonell felt taller.

The traffic lurched on, unaware of the drama just played out. MacDonell wondered about the tiny spark of life. How the devil had it come to be in the dead center of a busy four lane artery now being converted to an Interstate highway?

He arrived at work twenty minutes later, spoke to the security guard, and asked that the night shift supervisor be sent to his office. He parked the car, cracked the window an inch, picked up his lunch bag and headed for his office.

Duncan A. MacDonell, DVM., MS.
Chief, Bureau of Animal Regulation & Care…

…read the plastic nameplate on the door.

As big as this health department bureau was, (ninety-eight authorized employees) there was little glory in being Houston's head dog-catcher. A few dusty plaques and a half-dozen framed certificates decorated one wall, all from a prior life. Behind MacDonell's cluttered desk, in the shadow of a spindly, sun-starved Ficus tree, leaned a slender dart gun tube and a battered Remington .410 pump shotgun. A handful of dead leaves littered the floor. On the desk a stack of 35mm color slides had toppled over, some spilling to the floor. They were breed identification photos from the personal collection of MacDonell's Clinical Chief, Dr. Carol Clemmons.

On the floor was a fiber pad pulled from under the carpet when the city redecorated the health director's old office on MacGregor Drive. The restaurant inspectors got the rug, MacDonell got the pad. The ceiling lights had half their tubes removed in response to an edict to reduce power consumption. One fixture flashed at irregular intervals. An odd silence in the room indicated to MacDonell that the building's air-conditioning system was off. Reaching down, he propped the outer door open with a dead cactus in a clay pot. It was 7:45 a.m.

He hung up his coat, then knelt behind his desk and began picking up the slides and dead leaves. A minute later he was sorting through the stacks of paperwork on his desk.

MacDonell was a career public health officer with twenty years of prior military service. He was now nearing sixty, stubby, rotund, still energetic, but slowing down. Since he'd weeded out a startling number of drones and slackers he was feared by many of the older employees, yet at department headquarters he was respected by the lower echelons. Treat clerks and telephone operators decent, he often said. No telling where it'll get you.

He was recognized in the city courts too. Judges and prosecutors knew his silver-flecked beard and handlebar mustache, his boots, wide suspenders, big shoulders, and his ever-present Stetson, the narrow-brimmed Silver-belly model worn by cattle buyers.

A noise in the outer office caught his attention. It was Conrad "Connie" Oaks, his supply chief.

"You say something, Doc?" Oaks hollered through the closed door.

"We got any hot water?" MacDonell hollered back.

"Gimme five, Doc," came the muffled voice.

It was Thursday. Friday would be a city holiday, MLK Day, and everyone was looking forward to it. MacDonell had planned a trip to San Antonio.

Before he could go there was work to be done. 'Council actions' needed attention. A council action was a constituent service request or a complaint, forwarded without ever being read by a council-member or the health director. Throughout the year a full third of council actions would be poultry complaints; roosters crowing within the city limits. Another third were from people tattling on livestock owners. Horses were legal if space was adequate, but pigs and goats were illegal in any case. The rest were random animal problems or complaints about his officers. Today one reported a "fag's dog" running loose and ruining the neighborhood. He tossed it in the trash, and if asked, he would suggest it had been lost in transit.

Oaks rattled the doorknob and MacDonell let him in.

"Here's some hot…" Oaks announced as he reached back and clicked the door, "…and the AC is back on."

Serpentine scars decorated Oaks' big hands, reminders of the defunct kennel across the back lot where he had worked prior to MacDonell's arrival. Connie had a hitch in his stride and a tiny Purple Heart pin in his lapel. They were souvenirs from Vietnam, unnoticed by the other staff members. Oaks poured his boss a steaming cup of water while MacDonell took the potted cactus out of the door.

"Yesterday while you was in the field you had a visitor," Oaks said with a trace of irony.

MacDonell spooned some instant coffee in his cup, took off his glasses, rubbed his eyes and shook his head in disgust.

"You guessed it," Oaks said, grinning, "Doctor 'T.'"

Dr. 'T' was Sterling F. Trimble, MD, MPH, a toothpick-sized physician from Pennsylvania. So far Trimble had met with MacDonell only once in his three year tenure. It was eight months after the little man had taken over the department. The aristocratic health director had come on a Saturday. MacDonell assumed he was hoping no one would be there. Trimble had chatted nervously with a petrified junior supervisor in the front lot while holding a silk kerchief to his face. His ultimate complaint: absence of lawn sprinklers. MacDonell had hurried out to the parking lot and he still remembered the conversation.

MacDonell took a sip of coffee. "Why does he only come around when he thinks I'm out of the office?" he muttered.

Several of the council members were now referring to Trimble as "*The Shadow.*"

Oaks shook his head. "He stood in the parking lot again, Doc. Talked to a field officer for about fifteen minutes, then left. Never did come in the building."

"Anybody find out what he wanted?"

Oaks shrugged.

"Ridiculous," MacDonell said as he cracked his inner office door so his secretary would know he was in. He tried to keep the doors open to reduce the rumors that plots were being hatched.

Oaks sat on the couch and stretched out his legs. In the peaceful mornings he liked to come in, sit, sip a little joe, discuss budget strategy, or share a rare bit of office gossip. The two men talked for about twenty minutes, then opened the office door wide. Oaks was a gem and MacDonell knew it.

Nearby the fax began to hum. Telephone lights danced back and forth. People were moving around in the offices, turning on lights and machines. MacDonell's secretary, sixty-one year old Miss Willie Fish, had the phone poked in her ear. MacDonell watched her put up a skinny bronze finger for quiet. She listened then punched the hold button. "Talk to this lady, Doc. She ain't makin' no sense. Oh!" she added, punching the trans button, "…gots you a package." She handed over a cake-sized box wrapped in newspaper and held together with masking tape. "Man say it were personal." She smiled gold. "Light too. Angel food, most likely."

MacDonell was skeptical. "More likely two sticks of dynamite and an alarm clock."

Oaks laughed and went back to his office. MacDonell took the package back to his desk. He sat down, put the box on his lap and picked up the phone. After that he mostly listened.

The female voice had the ring of intoxication and MacDonell imagined he could smell juniper berries. "We don't give a care what it cost, Honey. We want all ya'll got. Every last one."

He tore a strip of tape from the cake box and examined it. He shifted the phone to the crook of his neck, shook the box, and held it to his ear. "Madam, what do you plan to do with all these animals?"

"In the first place, Honey, don't call me no madam. I ain't no madam." A clatter came over the line, as if she had dropped the receiver. When she came back, she was breathing hard. "See, all what we're tryna do is bring a drop of happiness to some sweet li'l orphans. We wanna 'dopt all them homeless pups, take 'em out to an orphanage for Easter. Them poor kids need sumpthin' to hug on, an stuff."

"We're only a couple weeks into the new year," MacDonell replied. He looked around his desk for a ball-point pen. "It's more than two months until Easter."

"We gotta give 'em a bath, put some ribbons round their li'l sweet necks."

"I see. How many do you think you'll need for this…project?" he asked, as he poked three tiny holes in the box.

"What I said. All ya'll got."

MacDonell reached around, punched a key and squinted at his computer. "Not all two hundred fifty-four, you don't."

For a moment the line went dead. "Two hunnert fifty-four?!" the woman said.

"Yes ma'am, two hundred and fifty-four." He punched three more keys and hit enter. "At forty-five bucks apiece that's about eleven thousand dollars. Of course, that'll include the licenses, worming, and all the shots."

MacDonell sniffed the package around the holes he'd punched, then leaned forward, gingerly setting the box on the far corner of his desk.

"That's ridiculous! They don't cost ya'll nothin'. Ya'll druther kill 'em! You sonabitch! I guess all that nasty stuff we hear about you on the TV is true. Somebody need to put *you* in that gas chamber, you bastard!" The woman slammed down the phone.

MacDonell twisted one end of his mustache, thought about what she'd said, then took hold of his wrist and felt his pulse for a few seconds. After a minute of thought, he interlaced his fingers, reversed his hands and cracked his knuckles out over his desk. "Williee," he called. "Ask Dr. Clemmons to come over here, would you please? Tell her we've got a snake."

A movement caught his eye and MacDonell sensed he was being watched. Looking up, he was happy to see that his clinic chief was already standing outside his door. "Come in, Carol," MacDonell called out. "Sit down. Sit down. Did you see that kitten I brought in?"

"We've already got a dozen that are much better looking."

"This one has a story."

"They all have a story."

"See if you can't find a place for it in the adoption ward."

"Is that an order, Colonel?"

MacDonell ignored her last comment and changed the subject. "You won't believe the call I just got."

"Something about a snake?" she interrupted.

MacDonell pointed at the box with his pen.

Clemmons puckered her mouth into a sour expression.

MacDonell recounted his last phone conversation. As he talked he was unconsciously measuring Clemmons against all the other female veterinarians he had known. Carol was very different. She was far from neat and not the kind to be asked to do a dog food commercial. She wore a white doctor's coat like a suit of rusty armor. With her endless animal skirmishes there was always a tinge of blood, and a hint of musk, anal glands, or vomit. Over in the kennel they joked that she doused herself with Mennen aftershave. This morning she was slurping black coffee and nibbling one of Willie's months old Christmas cookies. It was dusted with green sprinkles and shaped like a tree. Clemmons' French braid had come loose and strands of stringy black hair had fallen across her face. It was five minutes to nine and she already looked tired.

MacDonell had studied Clemmons over the years and concluded she'd been assembled like a Howitzer round. Her strength was of strong character, not beauty. A Cornell honor grad, her deep compassion for animals, especially cats, was well-disguised. What she couldn't disguise was a deep, unexplained anger, probably stemming from the fact that veterinary medicine in Texas had long been strictly a man's profession, and the Texas Board of Examiners had put her through the wringer.

No one, least of all MacDonell, doubted she was a good surgeon and a gifted clinician, but her New York tongue would aggravate a badger. Clemmons was hot-tempered, but in a morbid way MacDonell was thankful for. Truth be known, she kept him from losing his own temper.

At the end of his tale about the lady wanting to adopt all their prisoners MacDonell shook his head. "She offered to put me in a gas chamber."

"You're pulling my leg! Did you tell it was a decompression chamber, and that you took it out of here years ago?"

"I didn't get a chance to say much." He sighed, smiled, and leaned back in his chair.

"I just had a lovely call myself." Clemmons shook her head. "This nice lady wants to report a dog attack."

"Oh yeah?" MacDonell was curious. She had said attack, not bite. The bureau investigated an average of forty bites a week. Most involved children, usually boys under twelve. Bites in the face were common. He had all the statistics and quoted them freely to anyone who would listen. Clemmons supervised the quarantine, but the bite investigations were carried out by five of his best field officers.

An attack was something else. Aggressive breeds were gaining in popularity. Five pit bulls, a Rottweiler, and a Chow were already in the bite ward, and the week was young.

"This lady's name is Flannery," Clemmons said. "I know you've heard the name. Seems she's had a run-in with old man Pitkin. She said his pooches killed one of her favorite cats. She wanted to speak to you."

"What did you tell her?"

Clemmons grinned and dunked the last of her cookie in the coffee mug. "I said you'd call."

"Thanks a lot," MacDonell said. Leaning forward he poked at the box containing the snake. "How'd she figure it was Pitkin?"

"Who else could it be? He walks his whole pack through her neighborhood at night. They've torn up two of her cats in the last month."

A slender black woman in a starched white coat, one of Clemmons' euthanasia technicians, appeared at the outer glass door and stuck her head in. "Someone told me you got another snake," the young lady said, smiling as if she had just heard a good joke.

MacDonell pointed to the box on his desk. The woman stepped in, snatched up the package and headed out the door.

"Stick it in the fridge 'til I get there!" Clemmons called out before the glass swung shut.

Clemmons nodded toward the woman who was just now disappearing into the kennel building. "Don't let that grin fool you. She's quitting at the end of the next week."

MacDonell frowned. "Is it the work or the pay?"

"Both."

There was a long pause before Clemmons spoke again. "She's patient, and extremely gentle, but she says the only reward for killing all these animals is that she gets to do it all over again tomorrow. She can't see any light at the end of the tunnel."

"Want me to see what I can do?"

"God, yes. Talk to her."

"Can't do much about the wages. You could rotate her to the adoption ward once in awhile."

"Been there. Done that."

MacDonell stared out the window for several seconds.

Clemmons changed the subject. "You gonna call this Flannery woman about her cats?"

MacDonell took off his glasses and rubbed his eyes. "Did you explain that the city doesn't have the resources to investigate fights between dogs and cats?"

Clemmons smiled. "Of course I did. She said she wanted to talk to you, *personally*. Otherwise she'll call her councilman, or Dr. Trimble. I think she wants your job."

"Maybe Trimble ought to give it to her."

"Hmm. Yeah."

MacDonell stood, put his knuckles on his hips, peered deep into his big wall map, then sat again. In a minute he got up, walked to the outer glass door and looked out. The cactus by the door *was* dead, too much water. He thought about Pitkin's dogs and Flannery's cats. Clemmons watched him.

The solution was simple, reduce the stray population by increasing the adoption percentages, or so the department insisted. After nine years of hands-on experience MacDonell knew it was impossible, but he didn't argue anymore. He had seen it many times. Trimble, if he was like his predecessors, would consult with his favorite bleeding heart liberal, one of his public health nurses, or a city councilwoman who owned poodles, then announce some ridiculous new program of adoption. After that he'd journey down to the ghetto-situated Animal Control Center for a photo op. He'd have his picture taken with a cute pup, wait a few minutes for a flock of kindhearted adopters— who never showed—then trot back to 8000 Stadium Drive and leave MacDonell, Clemmons, and the technicians to face the reality of plunging the deadly blue euthanasia fluid into the veins of these poor abandoned little scabs.

MacDonell paced some more. Talk was cheap.

His thoughts shifted. Prudent to wait at least a half-hour, give this Flannery woman time to cool off.

It didn't work. Willie buzzed in and let him know the woman was on the phone. "Be sweet, Doc," she said.

He went to his desk, grimaced, and picked up the phone. Clemmons sat with green crumbs in her lap and a big grin on her face.

For Dr. MacDonell's benefit, Mary Kathryn Flannery took a deep breath and reviewed her long-standing love of animals. She went on to outlined her support of various humane societies and discuss her close personal relationship with council-member Annabel Mooney.

"This *Lemons* person" she said, "did not take my complaint seriously,"

In wasted detail, she went on to lay out her view of the sad Houston animal situation. She ended by reminding MacDonell exactly who it was that paid his salary, and then she requested an immediate and permanent solution to *the Pitkin problem.*

MacDonell restrained a sigh. He knew Alexander Pitkin probably better than anyone. He knew Pitkin's flea-bitten menagerie, too. The man lived in modest seclusion under a downtown section of the Eastex Freeway in a 1973 Ford van. MacDonell recalled all four tires being flat. Packing crates served as a lav and storeroom. The last time he'd visited the old man an atrium had been walled off on the open side by a collection of boosted shopping carts and stacks of mildewed newspapers. A wide sloping awning of plastic drop-cloths turned the eclectic collection into an exotic freeway Shangri-La.

Every year, Pitkin's animals had been rounded up and vaccinated against rabies. MacDonell had carried on long, bizarre conversations with the sixty-three year-old self-proclaimed world refugee, and found him to be shrewd, rebellious, and unpredictable. The press had once done a piece on Pitkin, hinting of a past, and labeling him an eccentric treasure. *"Part of the cultural quilt that makes Houston the diverse city that it is. A Houston tradition."*

The dogs were infected with mange and MacDonell suspected other parasites. They were worse off than Pitkin, but not by much. Still, the old man appeared to be relatively harmless: Relatively, since the story persisted he'd once stabbed an animal control officer in the arm with a three-cornered jeweler's file during an argument over a dog.

"Miz Flannery, there is just about nothing I can do to control Mr. Pitkin or his dogs. He's a squatter, and we've had zero cooperation from the Department of Public Safety or Houston's finest in getting him moved from his nest."

"His dogs are vicious! They run at large!" Flannery cried. "There's a law against that. I know you can ticket him or have him arrested!"

"We have ticketed him, many times. He pays them or his benefactor does."

"Who's his benefactor?"

"Damned if I know. Some River Oaks lawyer, I think."

"I'm *not* taking no for an answer."

"Have any of his dogs bitten a human?"

"They've killed three of my cats."

"I thought it was one cat."

"Two were badly mauled."

"I'm truly sorry about your cats, but as you probably realize, cats are free to run at large." MacDonell felt sure he had explained this to her before, or someone sounding exactly like her. "When you let your cats out of the house they're subject to the hazards of the street."

"That's just it! My cats are outdoor animals, they're legally at large. Your friend Pitkin is the one who's breaking the law!" Her voice was breaking. "Now you do something or I'll have your job!"

"Miz Flannery, I'm pretty sure you wouldn't want my job. Tell you what I will do. I'll send an officer down to the old man's...to his...to where he sleeps, have a good talk with him. Maybe we can work something out."

"Not good enough!" the woman insisted. "I want him and his dogs out of my neighborhood, and I'll give you twenty-four hours. My cats are within the law, they're harmless, and that's all you need to concern yourself with!"

"Ma'am, I'm sure the Audubon Society has a different viewpoint on how harmless free-roaming cats are."

"Well, the Audubon Society doesn't have the law on its side—*I* do!"

MacDonell was close to saying something he'd regret. "Miz Flannery," he said, "I'll admit I can't control all the dogs in this city, nor can the police prevent all the stick-ups and car-jackings. Dogs and cats are natural enemies and the ordinances don't protect them. It's a dangerous world out there."

"You mean you refuse to even *try* to prevent my poor kitties from being killed by that filthy man's filthy dogs?"

"Your cats' ultimate safety is your responsibility. In the meantime, city employees have tomorrow off." He thought a minute. "Tell you what—on Monday I'll go down and talk to Mr. Pitkin myself. Given the situation, that's all I can do."

"Well, I'm writing to your boss, and his boss, and the newspapers!" she screamed. "You haven't heard the last of me. I pay taxes...!"

After she slammed the phone, MacDonell gazed across his desk at the old leather couch. Two phone slammers in a row. The furniture seemed to be smoking.

Unfazed, Clemmons reached into the pocket of her lab coat and produced another cookie. "We need a full time training officer," she lamented. "I can't turn field officers into psychologists overnight. You can't even get them to recognize a beagle when they see it. It's like trying to make chicken salad out of chicken shit."

MacDonell scowled at her.

"Come on," she said, "I know damn well we've sent officers out there to talk to that old bat twice in the last month. She's got twenty-two cats for God's sake. I checked the computer, they're all vaccinated and licensed, which is pretty friggin' unbelievable. Her neighbors say she feeds them outdoors and lets them run all over the neighborhood."

"It shouldn't take a psychologist," MacDonell muttered, "just some practical diplomacy. Explain our capabilities. Can't Captain Bragg teach his officers to do that much?"

"Teach? Are you kidding? Frankie-boy couldn't teach a three-armed monkey to masturbate. Why he…"

"What did you do with my kitten?" MacDonell asked, trying to change the subject.

Clemmons grimaced. "My technician says her cousin is going to adopt it,"

He narrowed his eyes. "She better have a cousin."

"You heard what Bragg said about training blacks and women? He says that shit to me, I'll kick him so hard he'll find his crotch up under his sternum."

MacDonell held up his hands. "I heard what you told me. If he says something like that again, put it in writing and sign it. I'm not going to civil service with undocumented complaints. If I do, I'm just wasting my time. By the way, I'll be in San Antonio on Saturday doing some prospecting for that training officer you keep asking for. Connie tells me the time's right to fill a vacancy or two."

"Good luck," she said, and slammed out the door.

MacDonell thought about Frank Bragg for a second. As a retread ex-policeman he was probably the oldest employee in terms of longevity. Everyone had some little story to tell about him. No one would file a complaint. The man spent too much time getting cozy with the guard dog outfits, supposedly encouraging their compliance with the city's vague kennel ordinance. It was time wasted, but he couldn't prove anything on that score. Money and animals may have changed hands, but he couldn't prove that either. To Bragg, dogs were tools. To the guard dog companies, they were legal weapons, cheap to maintain, and a source of steady income. MacDonell made another cup of instant and returned to his desk.

The draft of MacDonell's monthly report was handed to Willie before noon. If there was one thing MacDonell knew how to do it was write a report. It was all there in black and white. Simple statistics, problems, solutions, alternate solutions, explanation and elucidation, all written in five cent words, everything necessary to justify the budget and the manpower. The problem was that no one read them.

Between the insane calls and one valid animal emergency, he endorsed eleven of last week's investigations. Four others he sent back for more detail. At noon he nursed a diet drink, chewed one of Jeannie's homemade ham sandwichs, and composed a letter to the municipal courts asking for clarification of the new arraignment system. After lunch he got back to the regular paperwork. A huge pile of council actions were now sorted and studied. Recommendations and comments were annotated and dispatched back through Bragg to his field investigators. At 5:00 p.m. MacDonell pushed back his chair, picked up a thick stack of paper and delivered it to Willie's desk. She smiled at him. A fresh stack had come in.

MacDonell hoped to be recognized for his management skills and promoted to assistant health director. He knew he had earned it. He reminded himself that his predecessor had made it into the thin-aired atmosphere of the department, even with the death dealing animal decompression chamber hanging around his neck.

At 5:15, MacDonell spoke privately with Clemmons' new euthanasia technician. The attractive young woman sat, knees together, hands folded, staring at the floor. He gave her the standard talk, including the cliché about putting animals to death. "Somebody around here—probably my predecessor—once said, 'if we can't give these animals a decent life then at least we ought to see they get a decent death.'"

"Can I ask a question?" she said.

Canis

"Sure."

"Why do you and Dr. Clemmons stay here?"

He shrugged, his gaze skittering around the office. "I think we make a difference."

"Dr. Clemmons says you get snakes sent to you all the time. She said last time it was a copperhead. She says you get dead cats thrown in your yard, and phone calls at night."

She had hit on the reason he moved out to Kingwood. It was a too-expensive bedroom community north of Houston, and the reason he wasted an hour on the Eastex freeway twice a day. He had no real answer. He gave her a faint smile. "The place needs a lot of help," he finally said.

She was quiet, polite, and left his office at 5:25.

MacDonell checked his calendar. Willie had added a note. An Australian was penciled in for Tuesday following the long weekend. What was that all about? He poured a cup of water on his cactus plant, filled his briefcase with paper, put on his Stetson and locked up the office.

With no tie-ups he could be home in fifty minutes. Jeannie had promised him a meat-loaf sandwich with hot mustard and a cold bottle of Shiner Bock. Then, if they waited an hour for the traffic to clear out, they could be heading west on I-10 by 7:00 p.m. There was a cold front over around Austin, so the sun would be no problem. They might even stop in at the Oak Ridge Smokehouse in Schulenburg for coffee and peach cobbler and still be in San Antonio by 11:00.

CHAPTER THREE

---

*I*t was 6:58 p.m. and already dark when MacDonell and his wife passed high over US-290 and turned south to catch Interstate10. Down below, on the Southern Pacific right-of-way, Lincoln Earle was hot-footing it, trying to stay on the ties.

Earle was pleased with himself. It had been a grand day. Maybe even spectacular. He'd washed only six car windows and picked up ten dollars, first crack. Then everything seemed to fall into place. He avoided his old lady and visited his two kids on the school grounds. Both were teenagers and too damn smart-mouthed and fearless for their age. Had a good talk, though. Gave each one a dollar bill, and to the girl he gave a pink plastic hair clip, something he found on the street. The boy got a Hershey bar, which he was instructed to share.

Later, Earle bought wine at the 7-Eleven and hooked a package of aged cheddar. He still had a couple bucks left and he'd gotten away clean. Catching him now would be a damn neat trick. He had tramped more than a mile and a half through the gathering dusk. The sun was long gone, leaving a ponderous deck of far-off clouds draping the horizon like funeral cloth. Earle shuddered, then filled his chest with a lung-full of free air. A shifting breeze brought the clear suggestion of pigs and fermenting potatoes. He wanted to go faster, but the uneven surface of the ties and rails made his feet hurt, and the right knee was swelling again. The sky, *and the swollen knee*; weather-wise it was an ominous combination.

Another half mile and he'd be needing a drink. It would soon be stony cold, but Earle was ready for it. As begets a man of talent and preparation, he planned to get home with a near full half-gallon of fine California Tokay.

He had already sniffed the cork, but just a whiff. The cheese was another matter; he had eaten half of it. Except for two sharp-eyed clerks working at the 7-Eleven, he might have been able to lift a package of crackers or a stick of jerky. Good money for the jug was fair, but these days the least little snack was more than he wanted to pay. It used to be he could buy a whole box of crackers for a quarter. Now they wanted a dollar and a half. He flexed his jaw muscles. The 'muthas, he thought, always rippin' off the poor.

Stopping to catch his breath, Earle peered over his shoulder. A pin-point of light—extinguished. On the off chance it was them from the store, he stuffed the last bite of cheese in his mouth and ditched the wrapper.

Earle turned and continued his hike. He carried the jug in a brown paper sack cradled in the crook of his left arm, praying he wouldn't drop it. Earlier, when he crossed the Hempstead Highway, he almost did—hell of a scare. He knew even good wine wouldn't take no crack on hard concrete. He cupped his free hand over the bottle and scrambled along the ragged stones for another hundred yards. Pausing, he listened a second time.

Nothing—not a sound.

At the crossing marker he spotted a faint, yet familiar, trace in the cobble, and began to work his way down the embankment. To Earle, proud descendant of a buffalo soldier, the path was clear and unmistakable. Despite being well within the sprawling city limits of Houston, Earle's destination was as wild and desolate as it was snug and safe.

Lolling around at night he could hear the mutter of traffic on the Toll Road, cross-country truckers, folks going home.

At the bottom he stopped, shifted the wine, snugged up his army field jacket, and peered up along the sloping path. It had been brighter at the top. Down here it was getting black. The musty scent of rotted leaves replaced the tang of the porkers. He stooped, lifted a springy branch, slipped under, and headed away from the tracks.

Approaching his thicket Earle paused one more time and looked back at the embankment. Something moved, clicking and scratching on the ties and ballast above him. He hesitated, shoulders hunched forward, realizing he could hear the thump of his own heart.

He picked up a fist-sized rock and backed into the shadows. Raising his head, Earle noticed the moon was riding just above the tops of the live-oaks. Tonight the moon would be full, much easier to travel. Right now, though, when he needed light, strings of dirty clouds drug themselves across the moon's face. If he waited a few seconds the clouds would pass and it would be as bright as day. Instead they surged, shifted, crested—then tore apart.

Somebody, or some*thing*, was still up there. The cops? Earle considered the stolen cheese and the mixed blessings of several nights in the Harris County Jail. Warm, he recalled, crowded, and the crappers always overflowed. If he could snake over a few more yards into the heavy stuff he would lose whoever it was.

A low shadow shot through the dewberry brambles. Earle's breath caught in his throat. What the hell was that? Were his eyes playing tricks? He turned, pushed through a knot of scrubby pines, and ducked around some broken strands of wire. Fifty yards and he would be home free. To hell with them. The cheese was gone, the wine was paid for. The receipt was in the bag. They could stick it.

Here in the forest tangle the trail became confusing. Earle stumbled, then caught himself. He walked, unblinking, into a branch, surprised by

the whip-sting on his cheek. He stopped, turned, went to the right, trying to get his bearings.

The clouds parted and the moon lifted over the clawing fingers of
that line of oaks. The trace became plain again. Earle tossed away the
rock, hugged his jug, and moved on. The moon revealed a darker blackness in the northwest, the cold front. His knee was never wrong. He
took a few cautious steps and here was the limb he had propped
between two lifeless sweet-gums. A glorious feeling of confidence
enveloped him and he hurried along. Under the canopy of a gigantic
magnolia tree was his shipping container, a sheet of corrugated steel
covering the bottom half of the opening. Here too was his tin bucket,
his plastic milk box, and at his feet, his fire pit. The clouds on the horizon meant rain, but hell he was home.

He moved to the steel sheet. With one hand he tilted the heavy metal
up on its end. Dropping to his knees he crawled to the far end of the
wooden shell. Inside it was snug and dry. He folded back the top of the
paper sack. His hands and arms trembled. Now, before anymore acci-
dents, he unscrewed the cap and swallowed a stiff welcome home. His
ribs warmed and he coughed a little. He slipped the bottle into the folds
of his blanket and fished for a small tin box. Snapping the lid with his
thumbnail he took out a book of paper matches, closed the box, and
replaced it under the blanket.

Outside he found his stockpile of dry twigs and rotted limbs.
Using his fingernails he scratched out some paper-thin underbark
and tore it into slivers. He reached for his milk box, pulled it near the
pit, and squatted. For the first time in hours his weight was off his
feet. He squirmed his toes around to stimulate circulation and bent
over the tinder.

Soft duff and dry leaves crackled nearby.

Earle stiffened and remained motionless. High up the moon lit the
tops of the pines, but down here the shadows magnified the darkness.
The wind was picking up. Leathery Magnolia leaves clattered in a

sudden gust. The pines swayed and their heavy trunks creaked. Earle held his breath and looked hard into the low-hanging gloom. Was he hearing things again?

Looking down, he arranged the twigs into a three-sided pyramid. The previous ashes were cold and a little damp. He pushed the dry slivers into the center of the pyramid with his thumb, and then fiddled with the matches. His hands quivered as he selected one, tore it out, and struck it against the book. It flared, and as it did he glanced across the firepit. From the shadows, two yellow-rimmed reflections stared back. Earle raised the match, squinted to see, strained to hear. Nearby, a second presence was breathing.

Lincoln Earle slowly lowered one hand, palm down, desperate to detect any vibrations in the earth. A tremor began in his shoulders and the vain light flickered. Earle started as the hot match burned his fingers. He flung it down and the glow was devoured by the darkness. The thin hair on Earle's neck prickled, and a frosty finger visited his spine. A new odor: wild, savage musk. He heard two metallic clicks, then through the leaves and brittle needles came rushing feet.

Something heavy, something with an overpowering stench, hit him in the chest knocking him backward. His head slammed into the wooden crate as he fell and twisted. Instinctively, Earle scrambled to the mouth of the box. In a cold frenzy, the dark presence slashed in under his ribs and wrenched at his stomach, tearing his ragged coat and ripping his thin shirt. Frantic, Earle pulled at the metal, and the slab thundered down over the opening. He was inside. He was safe. The metal had caught him across the ankle and his foot was numb, but still, he was safe.

Earle huddled deep inside the container. He was bleeding but felt little pain. Whatever the thing was, it was hurling itself against the metal, jarring the box with each blow. He tried to be quiet, to hold his breath, to be perfectly still. The corrugated sheet crashed again and again, shaking, slamming, jolting the container. Earle's stomach began to churn. What if it collapsed?

Claws—he could hear them scratching the metal. Then, above the steel, Earle glimpsed a black shape launched against the sky. It scrabbled, breathing hoarsely, over the top. It was in the box with him! Sweet Jesus!

Earle tried to scream but his throat was being crushed, air was not coming. He tore at thick fur with his blunt fingers. He kicked his feet and stretched back. Blood and foam spurted from his nose. An artery in his neck squirted high and something black ran down the box wall. Panic welled up in his chest. Outside, he thought. I gotta get outside and run like hell. Desperation claimed him. He struggled to crawl out, but the creature was upon him, holding him back, shaking him by the throat. The container rocked and rattled. Tendons snapped; he could hear them, feel them. His life was pouring out of his throat, and he could feel a numb sensation as the muscles and other parts of his neck were pulled away. He writhed and strained and kicked. The bones at the back of his neck began to twist. Fear began to fade.

Earle's last coherent thoughts were for the wine. Don't spill the wine. Please, don't spill the wine…

The clouds opened and Earle looked up, squinted. The moon was blinding. He closed his eyes. His mouth gaped but there was no sound. In the distance lightning flashed, in a few seconds came low, rolling thunder. Nearby a flash of dry light and a metallic whir, then another. The front arrived minutes later in a crash of thunder and torrential rain.

A fragment of stiff cardboard skittered across the pine needles and lodged in the firepit. The wind died and the rain slackened. Afterward raccoons would come to chirr and chitter and fight in the dark. In the bright morning crows and jays would squabble. Later the smaller animals would clean the bones, and in time the worms would polish them.

CHAPTER FOUR

Saturday morning was quiet at Lackland Air Force Base. MacDonell's nose leaked. He dabbed at it with a crumpled tissue. A slanting drizzle had pelted southwest San Antonio for an hour, but the overcast eastern sky looked like it might be breaking up. In this isolated corner of the base the 3260th Military Working Dog Training Squadron had already put in half a day. All eleven trainees were resting their dogs in a stand of mesquite. A few of the men had taken off their ponchos and draped them over the animals. Seven dogs were sleek new Malinois imported from Belgium, only four were German Shepherds.

Standing to one side MacDonell watched the men and dogs working together with a purpose. Down deep he was a bird-dog man and he always wanted something more from the relationship. Quail breast on toast was nice, but he also wanted his dogs to come into the house after a long outing in the field, to warm by the fire. Of necessity, these crafty devils would be stored away in a cold concrete kennel at the end of the day. He had to admit, though, the fawn-colored Malinois with their foxy black muzzles were impressive.

Jeannie sat reading in the family car. The brief visit with their daughter and the grandchildren had been refreshing, but soon they needed to get back to Houston. Their own family pet needed her medication and Jeannie didn't feel she could trust the young dogsitter.

The close-cropped trainees sipped water and whispered among themselves. They were a greater mixture of types than the dogs: four Airmen, four Marines, two DEA agents, and one beefy fellow in the uniform of the U.S. Border Patrol. The instructor, Technical Sergeant Lee Martinez, impeccably decked out in a set of sharp-pressed camouflage fatigues, called the first trainee forward. He was a short, pudgy lad with pale cheeks and the traditional white sidewalls. MacDonell studied the trainee as he plodded through the wet grass. To him the boy looked a little sick, and young enough to be in middle school.

"Okay, listen up," Martinez said as he scraped mud from his boot. "We'll run it again."

"Satan, SIT!" the young airman called out.

The dog, a four-year veteran, plopped its rump on the wet earth. With a quivering intensity, it fixed on the half-open door at the end of a narrow brown building a few yards away. The building was really just a glorified hallway with eight inside doors on opposite sides. The decoy, Staff Sgt. Orville Meriweather, waited inside one of the cubicles, his left arm protected by a padded sleeve.

"Poitrast, this time I want a thorough building search. And *this time* make sure you give your dog the proper reward." The sergeant's voice was firm. "And…" he added, rapping the side of his own head for emphasis, "…search the first two doors on either side twice." He paused. "Go fuckin' slow."

"Yes, SIR!" The boy's voice was still changing. He eyed the building, then the dog, then the building. The smooth, brown Malinois looked up at him, then back at the door. It leaned forward, panting, eager.

"Well, Airman?"

The dog held its breath. Its tongue froze, half out of its mouth.

"FIND HIM," the boy commanded. The dog lunged.

"BULL SHIT!" the sergeant roared. "Get your ass back here and read this building its rights."

"Heel," the boy said, and wheeled the dog back to the starting point.

A couple Marines, resting in the weeds, snickered.

"You'll get your turn," Martinez cautioned them, and the men fell silent.

"ATTENTION IN THE BUILDING!" the boy cried. "THIS IS AIR-MAN BASIC GAYLEN POITRAST, ACCOMPANIED BY AN ATTACK-TRAINED MILITARY WORKING DOG. THE DOG IS TRAINED TO ATTACK WITHOUT WARNING. YOU HAVE THIRTY SECONDS TO EXIT THE BUILDING OR I'M SENDING IN THE DOG!" The boy looked at Martinez. The sergeant scowled, but nodded his head.

"TIME'S UP!" the boy yelled, his voice cracking. "FIND HIM!"

The dog lunged again, this time dragging the handler through the outer door. The sergeant shook his head and the Marines laughed again. MacDonell and the sergeant studied the young man as he worked the dog at the bottom of the first door on the right. The airman banged on the left-hand door with his boot. The dog responded by bouncing across the hall and sucking a snootfull of air from under the second door. Whirling, it slammed back across the hall to the first door again. This continued up the narrow passage as the number of hiding places systematically decreased.

The dog stopped and half-sat.

The sergeant took a step toward the building. "YOU SEE THAT DOG SIT? DAMN IT, AIRMAN! READ THAT DOG! READ THAT DOG! NOW, GIVE 'IM A BITE—GIVE 'IM A BITE!"

"Yes sir," the boy croaked.

The airman pushed open the door and the dog disappeared inside. The muffled sound of canine retribution and Sergeant Meriweather's taunting screams filtered into the morning air.

"Do I detect a hangover?" MacDonell asked.

"Little puke got in at 3:00 this morning. Woke up half the barracks. I tol' him his dog don't really give a shit."

MacDonell shook his head. In a lull, he pressed his case. "You have a retirement date, Lee?"

The sergeant turned. "No sir, Doc, I ain't. I got more'n two years."

The pale airman marched around from the back side of the building and stood at attention. "Satan, sit," he said.

The armpits of his fatigues were stained with sweat almost to his waist. The dog sat and leaned comfortably on the young man's shin. Its long pink tongue was out about a foot, little drops of saliva flipping from its tip. The dog ran its right foot up over the side of its head and then licked the foreleg near where the dewclaw had been.

"Doc, would you take a look in this dog's ear?" Martinez asked. "I seen him scratching."

Without comment or encouragement, Poitrast went to one knee, looped the flat leather leash twice around the dog's charcoal muzzle, then hugged the animal tight to his chest. The dog knew what was coming and stiffened. MacDonell bent and carefully inspected first the depths of the Malinois' reddened right ear, then the left. The dog's dark mahogany eyes followed every move.

MacDonell went over to the car and spoke to Jeannie. Dutifully she dug into her purse. He returned with a skinny flashlight and a pair of eyebrow tweezers. He hunkered over the animal. After a little humming and whispering to the nervous dog, he stood up to report his findings.

"Here's your problem," He held up a fat gray tick. "I'd have them all checked," he advised.

The sergeant nodded. "I hear that." He turned. "Poitrast…no, Collins. Locate Major Fossburg. Ask her if she's got time to meet us at the kennel."

Airman Poitrast made a remark about female veterinarians. Both men ignored him.

"You might want to get this place sprayed, too," MacDonell observed.

Martinez considered it, then turned to the sweating airman. He stuck a stubby finger in the young man's face. "It's a good thing this dog is smarter than you are, Poitrast. Give him some water and take a seat in the weeds."

Martinez raised his voice and spoke to group. "When we get back, I want you people to check your dogs all over for ticks. In the ears and all over!" It was quiet. "GOT THAT?" he boomed.

"Yes, Sir," Poitrast said.

"YES, SIR!" the rest sang out.

The sergeant turned back to MacDonell, smiled, then signaled past him for a new team to step up.

MacDonell watched. "Anybody else about to cut the cord? Anybody looking for a civilian job?" he asked.

"What kind of work, Doc?"

"Training. I've got next year's budget review this month. If I found the right person I could hire somebody right now."

"Training dogs or people?"

"People, Sarge. Animal Control Officers."

The sergeant spit on the ground. "Dogcatchers, huh?"

MacDonell nodded. "We don't call 'em that anymore."

The sergeant blew air through his nose. "I know how it is on the outside, Doc. You yell at one of them shit-birds wrong and your ass is grass. Some work."

MacDonell kicked a rock at that, for he knew Martinez was right.

"WE AIN'T GOT ALL DAMN DAY, MEN. LET'S SEE ONE OF YOU JARHEADS OVER HERE, ON THE DOUBLE!" Martinez thundered.

MacDonell spoke again. "It takes a little finesse, but you could do it. The job, I mean…"

"YOU KNOW WHAT 'ON THE DOUBLE' MEANS—SHIT HEAD?" Martinez yelled. A marine was stumbling to his feet.

MacDonell tried not to grin, but at the same time had second thoughts. "You know anyone else? Anyone who knows dogs but can train people?"

Martinez looked down and MacDonell read his mind. The man was wondering how in hell a military veterinarian could wind up running an animal control outfit. Even one in a big place like Houston.

"Naw, Doc, not to work with dogcatchers." He hesitated and it appeared a thought had struck him. "Well, maybe there is somebody. You remember Longley? From back when we was in Germany? She had two tours here at the school, made Master. She's up at McConnell."

"Sure, I remember Janie," MacDonell said. "She's a great dog handler."

"Well, she got herself riffed," Martinez confided. "After sixteen years." Martinez folded his arms across his chest and frowned at the Marine who was still gathering dog and leash. "She tells people it's retirement, but the story is she braced a couple of drunks in civvies outside the NCO Club one night. Put her dog on this one guy and told him not to move while she cuffed the other one. They say the first guy moved," Martinez grinned. "Anyway, the dog showed him some ivory and the guy shit his pants. Bad luck, Doc. Guy turns out to be a second balloon and his father's a colonel." The sergeant shrugged. "She might want to talk."

MacDonell scratched his chin whiskers and searched his memory. "Blond?"

"Tall, husky blond. And feisty." The sergeant looked at his visitor. "I got her number back at the squadron. I can give her a call and leave yours."

MacDonell scribbled his home number on the back of a business card and handed it over. "Have her call either number."

Martinez tucked the card in his wallet. "Come to think of it, Doc, Longley's got people close to Houston. That might be a plus for you and her."

The next trainee came forward, a lanky, grinning Marine with a big Adam's apple.

"HOBO, SIT!" he said in a deep Kentucky baritone.

The sergeant turned his head. "You see what Poitrast done?"

The Marine blinked his eyes. "Yes, suh! I was watching, suh!"

MacDonell thanked Martinez for the lead, and started back to his car, feeling less than hopeful.

***

As MacDonell made his way out of the Lackland gate, Jeannie began pointing out landmarks. Giant Wilford Hall Medical Center on the right. On the left, Air Force Village, a retirement complex for military widows. She commented on it. Good God, he thought, he wasn't dead yet. Rain began to fall. He turned on the wipers.

Halfway around the 410 loop, Martinez' remarks began to sink in. MacDonell's choice of a second career nine years ago had been hasty and he knew it. Back then it seemed to be a challenge. In retrospect his decision was probably a mistake.

Houston's animal control had an ugly history. For decades cops ran the show. Not always the best cops. It wasn't unheard of for an itchy-fingered officer to pull out his revolver and shoot a yapping pup right on the owner's front porch. Then, in the early 50's, the city suffered an unparalleled rabies epidemic. At the same time the humane movement began to assert itself. Not long after that, animal control was moved into the health department. City government promised improvements and brought in veterinarians to manage things. A few were young bucks eager to move on to private practice. Most were tired or retired practitioners, looking for a 'position.' Like the city's promises, each of these vets lasted about 18 months. One poor soul had died of a heart attack at MacDonell's very desk. He shuddered.

Before they got to I-10, Jeannie asked to stop at the Randolph Exchange. Sunlight was shouldering its way through a streaking sky. The main gate guard, snappy in his dress blues and chalk-white gloves, shot a crisp highball salute at MacDonell and the world brightened.

Jeannie needed a large wok for a meal she was planning and the Randolph BX had a better selection than Lackland. She could also get directions to the skeet range where they might look at a variety of handguns.

MacDonell cruised up a broad esplanade. Two T-38's whispered across the back of the base, twisted, and made a wide arc up into the clouds. Sunlight reflected off stubby wings. On the right the massive tail of a C-5A rose above the flight line, and between the hangars a Lear Jet could be seen taxiing.

"You miss this, don't you?" Jeannie murmured, her eyes searching for even the tiniest evidence of the old mystique.

MacDonell cleared his throat and, glancing out the driver's side window, wiped the corner of his eye with his finger. She was right. Lackland had an efficient, sterile quality, but he loved Randolph. The old inner circle of two-story officer's quarters remained, steadfast with their screened porches, cracked sidewalks, and tall oaks. There was a kind of southern serenity about it.

After picking up the wok they drove to the gun club. Jeannie was about to invest in a purse-sized handgun. She had always been an excellent shot, but she only started carrying after a Kingwood real estate agent was raped and murdered. At the target range, on the previous Saturday, her automatic began ramming shells into the chamber sideways. She decided to replace it.

MacDonell watched her pick up a small stainless steel revolver with walnut grips. She checked the cylinder and held it out with both hands. Locking her elbows she aimed at a spot high on the wall behind the counter. The gun was a light Rossi five-shot .38 Special with a three-inch barrel. Nice double action.

"This one will hold sixteen rounds," MacDonell said, pointing through the glass at a blue 9mm Beretta.

"I'm not going after terrorists, Duncan." The lady behind the counter regarded the floor tiles and appeared to be suppressing a laugh. "Automatics are all springs and clips. I could put an eye out cleaning it.

This is much simpler and I don't have to put a round in every chamber. I load four and put the hammer down on the empty."

"Only four rounds?" MacDonell was skeptical.

Jeannie, a petite, delicately scented, grandmother of five smiled at her husband. "One should do just fine if it goes where I aim it. Now go see if they have that recoil pad for your duck gun, and get some patches, solvent, and a bore brush for a .38."

He shrugged. "It's your gun."

As Jeannie started filling out the paperwork, MacDonell meandered down the counter ogling the shotguns. After some early threats at the new job, even he had considered carrying a gun. Probably just asking for trouble, he thought.

The drive back to Houston was pleasant enough, with towering anvil-shaped clouds off to the north but keeping their distance. The car radio was tuned to a big band station. It had been a satisfying weekend. Grandpa had played with the grand kids and Jeannie had ordered a new weapon. Her peashooter would be shipped. It probably wouldn't stop much, but she might be a little safer. He'd be a lot more relaxed when she was out conducting real estate transactions in the combat zones of Space City, USA. He also had a nifty lead on a training officer. Jane Longley could be a great addition to the staff if it worked out. He would have to be charming.

MacDonell tried without success to concentrate on his driving. He remembered the week before his retirement, when he had visited in Houston. He had found the bureau in dire need of an infusion of esprit de corps. The new kennel was a marvel, but the people, the administrative offices, and the grounds were a mess. Unfortunately his retirement papers were already in.

Thus committed, he fought anguish and frustration with hard work. He came in on Saturdays, scraped paint, planted bulbs. He fired two lazy vets, hired six technicians in their places and began putting the multitudes of animals to death by lethal injection, rather than the despised decompression chamber. He needed to destroy more than a hundred animals a day. He tried to make it a personal, hands-on thing. Still, the slippery street dogs and frantic cats were dangerous. And it was also more costly, but it was an improvement he expected the city council to support. He even renamed the bureau. The Bureau of Animal Control became the Bureau of Animal Regulation and *Care*, or BARC.

Eighty-six percent of the employees were black, yet all the top jobs were held by whites. Within a year five of his six branch chiefs were minorities, each now with a desk and semi-private space to work in. He promoted Connie Oaks right out of the kennels, and the man's very first contribution was a functioning supply system. Later, Oaks developed standard personnel hiring criteria and came up with a computer-scored promotion system. Clemmons, his second in command, updated the training program. By the end of the second year his officers were passing the Texas Animal Control Officer certification exam.

Next, MacDonell set about to uniform and equip everyone. He got rid of the raunchy cowboy image by adding rank insignia, shoulder patches, neckties, and even Smoky Bear hats. He created a perception of calm, cool, forest rangers, decked out in green and tan. In spite of the increase in morale a few departmental big-wigs remarked on his military style of leadership.

On the radio Benny Goodman was finishing up a 1937 recording of 'King Porter Stomp.' Harry James, Chris Griffin, and Ziggy Elman were on trumpet, Krupa wailed the drums. MacDonell looked over at Jeannie. She had read the entire manual on the new Rossi.

"What do you think?" she asked, holding up the book.

"It's a sweetie-pie," he replied.

CHAPTER FIVE

6:00 a.m. Monday. MacDonell headed to work. He hummed a familiar melody from Gilbert and Sullivan as he regarded the traffic on the Eastex. The morning drive in was an uninterrupted opportunity to organize his day.

The whole household had been up an hour early. Jeannie called his attention to Diamond Lil, as if she needed to. The old bird dog was having a hard time getting started. She had gone to the back yard and hunted for exactly the right spot, sniffing, searching, sniffing. When she found it she squatted for a long time, her legs cramping up as she relieved herself. Wouldn't it be therapeutic, he fantasized, if she could find a covey of bobwhites in the back yard. Probably give the old girl another ten years.

Words came to the tune in his head. He tilted his head back, closed one eye, and opened his throat, "…aaand I am the ruler of the queen's na-veeee," he squalled out, bruising the notes. He peeked. The windshield held.

A well-dressed woman in a Buick Riviera pulled up on his left. She smiled and extended the narrow middle finger of her right hand, then hit her accelerator and slid silently away. He looked down at his instrument panel. His left-turn signal was flashing. He nodded to himself, turned it off, turned on the radio, and headed on down the Eastex, over the San Jacinto River, through Humble, and past the turnoff to Intercontinental Airport. Between Beltway 8 and Loop 610 heavy construction was progressing at a frantic pace. The radio news failed to report a chokepoint near Hopper, but did mention the killing of a 7-Eleven clerk, two carjackings, and a blurb on a League City boarding kennel operator reported missing by his wife. Inside the 610 loop, MacDonell sailed past the Collingsworth exit resisting the urge to turn off. He remembered he had promised to go see old man Pitkin and chance getting that wonderful Mrs. Flannery off his back.

He passed the George R. Brown Convention Center then dropped down and slanted to the southeast. He took the Fannin exit and immediately reversed his path, ducking back under the concrete speedway. In this neighborhood the homes were being wedged out by frontyard business ventures. Decades of fuel smudge had stained the houses a battery-acid gray. Here and there, dingy bed sheets dried on rickety balconies. Fungus grew on the damp concrete beams and revetments. The occasional plantings sprouted somber flowers.

Heading northeast along the access road he spotted Pitkin's palace; the burned-out hulk of a Ford van, a jumble of metal refuse, wooden shipping crates, stacks of newspaper, and a crooked row of shopping carts. MacDonell edged the car to the curb about fifty yards from the dwelling. He killed the engine and looked for signs of life.

A steady drone of morning commuters whirred above, but down here nothing stirred. He checked the rear-view mirror, then settled into his seat. After a minute, a movement caught MacDonell's eye as a shadow flickered under the axle of the van. A dog the color of dead grass. If it was a sentinel, it was doing a poor job.

Another minute and MacDonell made out a slumping form moving along the street on the far side of the freeway: Pitkin. The man hadn't changed a bit since MacDonell had last seen him. He was carrying a large brown paper bag. Dumpster donuts, MacDonell speculated. Free and plentiful, they were the standard fare of the homeless.

Pitkin looked left, and right, and left again, as he scuffed toward the shelter. Presenting the hollow-cheeked appearance of chronic illness, the man seemed fully alert to his surroundings.

As he approached, two dogs rose from behind the van, arched their backs, and sniffed the air. The dog under the axle maintained its position, but thumped its tail. In thirty seconds the bare-headed man was less than ten yards from the van. He stopped, straightened his shoulders, stretched his skinny white neck, and looked at MacDonell's car. The move reminded MacDonell of a turkey in the early morning dew, trying hard to hear the dry snap of a twig or the snik of a safety. Pitkin gave his head a finite turn, but kept his eyes fixed on the car.

This maneuver was a telepathic message for the dogs to do their duty. Alerted, three began to bark. As the mood struck them they would stop, scratch, and bark again. Their half-hearted racket signaled the advent of a horde of tan, rangy, half-grown pups. They spilled out of the back of the van in a wormy tangle and struggled to rise from the concrete.

Pitkin always had a pack of unruly animals around him. MacDonell counted ten: seven pups and three adults. He started his engine and eased forward. The faded man moved to his haven and was swallowed up in a pile of metal, boards, and newspapers. As MacDonell drew alongside most of the pups retreated under the van. Two big ones approached the car, and when it stopped put their feet up on the door, smearing it with a mixture of mud and feces.

MacDonell rolled down the window thinking he would pat the tops of their heads. The sour odor of seborrhea and acute moist dermatitis whacked him in the face. He looked at three or four wet, bulbous noses straining to reach him. Soon all seven pups had gathered around his car to smear it with excrement and pee on it. The three adults were tied with thin cord to the corners of the van. Counterpoint to the clamor of barking and coughing on the outside, there was spiteful silence within the dwelling.

"Mister Pitkin!" MacDonell called.

MacDonell's raised voice elicited a round of cheers from the pups. Soon, however, their itching claimed their attention and most of them sat to scratch or rub on the nearest solid object. A few of the larger ones could stand on three legs, scratch, and bark, all at the same time.

"HEY!…PITKIN!" MacDonell called out again.

Again there was no response. MacDonell could see the face of a tired man peering out at him. It was a sad, faded map, devoid of starting point or destination. Pitkin's eyelids drooped, revealing anemic pink linings. His dirty white hair was wispy, with wide yellow spaces between the scaly, random tufts. When Pitkin turned in profile, his prominent Adam's apple gave him the appearance of having a jointed neck. Three shopping carts filled with newspapers and aluminum cans stood between them. A few partially eaten donuts lay scattered on the damp concrete.

MacDonell motioned with his arm and called out again. There was only a cold stare. MacDonell recalled the grim story of the stabbing with a three-cornered file. He decided it was probably an exaggeration. He looked at the sick old man. Pitkin looked back. Texans would call it a Mexican Standoff.

Finally, MacDonell rolled up the window and reached for the door. Remembering how Pitkin's pups had once climbed inside a Channel 3 reporter's car, he knew he'd better only crack the door. He would have to squeeze out, while at the same time keeping these scrubs out of his front seat. He put on his Stetson and flipped his badge to the outside of his shirt pocket. Sometimes the appearance of authority did the trick. Often the Texas Exempt license plates and the big city seal on the door, with its steam locomotive and plow, were enough. Not today.

The grinding squawnk of the car door caused the pups to surge forward. MacDonell squeezed one foot out of the car and placed it on the concrete. Staying behind the door, he stood up, his head, hat, and shoulders clearing the top of the car. The pups, all seven, went belly-down on the concrete, licking under the door at his boot and chewing his cuff. "Git!" he spit out, moving his foot, trying to stay clean.

The pups scattered. From inside the space between the van and the packing crates, the sound of a foreign language came clear and crisp. The words sounded German, guttural "K's" and "H's."

Between the two men, a heaped up shopping cart started to inch forward. Surprised, MacDonell watched it. Stacks of newspapers tipped and slid away. As the cart crashed to the concrete, aluminum beer cans bounced like popcorn.

Exploding over the cart, a leaping, snarling form rushed at him. MacDonell stood motionless for an instant before he fell back into the car. Stunned, he held the door tight, but his left leg remained outside, wedged in the door. The dog, if it was a dog, slammed its front feet on the glass and seized the top edge of the car door with its teeth. It planted its hind feet on the pavement, tightened its grip on the door frame, and struggled backward with powerful thrusts of its shoulders.

MacDonell felt the door slip open and he yanked his leg in. Then with as much force as he could muster, he inserted his right arm through the steering wheel. Using it as an anchor he grasped the armrest with both hands and pulled hard. It didn't help—the door continued to inch outward. Now the animal altered its tactics and tried to shake the car door. The tiny compact rocked. The springs squeaked.

Unexpectedly, the dog released its grip and gathered itself for another onslaught. MacDonell used the split second to slam the door shut. Exhaling, he fell against the steering wheel. The raucous sound of the car horn blared. He straightened up and the sound stopped.

Looking out, MacDonell saw the beast had disappeared from view. So had all the pups. The adult animals, tied to the van, were now under it. Only their taut ropes were visible, straining against the bumper struts. MacDonell saw Pitkin scurrying, gathering up the spilled cans. Saliva and blood streaked the top of the car's window glass. MacDonell felt old. His arms and back were sore. His hands shook as he grasped the wheel. He wondered what to do next.

He keyed the ignition and eased through the cluster of pups who were now wrestling near his front bumper. Moving toward the curb, MacDonell looked in his rear view mirror. The tremendous animal, whatever it was, had vanished. The pups were quarreling and fighting over some tattered trophy. He left them to their squabble and eased on down the access road.

Up on US-59 the traffic had lost its immediacy. It was a relief to be alive and whole. He looked at the seat next to him: something was missing. He felt his shirt pocket for his badge. He looked for his map book. He touched a thin, stinging scratch on the top of his bald head: no blood. It was then he realized his hat was neither on his head nor on the seat. Those scruffy, oozing pups were dividing the dead remains of a one hundred and fifty-dollar Stetson.

***

"Willie, get Captain Bragg on the radio and tell him to come to my office! Please," he added. Then he rinsed out his cup and poured a little of the water on his cactus. His hands were shaking.

In twenty minutes, Bragg bounced in the door and collapsed into the first available chair. "What's up, Doc?" he said, grinning wide. He was out of breath. "Willie said you were hot."

After a cup of coffee, MacDonell was feeling close to normal. "I want you to go down under the Eastex and bust old man Pitkin."

"What for?"

"Exceeding the limit on adult dogs."

"I thought you wanted us to lay off the old buzzard. Didn't you say he was harmless?"

Bragg, the ex-cop, knew more about the law than the average animal control officer, and he exuded the confidence necessary to get the job done. MacDonell had wanted to throttle him a few times, but so far had not considered firing him. Retirement would soon relieve him of that task.

"Dammit, Frank, I just had the Kool-Aid scared out of me." MacDonell snapped. "Drag all his animals in here and see to it he's legal when he leaves. He's got four adults and seven pups over six months. That's at least eight over the limit, unless he has a kennel license, and that pile of crap he lives in doesn't qualify."

"What's the big deal?" Bragg asked.

"One of the adults is a big hound. I mean *huge*. It's as tall as a Great Dane and as heavy as a Mastiff. It tried to eat my car." MacDonell made gestures of height and size with his hands. "Must weigh 150 pounds!"

Bragg smirked and rolled his eyes.

"Look at my car door on your way out. Get Reyes and a shooting officer to go with you," MacDonell said. "I'd load two darts and have the shooter back you up with the .410."

"Reyes?"

"He's familiar with Schutzhund, he's quick, and he's as strong as a water buffalo."

The intercom buzzed. It was Willie's husky, Southern Comfort drawl. "It's a J.D. Longley, Doc. Says ya'll know her from the Air Force."

Bragg shook his head, mumbled something, and stomped out.

MacDonell scratched the fringe of hair above his ears. Martinez had made good on his promise. They had known her as Jane Longley at Bitburg Air Base in Germany. After Martinez left she became the non-com in charge of the largest military working dog detachment in Europe. He picked up the phone.

"Hello!" MacDonell spoke loud and strong into the phone. "Is this the famous Master Sergeant Jane Longley of the United States Air Force?!"

"Not anymore, Doc," a deep alto voice chuckled. "This is J.D. Longley, civilian. They just retired me out. How've you been?"

"Pretty good, pretty good. Apparently you heard from Lee Martinez?"

"Uh huh. Something about a training job."

"You looking for work?" MacDonell asked.

"Well, no, not really. I've got something lined up. It's temporary, till something permanent comes along, but the money's good."

"When did you get to town?"

"Oh, I've been here. Right now I'm staying with an uncle up in Liberty County. I had thirty days terminal leave coming so I came down awhile back to take this job. Then I went back up to McConnell a few days ago so they could cut the final retirement orders. Had a nice visit with my mom before coming back."

That was twice she had made reference to retirement. She was putting a good face on a bad situation.

"What are you doing for dinner tomorrow?" MacDonell asked. "Jeannie and I would love to have you over."

"Well…"

MacDonell didn't let her temporize. "Come on. We'll just toss on another steak. Jeannie'd be hurt if you turned us down."

They confirmed a 6:30 p.m. dinner. She would come over for a tour at 4:30 and follow him home.

MacDonell was pleased. Even if he couldn't talk her into a job it would be good to see an old military acquaintance. Not many of his officer buddies lived closer than San Antonio. Having once been enlisted himself, MacDonell knew it was awkward for the non-coms to rub elbows with officers. But now he and Jane Longley were civilians. Before lunch he called Jeannie; indeed, she recalled Longley. Dinner would be no problem at all and, as Jeannie stated quite succinctly, she would welcome the intelligent conversation another female would provide.

In the afternoon Bragg slid sideways into MacDonell's office. He perched on the arm of the chair by the door. "We got Pitkin's scrubs," he said. "Want to see them?"

God no, he didn't want to see them. MacDonell was writing and didn't look up. "You get them all?"

"All he had," Bragg replied.

"Great," MacDonell said, still looking down at the papers on his desk. "Anybody hurt?"

"Not unless you can die from the smell."

"What about the big one? Where did you put it?"

"There wasn't anything very big, Doc. The biggest thing we picked up was about thirty-five or forty pounds."

MacDonell looked up. "You didn't see a mastiff?"

"We got three smallish adults and seven big greasy pups. The old fart's about to bounce off the ceiling, if that's any consolation."

"No big mastiff?"

"No, Doc. We got all there was. No mastiff."

MacDonell leaned back, lacing his fingers behind his head.

Bragg grinned. "You sure this hound from hell wasn't all in your imagination?"

MacDonell ignored the smirk. "First thing in the morning go talk to that Flannery woman. Ask her if she can describe the dog that killed her cats. Get it in writing." He thought for a few seconds more. "If you want to, take another look. Have a talk with the old man. If he's gone, look around anyway."

"Won't I need a warrant?"

MacDonell shook his head. "You know the legal definition of probable cause. If you need a warrant, you know how to get one."

MacDonell thrived on action. He would sleep well tonight.

CHAPTER SIX

---

*E*arly Tuesday morning MacDonell stood on the curb in front of the new kennel building and peered through a smoky vehicle, past the driver, to the passenger side. A frail woman was leaning against the headrest. Her hand shook as she pressed a bloody towel against her cheek.

Behind the wheel city councilman B. F. Dockery twisted his half-smoked cigar between blue lips and fumbled with his keys. A dense gray haze filled the car's interior.

MacDonell looked up, away from the car, and out onto the decaying neighborhood. The roar of mowers and the scent of freshly cut weeds drifted from a city crew working outside the fence. He wished to heaven he could have stayed in San Antonio a few days longer. Leaning forward, he put the fingertips of both hands on the window frame. "If you want some free advice, Mr. Dockery, get your mother a canary. They sing, they don't eat much, and they're not likely to disturb the neighbors." MacDonell thought for a second, "...and they sure as hell won't try something like this."

"Mind your own business," Dockery muttered.

"Dog bites are my business, councilman."

Dockery spewed a deep lung-wrenching cough, started the engine, and spit past MacDonell's outstretched arms. For a second the councilman hesitated, looking at MacDonell's belt buckle. It seemed as if he might say something, but without a word he ran the window up, jerked the big sedan into reverse and backed out. The heavily-tinted windows hid the woman's face, but MacDonell could distinguish her outline. She still held the blood-stained towel to her face. The car pulled out of the lot, dodged a looming Texaco tanker, and was gone.

Across Carr Street the echoing boom-clang-boom of a steam hammer pounded at the back of MacDonell's head. Past the foundry a string of rusty chemical rail cars shuddered, then jolted forward with a cat-like shriek. In the adjacent salvage yard, the sputtering blue glow of cutting torches welcomed the bureau chief to another happy day.

Carol Clemmons stood nearby on dead grass, trying to hang on to a frisking animal. MacDonell stepped back and took a deep breath. The sharp odor of burnt metal percolated through his lungs.

Clemmons looked angry. "Sorry about the radio call, but I figured you needed to know."

He turned. "Did you cancel the ambulance?" He had to yell to be heard above the din of the foundry and the rail yard.

She looked at him and nodded her head. "I told that idiot this dog wasn't adoptable," she yelled back. "I told him we had no history on it. It's obviously never been socialized. I don't think the damn thing's got two fucking neurons to rub together."

"You tell him that, too?"

"Hell, yes. I told him it was way too much dog for a woman her age. She's in her seventies, for God's sake! I made sure he signed a waiver before I even brought it out." Clemmons struggled as the dog lunged hard against the leash, leapt, and snapped up a mouthful of empty air. She jerked back harder. "HEEL! you brainless clod."

MacDonell looked down at a fat, blue-eyed Siberian Husky mix. Its tail curled up loosely, and it was tall, too tall for the show ring. He guessed the animal was about four years old. It strained sideways against the leather as they made their way back up the cobblestone walk.

He held the door, Clemmons pulled hard, the Husky gagged and wheeled backward. Reaching out with the side of his boot, he gave the dog a gentle nudge forward. They passed through the glass-walled entry, into the quiet.

"Lupe showed him smaller dogs; a couple puppies, and a half-dozen nice little kittens." Her thin voice echoed in the high empty arch of the domed lobby. "They've already been neutered, have their shots, and are ready to go. But oh no, he had to have this particular nitwit for dear old mom."

A smile flickered in MacDonell's eyes. He rubbed his ear as he guided the conversation to a softer level. "He was looking for a guard dog, then?"

"He wasn't interested in anything small," she said, "or *deflowered*—his words. You'll notice the horny thing's hung like a draft horse."

"You tell him the law?" MacDonell asked.

"You don't tell an asshole like that anything."

"Where'd we pick it up?"

"Running down the middle of Memorial Drive. Some yuppie lawyer called after he caught it hiking its leg on his Miata. Not on the tire, mind you. On the hood."

The dog pulled hard and MacDonell looked it over again. It weighed a hundred and ten pounds, maybe more. The tongue lolled out to one side and its black-rimmed lips pulled back revealing long, perfect, snow-white canine teeth, and equally perfect premolars. The soft fur on the face and above the eyes was white, highlighted with smoky markings changing rapidly to black. The eyes were rimmed in black, the lashes inked, as if eye makeup had been applied. The chest was deep, the body much too long, the tongue glistening. The smell of it was fresh, exciting, alive. An attractive, if not quite perfect, specimen. For an instant MacDonell was angry but he forced the feeling away.

"Haven't you told your people to keep visitors out of the wards unless they're looking for their own animals?"

"The man's a city councilman, Doctor. He let everyone know that." She hesitated for a second. "Showed up at 7:00 on the dot and knew where he was going."

"How'd he know about this particular dog? He didn't just wander in here at 7:00 a.m. with his mother."

"I'd like to know that myself," Clemmons said, scowling. "The old lady didn't say two words."

"I told him to get her a bird."

Clemmons nodded. "I heard. What he ought to do is spring for an electronic security system and go visit the sweet old thing more often. Oh, listen. Guess who she's related to?"

"Who?"

"She's old man Pitkin's sister."

"Oh God, the dumpster maven? Did you explain what we'll have to do next?"

"I talked to her while I was cleaning the wound. She's not much like her brother. Not proud of him, by the way, but he is family. I explained to her the face and hands were the worst possible place to get bitten, rabies-wise."

"She object?"

Clemmons shook her head. "Not when I told her we had no owner and no vaccination history on the dog."

MacDonell looked at the straining animal again. "A little snappish," he said, bending forward and studying the animal carefully. "And it could stand to lose some weight."

"It's getting ready to lose about ten pounds…The friggin' hard way."

"I know."

Clemmons jerked the lead again. Turning to the animal she whispered, "Heel, you stupid sonofabitch!" Then to MacDonell, "I don't think dumb-shit here has had a collar on in it's entire fucking life. SIT!" The dog's tail bounced and flared. The dog skittered sideways, pawed the collar, and made clicking sounds with its teeth, but remained standing.

MacDonell cleared his throat. "Be careful with it, Carol," he said, then changed the subject. "What about brother Pitkin's critters?"

She wiped the back of her free hand across her forehead. "They're all eaten up with parasites, and one of the pups has a wet-sounding pneumonia. It may not make it."

"Worm the ones that can survive it, vaccinate them all, and make sure they eat."

"The one pup was too weak for the swim so we had to dip it by hand. I never saw so many fleas. And stink? My God."

MacDonell edged toward the adoption windows. Four cats sat preening and a fifth rubbed the bars. "Has he been around to see them?" he asked.

"Late last night for about an hour. He was pretty subdued."

"Did Frank ever go back out and pick up the big one?"

"I don't think they went back."

MacDonell rolled his eyes.

"Why?" she asked.

MacDonell gazed toward the windows. "Oh, nothing."

Clemmons looked skeptical. "Did it…?"

He lifted his hat and rubbed his fingers lightly across the top of his head. "Besides, my shots are all up to date."

"You sure?"

"Positive," he said, screwing the hat on again.

The Husky danced and scratched the epoxy floor as Clemmons fought the lanky beast down the security passage. A slender Siamese cat ignored it through the glass.

MacDonell shook his head. "I'll have an officer fill out a bite form and you can send the head-to-lab card over after you've put it to sleep. I'll be in my office."

He hustled along the colorful front passage, striding to keep up with the broad green and yellow arrows emblazoning the walls. Wide, bright windows flashed by, feed pans rattled, water was running. A door opened ahead of him. His chief cashier stepped through in a brilliant shaft of sunlight. She had a look of amazement on her face.

"Doc, what happened to your new hat?"

"It's a long story. Let's just say it got 'et."

"Well, that one looks like somebody ran over it."

He smiled. "This one's probably older than you are."

She smiled back, pushed in a door with her hip and disappeared.

Stepping out of the most sophisticated animal control building in North America, MacDonell let the heavy outer door slam behind him. From a distance he heard the steam hammer again. He moved across to the old administration building and unlocked his office.

Inside, the clang of the hammer faded but refused to die. He collected his thoughts. What a way to start the day. MacDonell lay the grubby old Stetson gently on the credenza, cursing Pitkin's soul. Then, like a thousand other mornings, he hung his rumpled coat behind the inner door, clipped off the tie, and rolled up his sleeves. His arms were tanned and strong. He opened the inner door, spoke to Willie, asked who had hot water. She smiled and pointed to Connie's office door.

Would he proof-read the report today?

He would.

Three neat stacks of bite investigations were lined up across his desk, and a half dozen forms had been stuffed under the inner door. He gathered them up. The ritual was followed as surely as if a groove existed in the earth; complaints, reports, complaints of reports, reports of complaints.

***

At 10:00 the sunburned entrepreneur from Australia showed up: John Neville Martin-Robertson, read the business card. He was slender, with bright blue eyes, a shock of blond hair, and miserably arrayed in a three piece suit.

MacDonell was intrigued by his letter. He was asking for a trial of a high-tech dog tag, a spin-off from a cattle tag now in production in Sidney. In the beef and dairy industry, the idea was for the tag to transmit signals opening feedlot gates, activating scales, measuring milk production, and triggering a computerized data base.

The man had a lopsided jaw, spit his words like a machine gun, dropping H's like confetti. MacDonell listened intently. The dog tag he was touting was about the size of a quarter, but three times as thick. It was sturdy gray plastic with a small clear window, smaller than a grain of popcorn, and sensitive to UV light.

Martin-Robertson grinned. "It's all done remote, without laying 'ands on the bloody animal. Look 'ere mate, anyone can see the value of that."

"Show me," MacDonell said.

They took the tag outside and hung it on the fence. The Aussie produced a UV light. The beam came from a small box-like device with a pistol grip on the bottom and a barrel on the front. The barrel was the size of a soup can. "Adapts to the cigar lighter," said Martin-Robertson. "The tag contains the transmitter, about nine mil." He held up two fingers with a small space between. "Sends out a coded nine digit number." He aimed in the direction of the tag and pulled the trigger. There was an audible beep.

"So?" asked MacDonell. "What have we got?"

Martin-Robertson showed the light source to MacDonell. "Here's what we 'ave, mate."

On the back a dial read 000,010,114.

"And this number corresponds to just one tag?"

"Right-o," the man said. "With more development and a link to your database, you Texans could tell if a tyke has its rabies shots, where it lives, who owns it…and you could 'ave it all right in the cab of your dog wagon." He passed the light to MacDonell. "Broadcasts for twenty seconds."

"Nifty."

"And our prototype has a twenty-year life span. Rather than posting a new tag each year, this one might well last the lifetime of the doggie."

MacDonell was impressed.

"It contains a lithium wafer which we project will have a useful lifetime of ten years.

MacDonell cocked his head. "That's pretty slick. We have a similar device that vets inject under the skin. It's used for racehorses and expensive dogs. Costs about twenty bucks a pop. Trouble is, it uses a hand scanner and you have to catch the animal to read the tag." He looked at the man. "I know this sounds cynical, but a lot of Texans find it cheaper, and a lot less trouble, to get a new pooch. They'd rather do that than come down here and bail one out." MacDonell watched the man's eyes. "You mentioned a test. Is that what you want from me?"

The Aussie nodded. "No cost, mate. I'll provide an 'undred prototypes and a scanner," he explained. "In six months we'd like to 'ear. A page, maybe two, of your impressions. We'll pay the return down-under."

After he left MacDonell stowed the equipment in a file drawer and proceeded to read the technical data. He was cheered by the colorful accent and the lighthearted attitude of Mr. Martin-Robertson. MacDonell wasn't sure how he would structure a valid field test, but he knew he could.

***

At about 3:00 p.m. MacDonell's blood sugar plummeted and he snatched a minute to visit the candy machine. Back at his desk, Willie put through a call from councilmember Dockery.

"Listen, MacDonell," he started out.

"How's your mother, Mr. Dockery?"

"She's okay. Now listen. I got a friend who wants that big Husky. You probably know him—Robin Paine."

MacDonell exhaled and ran his hand across the top of his bald head. He'd assumed Clemmons had explained the procedure. "I'm sorry, Mr. Dockery, but the animal's not available."

"What do you mean, 'not available?' It was available this morning."

"Well, no sir, it wasn't. It wasn't in our adoption ward and therefore it was still legally the property of its owner until 8:00 a.m."

"So the owner picked it up?"

MacDonell was wishing he had taken Willie to a late lunch. "No," he said. "We put the dog to sleep shortly before 9:00 this morning."

There was a pause. "And just who the hell authorized that?" Dockery asked.

MacDonell bristled. "That's a decision I made. It's one I have to make several times a day."

"I thought you held them ten days."

"We do if we have an owner."

"Hell, MacDonell. You know damn well that dog didn't have rabies!"

"I'm sorry, Mr. Dockery, but knowing isn't the best evidence, especially if the city gets into a lawsuit."

"That was a good pooch and I had somebody who wanted it. Next time you get one like that, you call me—understand?"

"Mr. Dockery, the dog was not a good candidate for adoption."

"How the hell do you know?"

"After thirty years I can pretty much tell."

"Aw, bullshit!"

***

At 4:00 MacDonell remembered dinner. Jeannie promised chicken-fried steak, hash browns, and a nice cream gravy. He put the final draft of his activities report off to the side and signed a few supply requests for Connie Oaks.

Willie Fish buzzed in. "Doc, there's a Miss Longley here to see you."

MacDonell stood up as his visitor stepped in. Longley looked taller than he remembered, and in her cream-colored riding pants and high leather boots she looked attractive and stylish. She was in a long-sleeved white blouse with a small loose bow at the neck. A brown leather riding crop sprouted from the top of her left boot. The blond hair was cut short around the ears and tapered in back. She smiled broadly and extended her hand. Longley's chin was square, and she had lots of straight white teeth.

"Janie! You look great. Been riding, I see." He grasped her strong hand with both of his.

"'J.D.,' Doc. It's 'J.D.' these days."

"Since when?"

"It's all a part of the image. The clothes, the name. New life, new beginnings. I see you did the same thing." She nodded, indicating MacDonell's grizzled chin.

"Oh, the beard. Well, no…for me it's sort of a disguise." He motioned her to a chair. "After the hair on top went, I thought I needed a more impressive countenance."

Longley laughed. "Same difference. I wanted to make a clean break from the Air Force."

"Well, something must be going good for you. You're not the same skinny kid I remember." He recalled the stubborn, slender young sergeant fighting to make her authority stick in an almost all-male career field.

"That was more than ten years ago, Doctor Mac."

"What have you been up to for the past ten years?"

She beamed. "Well, I pulled two consecutive three-year tours with the dog school at Lackland after I got back from Europe. Then I got transferred to McConnell. I spent three years up there until I retired."

MacDonell nodded. "You said on the phone you already have a job here in the big city?"

"Yeah, sort of," Longley replied, smoothing her riding pants. MacDonell noted the strong hands again. "I'm really doing a lot better than I thought I would."

"Tell me about it," MacDonell said with sympathy. Martinez told him she'd been riffed after the incident with her dog. He tried to keep the doubt out of his voice. Retirement was one thing, a Reduction In Force was another.

Longley paused, indicating it was really not his business, then asked, "So, what's the poop on the job here? Sgt. Martinez was pretty sketchy about it."

"I need a training officer," MacDonell replied. "My field chief doesn't have the time or the talent." He leaned back and looked her up and down. "We're planning to convert one of my existing field positions," MacDonell said, turning the notion over as he spoke.

Longley nodded.

MacDonell continued. "The old-timers are going to raise hell when I do. I've already been accused of military bias." He gave his head a brisk rub with his knuckles. "Still, six years at the dog school? Experience like that is darn hard to come by," he mused. "It'll be worth the fight."

"Let's just think about it, okay?"

"Sure. Now tell me more about yourself. Want to look the shop over? We can walk and talk."

The conversation ebbed and flowed as he conducted her on a grand tour. On the second floor he pointed out where his predecessor intended to build an elaborate surgery, classrooms, and new office space. He showed her the empty elevator shafts. The third floor, he said, contained space for a year's supply of bulk dog food, which could be gravity-fed to the first floor feed room. "It's never been used," he said.

When they stepped out of the empty second floor onto the wide landing, the sun was a dull orange ball. She had been fascinated by the size, shape, layout, and dynamics of the building, as well as all the labor saving innovations. She asked all the right questions, said all the right things. He could tell it was the most imposing animal shelter she had ever seen, and her concise observation from the second floor balcony said it all. "Looks like the Starship Enterprise landed at the city dump."

MacDonell grinned.

"You should be proud," she said.

"It's got problems. In spite of all the planning there are a few leaks around the upper windows. Nothing like the old place, though."

"It's the best shelter I've ever seen."

"I can't take any credit. My predecessor designed it and went through all the labor pains."

"How come it's only half done?"

"The city authorized bond funds, but waited years to approve the spending. By that time the money would only buy half as much. He had to make some tough choices, so he decided to solve the animal problems first and sacrifice a lot of the people areas. He'd actually talked about a day-care center and a weight room on the top deck."

Longley stood on tiptoes and squinted. "What's that?" she asked. Beyond the roof of the administration building, the gabled end of a long tin barn arose.

"That's the old kennel building from the fifties. The monstrosity on the right is the one I told you about. It was built in the seventies."

"And he really sprayed water on the roof?"

"He sure as heck did. The council never came around, and when they finally said they would, it hadn't rained for two months. He wanted them to see what these people had to put up with."

"And…?"

"Water poured in like the boiler room on the Titanic."

In a few minutes MacDonell led Longley to the parking lot and got into his oxidizing city car. "We better hit the road. Jeannie's probably waiting dinner." He sat until she pulled up in her shiny red Bronco, then they moved in tandem through the gates and up onto the Eastex.

The trip north was smooth, no tie-ups, no fender-benders. The heaviest traffic leaked away at the big airport, and in tiny Humble the streets were quiet. Above the strings of dim headlights, two fish ducks, slender-billed mergansers, shadowed the San Jacinto River looking for a roost. To his right, MacDonell saw the river's shallow brown water, bordered by a thin ribbon of *Liquidamber* sweetgums, the burnt orange leaves barely visible in the failing twilight. Together the vehicles skimmed over the bridge, up and off at North Park Drive where bursts of red sumac and florescent yellow willows dotted the route. Kingwood itself, or "The Livable Forest" as it was advertised, was lush, murky green, and getting dark.

The radio sputtered and the dispatcher asked for double O three. MacDonell answered it.

CHAPTER SEVEN

"I don't envy you that trip every day," Longley said as she clicked the door of the Bronco.

"Twice every day," MacDonell replied.

They sauntered up the driveway, he a half-step ahead. He glanced back, a bit envious of her flashy off-road wheels. A monstrous black cat with back-lit yellow eyes met them at the front door. The long tail twitched and a serious warning rumbled in the cat's throat. MacDonell scooped her up.

"What's her name?" Longley asked, reaching to stroke the long glossy hair.

The cat hissed.

"Carbon Copy," he said with a tired grin. "I'll put her up. She can be a booger when she wants to."

In a second Jeannie appeared. Her newly-auburned hair was piled on top of her head, her face pink from cooking. "My goodness, is that Janie Longley?"

"It's J.D. now," MacDonell said, then watched as a perceptive look slipped across his wife's face.

The women shook hands and smiled, then Jeannie encircled Longley with a warm hug. "Well, J.D., you've gotten all grown up, haven't you?" she said, looking her guest up and down.

Longley shrugged. "I ought to be. I'm thirty-four now."

"It doesn't seem possible. Come on, come inside, supper's almost ready." She pulled off her apron. "I must look like Betty Crocker's grandmother."

"You haven't changed a bit," Longley commented.

"Certainly not," Jeannie laughed. "And I hear pigs are now running their own airlines."

MacDonell put the cat in the study and closed the door. He retired to the master bedroom, hung his coat, took off his tie, changed from boots to loafers, and proceeded to wash up. "What smells so good?" he hollered.

As promised, Jeannie had prepared the typical Texas fare, but with a few touches of her own. The good china was out and a pair of dark green candles graced the center of the table. It was a rare occasion. A light, thinly-sliced cucumber salad with a sweet vinegar dressing started off the meal. The chicken fried steak was tender, and at the same time crisp. The hash browns were golden and the cream gravy was smooth and thick; white pepper, no lumps. Jeannie winked at MacDonell about that. The iced tea was sweet, but with no one looking MacDonell added another half-teaspoon of sugar to his glass.

Conversation brought back a flood of memories of their years in Europe. Food was a prime topic. They talked of sauerbraten, sweet red cabbage, and heavy bread. MacDonell mentioned the delicious trout, classic poached Forelle blau and crispy Müllerin, the wursts and sausages, ahh yes. His wife recalled the delicate sauces, hot pommes frits, nutty Dutch cheeses, and Belgian waffles. Their diplomatic guest praised the local fare.

After the meal they moved across to the living area of a spacious multipurpose room, leaving the dishes on the table. Longley sat on the raised hearth and hugged her knees. Above her a .30-.30 Winchester hung over the fireplace. Above that a four foot eagle, hand-carved from Philippine monkey pod, loomed over the room. Porcelain plates displaying European game birds decorated the walls. The room was bright, even with its dark oak furnishings.

MacDonell selected a heavy leather-covered oak chair. Representations of wild boar, Hirsch or German red deer, and the smaller roe deer decorated the dark blue and brown salt-ceramic tiles inlaid into flat spaces on the heavy turned legs. Jeannie sat on the matching couch and looked past Longley into the flames. Another magnificent red deer, this one in bronze, dominated the tiled coffee table. Rich brown flocati rugs from Thessaloniki covered the wall-to-wall carpet. Animals seemed to be everywhere. Even the carved chess pieces were lions and cougars, kangaroos and bears. Nobody but a veterinarian would live here.

At about 9:00 p.m. Longley asked about the dog. "Where's Diamond Lil?" she said. "I haven't seen her yet."

MacDonell looked at Jeannie.

There was a flicker of unspoken gloom, then Jeannie brightened, "Bring her in," she whispered.

"Let me show you her latest old-dog trick," MacDonell said, slipping off his loafers. He padded to the kitchen and out through the connecting garage door. Diamond Lil was curled up on her thick pallet. She raised her head.

"Come," he whispered.

The old German Wirehaired Pointer struggled up. It took some time getting through the kitchen. Her toenails clicked on the tile and she slipped a bit as she rounded the corner into the dining room. She stopped at the edge of the carpet, looking first to Jeannie for permission.

"It's okay," Jeannie said.

The dog hesitated, then came on in. Seeing the guest she slowed, then quivered a warm greeting.

Longley rested on one knee and beckoned. "Come here, old thing."

Unsure, the dog looked again at Jeannie, then brushed her lightly as she passed and headed for the young woman. She sat before the stranger, put her chin and big nose on the knee of Longley's riding pants. She was out of breath.

It didn't take much time for Longley to recognize a problem and look over at MacDonell. "Heartworms?" she asked.

"She's been negative for years," he replied.

"But congestive heart failure?" Longley asked.

"She's been on Digoxin for about two years now. We're considering combining it with Milrinone if things get worse."

Longley showed the dog her hands, palms up. A soft snuff and Lil cocked her ears. The woman rubbed the supple, paper-thin ears, stroked the dog's head, then ran her hand down and patted her side. "You don't remember me, do you, sweetheart?"

The dog responded by lifting one front foot and placing it on Longley's knee, no weight, almost not touching, then removing it just as quickly.

Lil turned her head and looked back at Jeannie. The ears drooped and the tail moved with a slow steady pulse.

"Here's her trick," Jeannie said. She pointed at MacDonell's shoes. "Get grandpa's slippers," she said. "Go on, get grandpa's slippers." MacDonell stood by the dining room table, watching.

The dog rose and started for the shoes, missed a step, then went on. Picking up the first shoe in her teeth, she ambled to the hall, swayed on unsteady legs, and disappeared. In a moment she reappeared in the door. Head up, she carried a soft leather moccasin. She deposited it at MacDonell's feet, then repeated the process. Task completed, she came to Jeannie for her reward.

"Watch this," Jeannie said, rubbing the dog's neck.

The dog sat on Jeannie's foot. After a minute of having her shoulder rubbed, she leaned against Jeannie's leg. In another minute, the grizzled body was lying flat on the heavy flocati rug, but her head was still in intimate contact with Jeannie's foot. Chocolate brown eyes kept everyone under warm surveillance. Every so often she would twitch her eyebrows toward MacDonell or back to Longley.

"I don't know what to do," Jeannie remarked in a whisper. "I have to sit here for half an hour sometimes before I can get my foot out."

The three talked late into the evening about a wide variety of things: MacDonell's and Jeannie's bird watching, Houston's crime situation and the problems of the homeless, politics and taxes; Longley's plans for the future and theirs. J.D. wanted to train horses and dogs and have a stable of her own. MacDonell confessed to wanting to write a mystery novel and do a little fly fishing. Jeannie would have liked one more tour of duty in Europe.

"I hope you can come to work for Duncan," Jeannie said. "He needs all the help he can get."

MacDonell winked at his wife. "I think things are going pretty well, if you consider how far we've come."

"Duncan, they're a thankless…well, except for Mr. Oaks and Dr. Clemmons. And, of course, there's his secretary, Miss Fish. She's Duncan's real boss. Have you met Carol Clemmons?"

"Did I?" Longley asked. "No, I don't think so."

"She's different, to say the least," Jeannie said. "How about Mr. Oaks? He's such a sweet man. He needs to relax, though. He's so rigid."

"I don't think Connie would like to hear you call him sweet," MacDonell said.

"He's the black man, right? The supply chief?"

MacDonell nodded and looked into the fire.

Jeannie picked up the conversation. "There was a lot of bickering when Duncan first got there, and none of the female officers had ever been promoted. He's had his hands full."

"She makes it sound pretty bad," MacDonell said. He rubbed his hands together and smiled. "Truthfully, J.D., I find more interesting things going on down there in one day than I could find in a month if I had a practice. Crazy, weird things. One day we'll get a Bengal tiger and have to figure what we're going to feed it; the next thing you know, I'll have a half dozen cops in the lobby, arresting one of my clerks for food stamp fraud." MacDonell shook his head. "Pay was a big problem. Still is, but we've made progress." He stretched his legs and wiggled his toes. "We'll pick up forty cats living with an old lady in a one-room shack, five minutes later the phone rings and some fruitcake's been caught sacrificing chickens to Haitian fertility gods. It's nuts."

MacDonell stretched his arms. "We've pulled ten-foot snakes out of toilets, and alligators out of bathtubs. Once we found a Indian cobra hidden in a man's washing machine." He leaned forward and put his elbows on his knees. "Had a knife fight in the lobby one morning over a coonhound. And did you ever try to get a horse out of a glass elevator? I have. To top it off, and this is painful, three of my former employees are guests of the Texas Department of Corrections for selling cocaine."

"Like I said, it's a zoo," Jeannie put in.

They all laughed.

"Sounds like fun, all right," said Longley.

"I just wish he could find a little time to relax," Jeannie said, displaying a bit of worry.

MacDonell plunged forward. "The law enforcement is the most interesting. We get involved in a lot of court cases. Everything from animal cruelty to numb-heads selling smuggled parrots along the road. We've even had cases where we've had to go into somebody's backyard to dig up a bite suspect."

Jeannie got up and started for the kitchen. "If it's so much fun, how come your blood pressure's up and your doctor has you on medication?"

"That's not the job's fault," MacDonell called after her. "It's lack of support," he said to Longley. "Eighty percent of my expenditures go for salary, and the department's cut my budget almost every year."

Longley stretched and looked around the room. "Your sweet secretary told me you wheedled a brand new computerized animal management system."

"The secret is to spend all your equipment money. Most bureaus budget more than they can spend. Connie worked out a system. He stuffs purchase orders in the pipeline, then runs down to the other end and fishes them out. Every other supply chief sits on his prat and hopes things will work out. Last year Connie got equipment money from two other bureaus because they couldn't get it all in the pipeline."

"You had something to do with it."

"I'm the talent scout."

"Don't believe that," Jeannie piped from the kitchen.

MacDonell went on for several minutes explaining how he maintained his managerial sanity in an insane system. Jeannie brought in ice cream with a splash of Kahlua. They talked some more. Then it was time for Longley to go. Employment, she said, was the last thing on her mind right now. MacDonell showed his disappointment, but couldn't hold it against her. To his surprise, though, Jeannie exchanged phone numbers with the younger woman and extended another invitation.

"It's been good seeing both of you again," Longley said before driving away. "Thanks for the supper, too."

MacDonell stood in the driveway with one arm around his wife. He watched the red Bronco disappear into the pine-scented Kingwood evening. The night would be cold.

"She's the same, but different," Jeannie said, as they turned to go in. "I'm not sure how, quieter maybe, more serious than in Germany. Of course, she's older."

"So am I, apparently."

Jeannie gave him a puzzled look.

"*Grandpa's* slippers? Jeez-Louise."

"Well, she definitely *looks* older," Jeannie said, jabbing him in the ribs. "And she's got problems. While you were changing your clothes she told me her mother is very sick."

MacDonell had the real answer. "How would you feel if you got bounced out of a twenty-year career? It's no fun getting riffed."

"I thought she said, 'retired.'"

MacDonell rolled his eyes. "A rif is a reduction in force, downsizing and weeding out problems at the same time. No retirement check either."

After awhile MacDonell brought Lil's pallet from the garage and put it in its usual place on the kitchen floor. He talked to her for a full five minutes, stroking the top of her head, massaging her ears. After he got her settled he went to his study and fiddled with his computer. That morning, before he'd left for work, a squadron of Cedar Waxwings pulled a raid on the pyracantha bush next to his feeder. The birds weren't unusual this time of year, but the numbers had been breathtaking. And, true to form, they got plastered on the fermented berries. Before he went to bed he outlined the event in a text file, set the alarms, and locked up the house.

"It's going to be another humdinger of a day tomorrow," he said, as he strained over the convexity of his belly to pull off his socks.

Jeannie was already in bed. "How do you know that?"

"Radio call on the way home," MacDonell said. "Just after I crossed the bridge, Sergeant Gallegos called to tell me Pitkin has taken up residence outside the back gate. He wants his dogs back with no out-of-pocket expense. Gallegos said one TV station sent a crew. I expect they'll have film at 10:00."

"It's already after 11:00. We missed it," she said.

"Good," he said, clicking off the light.

"My Rossi came today," she said. "UPS delivered it."

"Good," he muttered.

"Went out to the range," she whispered.

He was asleep.

CHAPTER EIGHT

"*D*OCTOR MENGELE! DOCTOR MENGELE!" Alexander Pitkin screamed. "IF YOU HARM MY DOGS, HUMAN BLOOD WILL FLOW!" To his once-white shirt, soiled pants, and unraveling sweater, the man had added a battered top hat. Around his neck on a string, a hand-lettered placard. It read: City Killers!

"Dr. MacDonell, do you have a comment?" a Channel 2 reporter asked, extending a microphone up to the car window.

MacDonell hadn't seen this one before. A young face, short shiny-black hair and Asian eyes. She's beautiful, he thought. With looks like that and assigned anyway to the dog pound beat, she had to be a rookie.

Rolling down the glass, MacDonell answered. "Can't say I appreciate being called a Nazi. Other than that, no, I don't have a comment."

Pitkin hobbled over to the car, bent forward and spit an unhealthy gob of green phlegm on the windshield. The reporter stepped back, rubbed a Kleenex on her sleeve, and wrinkled her nose in disgust.

MacDonell drove on through the gate and over to the truck wash. He applied a little soap and the power nozzle, then parked the dripping car in its usual space.

Inside, Willie had already received the first call of the day. "Starting early," she said, handing over the receiver. "It's Dr. Trimble's information lady."

He took the call standing up.

"How are you this morning?" the young voice whimpered. It was the Public Information Officer's standard conversation starter. When she put her mind to it she had a Boston accent. And it always intrigued MacDonell for about fifteen seconds.

"Fine as frog's hair," he replied, a touch of Texas color.

"What?" she said.

"Fine. I'm fine."

"What's going on over there now?" she asked.

Feisty after the incident at the gate, he came back with, "who wants to know?"

"The director wants to know, that's who."

"Oh yeah. Put *him* on."

The voice sounded like bored royalty.

"Duncan, this is Sterling. What's going on? We understand a TV crew is over there, and some fellow is yelling and walking around with a sign."

MacDonell recognized the nasal drone. He felt flattered. He'd heard his boss's voice only twice in three years. "It's old man Pitkin," he answered, staring at the clock on Willie's wall. "Monday we picked up his dogs. Now he wants 'em back."

"Who?"

"Alexander Pitkin."

"And just who is Alexander Pitkin?"

Here was a dangerous opportunity to sink his own boat. "He's what we call a troll," MacDonell said. "He lives under one of the elevated highways with a pack of mangy mutts."

"You mean dogs?"

MacDonell wanted to chuckle. "Canines, yes. But in this case there's no question. They're mutts, sir."

"Are you going to let him have them?"

"Of course, after the usual formalities. Vaccinations and licenses, and he's also exceeded the ordinanced limit on numbers. City Code,

Chapter 6., he needs a kennel license if he wants to keep more than three adults."

"I see…and why is the media over there?"

MacDonell rubbed his temples with the thumb and little finger of his free hand. "I don't know why they're here. I suppose because the old coot called them. He usually wants to make his point with a high profile."

"Usually? You mean this has happened before?"

"About once every eighteen months," MacDonell answered. He closed his eyes, waiting.

"Dr. MacDonell," Trimble began, "I want you to take care of this matter as quickly and as quietly as possible." His thin voice lowered almost to a whisper. "We can't have our department picketed. And especially by street people."

"May I ask who called you about this?"

"That isn't important."

"Are you asking me to give this bird some kind of special handling?"

"If that's what it requires, yes. It's important that you get him and his sign out of sight."

"What about Mrs. Flannery's cats?" MacDonell asked.

"What?"

"Mrs. Flannery. She's the lady who complained about his dogs. She said they'd killed two of her cats. Which is why I went out there in the first place. What do I tell her?"

There was a lengthy pause in the conversation.

"You do understand, sir, the lady threatened to call Annabel Mooney if I didn't do something." MacDonell smiled to himself. He'd been doing this job for six years before Trimble came along.

"I've heard of her," Trimble admitted.

"So what would you like me to do?"

"I want you to go ahead and handle it, I guess." MacDonell could almost hear the wheels grinding. "But make sure you keep the department out of it."

"That won't be easy."

"I'm not concerned with how easy it is, doctor."

MacDonell was quiet for a few seconds. "It would help, sir, if I could get some support in these situations. We are a part of the department,—last time I looked."

"We're talking about dogs, Dr. MacDonell."

Bragg and Clemmons slipped in during the last half of the conversation. They stood around in Willie's office with grins on their faces until MacDonell dropped the receiver into its cradle. He scowled. "Who told him Pitkin was over here?"

Clemmons looked at Bragg. "Probably saw it. He's got a big TV in his office."

Bragg shrugged.

MacDonell retreated to his office, sat, put both feet on his desk, and held his head. "Wants to avoid confrontations, and above all keep him out of it."

"How in hell are we supposed to hear people's complaints, lock up other people's pooches, enforce the law, and not be a little confrontational?" Bragg scoffed.

MacDonell leaned back, extended his arms, palms up, and then clasped his fingers atop his glistening pate.

"I suppose he wants us to waive the charges?" Clemmons asked, pursing her lips.

"No, no. Standard fees," MacDonell replied, coming to sudden attention and putting his feet down. "Ask the old man to apply for a separate kennel license and furnish addresses for each group of three adults animals. They're all more than six months old."

"Can we do that?"

"The ordinance doesn't say we can't."

"He won't do it," Clemmons said. "You know what the old bastard is like."

"Yeah, I know. He'll do it or surrender a few."

MacDonell looked up. Willie was at the door, signaling to Bragg. He saw her, seemed annoyed, and stalked out.

"The charges are already \$470," Clemmons reminded her boss. "Pitkin can't pay that kind of money unless he gets help from his angel."

"Trimble said to handle it." MacDonell waggled his head. "I'm handling it."

"I'd tell Trimble to get his skinny little ass over here and haul off the friggin' dogs himself," Clemmons announced.

I bet you would, MacDonell thought. "I think I've pushed it about as far as I care to, Carol. Next time he calls, you talk to him. Tell him he can come over and help you ice a few cats, or unload the cooler in the morgue."

"Oh, I'd love to," she grimaced, then stuck out her tongue.

Bragg stomped back in. "Doc, I gotta go out to the south side. Some high school FFA project got wiped out last night. Lady says she seen a pack of dogs running the neighborhood. Gallegos sent a truck, but nobody could get close enough to dart one."

"What kind of project?"

"Pigs."

MacDonell couldn't hide his frustration.

"Try a primal scream," Clemmons said. "Works for me."

Bragg looked back, puzzled. "You people are nuts," he called over his shoulder. "I'm outta here."

"This really isn't very funny," MacDonell said after Bragg left.

"I don't know how you stand it," Clemmons said. "I'm glad you've got the stick, albeit the shitty end."

***

For most of the early afternoon the director's PIO kept MacDonell's phones warm trying to learn the city ordinances governing animal licenses and kennel limitations. The first half-dozen explanations may have been too complex. At 1:59 MacDonell instructed Willie to fax the city's entire thirty-page animal ordinance to the health director's office.

Except for Pitkin marching up and down and yelling at the trucks, the day progressed without further incident. A little after 3:30 Willie buzzed. "Dr. Clemmons called over. She say to tell you Robin Paine is in the building."

MacDonell's shoulders fell. Paine, the pal of councilman Dockery, had been a deputy constable. Now he ran a school for protection dogs and served as spokesperson for fringe elements of the animal rights community. He was thick with the Ft. Bend County constable's office, and loved to go on dog fight raids with a TV camera.

Two or three years ago Paine got a lot of press by referring to an underfunded animal control agency in Waco as the Auschwitz of animal land. The woman running the place got fired.

MacDonell fixed a serious look on his face. He needed a sugar fix. His hands quivered.

"Comandante," Paine boomed, as he came striding into MacDonell's office, "…mind if I come in?"

MacDonell gave him a stern look, but didn't stand up. "Don't give me that 'Comandante' crap, Robin."

"You run this death camp, don't you?"

MacDonell ignored the remark. "Your pal Mr. Dockery was in yesterday trying to adopt a pet for his mother."

"So?"

"So it nipped his mother in the face."

"Too bad."

"This morning he said he wanted it for you."

"Oh really? Where is it?"

"Where do you think?"

"You know, you'd scare up a lot more suitable adopters if you'd move this place out of the ghetto and into the country."

"That's brilliant."

"Yeah…the neighborhood is holding you back…" Paine lowered his voice and glanced out at Willie, "You should try to thin out the spooks and españolies you have working for you."

MacDonell boiled. He knew Paine was right about the neighborhood, but he didn't like the disparagement of his employees. He thought the young man was trying to instigate something. "Speak up, Mr. Paine. You have such a clever way of expressing yourself. Maybe I could get you on tape."

"Adopters are mostly middle-class whites, Doc."

MacDonell strummed his fingers on the desk top. In spite of the bold approach, Paine was a thin, pale, college type. His clothes didn't fit and his shirt had just come from the laundry. A tag was still on the sleeve and the folds showed. MacDonell stared at the young man. "Do you have some business with us?" he said.

Paine smirked. "You picked up old man Pitkin's animals. We'd like to know what you're going to do with them?"

"Who's this *we* you're referring to?"

"The Coalition of Humane Associations of Greater Houston and Harris County," he said, ballooning out his chest.

"Training protection dogs is just a sideline with you?"

Paine's expression remained cool. "I have multiple interests. Right now I'm here about your friend Pitkin."

MacDonell leaned back in his chair and put his hands behind his head. "So you're a humane society *and* a killer dog trainer. What hat are you wearing today?"

"For openers, I…we…don't want you to give those dogs back to the senile old sonovabitch," Paine said. His stringy hair flared as he spoke. He had the complexion of raw buttermilk, and the glossy black stone on his loose-fitting string-tie matched his beady eyes.

MacDonell raised his eyebrows. "What makes you think he's so terrible?"

Canis

Paine smiled through yellow teeth. "The old man has never been dealt with properly. This time we're demanding you solve his problems. Before we have to do it."

MacDonell eyed him. Did he not know of the relationship between Dockery and Pitkin? Was he being set up? "In case you forgot, the old man's got rights like everyone else. I can't keep his animals without going to court, and neither can you."

"Take him to court. Charge him with cruelty."

"That's your solution to everything."

"He's homeless, for Christ's sake. He can't even take care of himself."

"Fifth amendment, Robin—due process. Homeless people have rights, whether you like it or not."

"Anybody who lives like he does and treats animals the way he does shouldn't be allowed…"

MacDonell interrupted. "Have you seen them?"

"Yeah, I went back there. They're skin and bones. He don't provide veterinary care. He sleeps with them. Plus, there's been rumors. You know what I mean."

"I don't care what you mean."

Paine clenched both fists and raised his voice. "The old man's a pervert. You know what he does. Charge him with cruelty."

MacDonell shook his head. "The pups are skinny, but they're not starved. We've no indication he's beaten any of them. And as far as the rest of it, it's called buggery, you little twerp, and it's all in your filthy little mind."

"In your heart you know I'm right," Paine added.

MacDonell smiled. This kid had never heard of Barry Goldwater. "Robin, Robin, Robin, I can't run this place with my heart. I have to follow the city ordinances and the laws of the state. I've got to prove intent to make a cruelty charge. You know that."

"You don't have to make it stick."

"In other words, harass him more than I already am?"

Paine sat, took a solemn breath, and wet his lips. "Dr. MacDonell, let me make a suggestion."

"I'm tired of your suggestions. Take a hike!"

"Hold the dogs," he said, "until we...until our coalition...can find them proper homes."

"Is your place full?"

"Temporarily we are full, but…"

MacDonell interrupted. "Don't you have some respectable white people just dying to provide foster homes."

"No, but…"

"I see," MacDonell said. "Well, I'm not holding them at taxpayers expense, and that's that. Now hit the road."

Paine stared at MacDonell.

MacDonell stood up. "I don't have time for this, Robin."

"You're saying you refuse to help these animals?"

"Listen, you…" MacDonell sucked in some air and re-thought what he wanted to say. "When and if they leave, these animals will have been vaccinated, dipped, and had a balanced ration for however many days it takes."

"I thought you cared about animals."

MacDonell folded his arms across his chest. Across the street the steam hammer began pounding on a hot ingot.

"Hit the road," MacDonell whispered.

Paine snorted and huffed out the door.

MacDonell visited the machine for a diet Dr. Pepper, then returned to his desk. He studied a milk goat application and tried to relax. Later he signed a few letters and read a draft proposal for some new statewide animal legislation. At exactly 4:25 p.m. the phone buzzed and he listened to the health director again, this time compliments of Robin Paine. Trimble expounded at great length on Paine's sympathetic feelings for the animal world. Although he couldn't put his finger on exactly what Paine was offering, Trimble concluded that Pitkin and his animals would be better off if a private humane organization was handling things. MacDonell took a roundabout, poorly-organized ass chewing. He explained one more time that the dogs had been picked up on a dangerous animal complaint, the kind of thing humane organizations always steered away from.

"I don't care about that," Trimble said.

"What can I do to make you happy?" MacDonell asked.

"Just listen..." Trimble talked on, philosophizing. In the future MacDonell would consider all offers of assistance from the humane community. He would accept them in the same gracious manner in which they were presented.

"The man's a bigot," MacDonell said.

"We're talking animals here," Trimble cut in.

"I'd love to give him the whole damn works."

"He told me he doesn't have room."

"Of course he did." MacDonell took a deep breath.

"I suggest you come up with something."

"I've got Pitkin and the press, or Flannery and Paine."

"Stick with the law."

"That's what the hell I'm trying to do."

"Don't get flippant with me, Doctor."

MacDonell listened again in silence, burning over the idea that Paine had better access to the director than he did.

Clemmons came across from the clinic late in the day. She had escorted Paine on his visit through the hospital ward and agreed he was up to no good. He seemed to be taking an unnatural interest in Pitkin's larger animals, she said, but she couldn't see how he would ever make a buck from the pups.

"He's a friend of councilman Dockery," MacDonell said.

"We've all got something to be ashamed of," Clemmons said, after giving the matter some thought.

***

Bragg got back at 5:15. He had six Polaroids of FFA feeder pigs, their throats ripped out, probably by large dogs. Bragg was enthusiastic. The high school and the homeowner's association, he reported, were outraged, both demanding MacDonell issue firearms to all district officers.

MacDonell was relieved when Willie's clock signaled the end of the day. Halfway across the San Jac bridge, Gallegos relayed a message from Dr. Clemmons: one of Pitkin's pups had taken a turn for the worse.

Chapter Nine

---

*E*arly Thursday, Clemmons asked for permission to euthanize Pitkin's sickest pup. "I'm the one licensed to practice around here," she said. "If the damn city won't authorize a modern approach to veterinary medicine, I say we put the poor thing out of its misery."

Meanwhile, a Chronicle editor recommended the dogs be released to their owner without any penalties. Nine Val Verde East homeowners, calling in to the health department, demanded the dogs be destroyed. At the same time, Paine and his group kept the city attorney's phones tied up talking about bringing cruelty charges against Pitkin.

The department's PIO called and informed MacDonell that Trimble was studying the various issues.

While controversy swirled, MacDonell sweet-talked his friend Gordon Summerfield, a Kingwood practitioner, out of five bags of IV fluid and some antibiotics. MacDonell handed them over to Clemmons and suggested she abandon practicality.

Friday came. After a full day of wrangling, someone in the department suggested Pitkin's animals be released via some type of positive media event. The director's office made it official. Instructions were simple: stick to the law, avoid controversy, and make sure the department didn't come off as the heavy. In other words, the PIO said, make the old man pay a reasonably stiff fee, but don't be a hard-ass.

"I think Trimble ought to do this," MacDonell said to nobody in particular. "It had to be his idea."

Since it was clear and cool, MacDonell decided to do the deed outside. Even the media could see (and smell) why the bureau chief didn't want Pitkin in his office. They sacrificed the best light and arranged their cameras upwind. MacDonell's staff stood by and watched.

MacDonell put on his coat and tie. In a clear voice he explained the bill. There would be no charge for veterinary care and no court citations would be issued. "The total is now $670, immunizations, licenses, and five days board. Payable immediately," he concluded.

"You bastard!" Pitkin screamed. "You kill three my dogs!" His voice was high-pitched and excited. "I have already dreizehn!"

"Nicht dreizehn. Speak English," MacDonell insisted.

"Ya, I have already thirteen."

"Mr. Pitkin, on Monday we picked up ten very miserable dogs. We killed none. Today we are releasing the same ten, all vaccinated, all licensed, for $670. Today. If you wait until Saturday it will be another fifty dollars. I suggest from now on you keep them home, feed them better, and provide proper veterinary care." Then MacDonell tapped his temple with a forefinger and in an almost inaudible voice he added, '*Sie haben einen Vogel.*'"

Pitkin stared at him for a few seconds, then turned his head, robot-like, and looked at the cameras.

Clemmons snickered.

"What did he say?" Bragg asked.

"It's German," she whispered. "*You have a bird in your head*,' is the literal translation. Pitkin knows what it means."

The wrangling continued in subdued tones. After half an hour, ten became the agreed number of animals. Soon the argument centered on how the city counted days. Two or three times Pitkin raised his voice. At least twice he injected the word 'pogrom' into the negotiations.

After an hour they were no closer to a solution. The camera crews turned off their equipment. Pitkin added a demand for written apologies from MacDonell, as well as the mayor, the health director, and the city attorney. Feeling the harassment and the futility, MacDonell broke things off. He went to his office, and began signing a large folder of supply requisitions. He tapped Clemmons to stand in.

"Get this over with, Carol."

Clemmons straightened her back, squared her shoulders, and took a deep breath. "Can I tell the reporters who the old fart's sister is?"

"Keep the old lady out of it."

"Is this what the department expected?" she asked.

"I doubt it. Trimble and his PIO aren't taking calls."

By 10:00 a.m. Clemmons had formulated a potential solution: no apologies, and the city would knock off seventy dollars. That would make it an even six hundred owed. But Pitkin claimed to have no more than three hundred. The TV crews passed the hat and scraped together another hundred and ten. Clemmons, on MacDonell's okay, agreed the last hundred and ninety could be paid off in a week. The cameras were turned back on and Pitkin, tilting his head back like a pelican and squinting his tiny bloodshot eyes, handed MacDonell's clerk a fistful of wrinkled bills. She counted them out and pronounced him exactly one hundred dollars short.

Clemmons counted the bills again: $310. The lights were bright, even for being outside. As the cameras stared at him, Alexander Pitkin reached into his sock and produced a small roll of additional green. With an exaggerated flair he peeled off a soiled hundred dollar bill and handed it to Clemmons. Balancing on one spindly leg, Pitkin returned the stash to his sock. The cameras caught it all. MacDonell, stepping outside at that moment, did too.

Rhonda "Red" Ryder of Channel 12 asked what was supposed to be the final question. "Doctor MacDonell, how do you feel about taking so much money from such an obviously destitute old man, just so that he can get his beloved animals back?"

"Red, his animals are now vaccinated against four diseases, including rabies. That protects the rest of our citizens, even the non-destitute ones. They're all licensed with the city. That'll give us the ability to return them to Mr. Pitkin should they become lost. And we now have his assurances that he is going to keep them in compliance with city ordinances. That means they shouldn't be running at large and terrorizing his neighbors' cats. I'm perfectly content with this arrangement."

"Will he abide by it?"

"Six months—if we're lucky," MacDonell mumbled.

The reporters pressed, squeezing in follow-ons. "But he's taken refuge in a van. Obviously he's unable to pay."

"Come on. You saw the wad in his sock just like I did." MacDonell smiled. He knew this was all being picked up by the camera.

"What about the kennel ordinance?" asked the man from the Chronicle.

"My boss is giving him a year to comply."

Another reporter chimed in. "Does the city really need this old man's money to keep operating?"

"I'm not in a position to waive fees and fines that are legally owed to the city." MacDonell moved away from the cameras. They followed.

"Didn't you waive seventy dollars? What was your authority for doing that?" another reporter asked.

"I decided not to count today, since he's picking them up today."

"Well, that's not exactly right, is it? You waived seventy and that's…" MacDonell moved toward the building. "That's all the questions I have time for," he said.

Ryder turned off her mike and handed it to the cameraman. "I've seen the dogs," she said. "I don't see why you let him keep them anyway."

"Maybe you and the editor at the Chronicle ought to get on the same page."

Ryder smiled.

They talked a little more and MacDonell got the impression Ryder was fed up with the Pitkin affair, too. The rest of the TV people began rolling up their cables. For a day in January it was suddenly warm. MacDonell wasn't sure why, but he carried the cameraman's tripod to the van, then went back inside.

Captain Bragg and a Mr. Cleon Soames were waiting in MacDonell's office. Soames was taller than Bragg, who was himself six-four. He wore blue overalls and a starched shirt. His thin red hair stuck up in back, he was big in the belly, and his cheeks had a ruddy glow. Vessels, both red and blue, laced a prominent hook of a nose. It was the problem of the assassinated pigs.

MacDonell took off his coat and tie and got a diet Coke out of his small office refrigerator. He offered them one. Both men turned him down. Soames was impatient and wanted to get his concerns across in the most convincing manner. He had his own Polaroids of the slaughtered pigs and he spread them out on MacDonell's desk. MacDonell sipped and looked. "Yes, I've seen the pigs," he said.

"The question is, what are you going to do about them?"

"Do?" MacDonell asked. "What would you like me to do?"

Soames raised his arms like a giant hovering bird. "The kids who raised them pigs put in over a hundred hours feeding and grooming and all that. Then the city lets this happen."

"Mr. Soames, I was in the 4-H Club when I was a kid. I know the effort that goes into animal projects. My question is, what do you want me to do?"

"Can't the city replace the pigs?"

"Come on, Mr. Soames! This is the Animal Control Center, not a farm."

"I know what it is. But it was the city that caused all this."

MacDonell slammed a folder down on his desk. "The city?! Next time you want the city to solve all your problems, try substituting the word *taxpayer*." The room was silent. Bragg scratched his backside. MacDonell walked around behind his desk and sat down. "Look," he said, taking a new tack, "do you realize we have a city ordinance which forbids the keeping of swine?"

Soames swallowed, surprised at the sudden turn in the conversation. "We've raised pigs out there as long as I can remember. Since before we got annexed."

"I don't doubt it, but it doesn't change things. You want me to babysit pigs that were voted out years ago."

The big man saw he had better give up on this part of his argument.

"I come in here for some help. Your captain said you could give us some assistance…prevent this from happening again."

MacDonell frowned at Bragg.

"I've already asked the captain to have his district officer patrol in your neighborhood when he's not otherwise occupied. That's the best I can do right now."

"You gonna' let yer dogcatchers shoot them wild dogs?" Soames whined. "…or what?"

MacDonell looked down at his littered desk. "Why don't you try to find out where these animals are coming from?"

"That's your job."

MacDonell folded his arms and put one hand on his chin. "I know my job," MacDonell whispered. "But I could use a little help."

"I work full time," Soames informed everyone.

Channel 12's early evening news broadcast featured a human interest piece at the end of the hour. The anchor looked into the TelePrompTer and read the following: *"Today Mr. Alexander Pitkin, a down-on-his-luck Houston citizen who temporarily makes his home under a downtown freeway, lost a substantial part of his life savings after a run-in with the city administration. Here's Red Ryder with the story.*" Fade to Ryder: "*Dr. Duncan MacDonell, director of Houston's animal control bureau, today…*" A close-up of Pitkin seated flat on the epoxy floor and surrounded by leaping, licking, peeing pups dominated most of the three minute piece. Pictures of TV cameramen ponying up a little cash were featured. MacDonell's statements were severely edited. His lips moved but nothing came out, until, "*I'm perfectly content with this arrangement.*"

He stayed up, hoping the late news would present a more sympathetic story. Instead it started off with an ambiguous reference to a mutilated body found on Galveston Island. A distant shot showed a body under a sheet with plain-clothes policemen standing around in blowing sand. It wasn't that uncommon. MacDonell's eyes got heavy and he blinked a few times. When he came to, a late night comedian was making lawyer jokes.

CHAPTER TEN

A day passed. Late in the afternoon on Tuesday, January 14th, Annabel Mooney's office called. MacDonell was invited to a palaver in the basement at 900 Bagby Street. It was the first meeting of the city's animal control committee in almost three years. Lonnie Kenner was there, standing in for councilman B. F. Dockery. Don Simpson represented Marjorie Reed and councilmember Mooney, the chairperson, represented herself.

Because of the Texas Open Meetings Act, several members of the public had been notified of the get-together. Robin Paine was there; MacDonell blinked at his conservative dark suit. Mercy Smith represented the HCSPCA. The Houston Humane League, Citizens for Animal Defense, and Special Friends were represented by new faces. Cleon Soames, 4-H father and FFA agriculture instructor, was there along with a Mr. Curtis Rebarger representing a Val Verde East homeowner's group. The Chronicle and the Leader were both represented. Channel 12's Rhonda Ryder and the pretty young TV reporter from Channel 2 set up in opposite corners of the room, near the wall plugs. Ryder gave MacDonell a weak smile but avoided verbal contact. Both cameramen had short conversations with MacDonell and he loaned one of them a piece of white paper to calibrate his color lens. A half-dozen citizens/observers found chairs in the back of the room.

Annabel Mooney started out by asking MacDonell to sit across from her at the table. He hesitated for a moment, anticipating that Trimble or his PIO might show up. The two council reps sat on either side of Mrs. Mooney and studied the contents of the blue folders they were carrying. Mooney was a soft-spoken woman, representing River Oaks and most of the affluent neighborhoods on the west side. "Dr. Mac," she began, "where's Dr. Trimble?"

MacDonell shook his head and shrugged.

"No matter," she said. "What we need to discuss is what we are doing to control packs of wild dogs in the city?" She was a plump, pleasant woman and wore a flowered dress with ruffled sleeves that covered her upper arms. Her face flashed off and on, knotting up her cheeks like neon cheese puffs. MacDonell suspected it was a nervous tic.

"Miz Mooney," he began as he gathered his thoughts, "I've assigned one officer to each district on the day shift. When they are not answering calls from citizens about specific animal problems, they're free to patrol in their district."

"And refresh my memory. How many districts?"

"Yes ma'am, twelve."

"And how many calls a day?"

"We average about 400." He could see her calculating in her head. "And we dispatch out about half of that."

"And if you receive a report of a pack of dogs?"

"Other than my regular district officers, I have two special officers I call field investigators. I direct them to various locations in response to requests for assistance from the district officers or their regional sergeants. Or they're sent by the field supervisor to investigate specific problems. It's a lot like the Fire Department. You call—we haul. The difference is the city has seventy-five fire stations. I have two investigators."

"How many district officers do we have on a typical day?" she asked again.

"Twelve…" MacDonell wondered how many times he had answered that question for her in the past nine years.

"Every day?"

"Miz Mooney," he sighed, "on the regular day shift, if everybody comes to work, I have twelve. Twelve districts, twelve officers. That's one for every fifty square miles…" He paused. "When they all come to work," he repeated. "People get sick, go on vacation."

Mooney looked down at her papers, and Kenner suddenly straightened up in his chair.

"Twelve? Your personnel roster indicates more than sixty uniformed spaces," Kenner inserted.

"That number includes kennel personnel, Mr. Kenner. I still run three shifts a day, twenty-four hours a day, seven days a week. Add in the bite investigators, dispatchers, and, of course, I also have several unfilled spaces."

"What about clerks and the people who answer the phone?"

"They're separate."

"How are your dogcatchers equipped?" Kenner asked, changing the subject.

MacDonell paused. "We call them Animal Control Officers, Mr. Kenner. They're each equipped with a vehicle, radio, ticket books, uniforms, and they have an aluminum pole about six feet long with a cable loop on the end. They're also issued rope, a first aid kit, small cages, heavy leather gloves…"

"No, I mean, don't they have…you know, tranquilizers?"

"The two investigators and the captain have access to an air-driven dart gun. But not my regular field officers."

Now it was Simpson's turn. MacDonell turned to face him.

"Doctor Mac, I have no experience with your organization. I'm representing Marjorie Reed. What I want to know, I guess, is are your officers issued firearms? From what you've already said, I think I know the answer."

MacDonell nodded. "As I understand it, .38 caliber sidearms were taken from our ACOs when we were separated from the police department and became health officers. That was back in 1969 or thereabouts." MacDonell hesitated, then completed his answer. "My two investigators have access to three different types of firearms, but they're kept in a locked cabinet. They're only used if all other attempts at capture have failed."

"What are those firearms?" Simpson asked.

"We have a .22 rifle, a .30-.30 Winchester, and a .410 shotgun using rifled slugs. Actually two of each."

"Who authorizes their use?"

"I do," MacDonell replied, "or the field captain if I'm unavailable. And then only if the situation warrants."

Soames stood up at the back of the room and shook the room with his loud voice. "Don't you think the killing of livestock warrants it?"

No one said anything.

"What about that, Doctor?" Kenner interjected.

MacDonell smoothed his chin whiskers. "We're concerned with threats to human safety, Mr. Kenner. Livestock, of the type Mr. Soames is referring to, are not permitted in the city."

"What type is he referring to?"

"Pigs."

"And these little pot-bellied things people keep in their homes?"

"Not legal, sir."

Kenner pressed his point.

"Dr. MacDonell, don't you consider the fact that these children were engaged in a school project?"

"Well, sir, these animals were inside the city, which violates the ordinance. Because I didn't get a complaint, I didn't issue any citations. On the other hand, I can't go around standing guard over every school project."

"In other words, you didn't know about them?"

"I didn't get a complaint."

"You get complaints about livestock?"

"Everyday, Mr. Kenner."

Mooney reasserted her position as chairperson. "Dr. Mac, could you explain bureau policy on the matter of livestock and the enforcement of that particular part of the ordinance?"

"Sure," MacDonell said, leaning back in his chair. "I only have enough officers to handle complaints. When we get one about livestock we investigate. If the animals are in violation, we enforce the law by issuing court citations."

"Nobody complained about these little piglets?" Kenner asked with a touch of indignance.

"Not to my knowledge," MacDonell replied.

A chair scraped in the back of the room and Robin Paine stood and raised his hand. Mooney ignored him and asked the next question. "Doctor, is there a problem with wild dogs in this city?"

MacDonell stared at the floor for a second, then looked up at her. "I'm certain there's a problem, but I don't think I'd label them wild dogs. I'm sure you remember the time a pack of strays got into the zoo. Killed some wallabies. Left to their own devices dogs pack up, cause damage, even chase children on school grounds, and then return home. Often the owners don't realize their pets have been out bothering people."

"Bothering, hell!" Soames shouted. "They're killing! The next thing you know they'll kill some innocent child!"

"That's enough!" Mooney snapped. "Sir, I have to ask you to sit down and be silent. If you make another outburst like that, I'll have you removed."

A solemn-faced police officer stood up and put his thumbs in his utility belt.

Glowering, Soames sat down.

"Miz Mooney," Robin Paine said. "Could I say something?"

"If it's relevant, but keep it short and to the point. What's your name and who do you represent?"

Paine identified himself and announced his affiliations.

Mooney rolled her eyes.

Paine cleared his throat. "Recently Dr. MacDonell chose to release some animals to a homeless man, knowing full well the man couldn't take care of them and that he—that person—allowed them to run loose. The man's a derelict. He doesn't take care of the animals. They're sick and diseased and…"

"Get to your point, Mr. Paine," the councilwoman said, drumming her note pad with her pencil.

"The man's an irresponsible owner." Paine raised his voice. "It's our organization's position that Dr. MacDonell is not doing his job. He should file cruelty charges against all these irresponsible owners and hold animals like that, at least until he can find good homes for them. When he releases big vicious dogs to people like that, they can go out and kill cats and livestock."

Paine left the thought hanging.

Mooney nodded dismissively. "Is that all, Mr. Paine?"

"Well, maybe the committee might give some thought to replacing Dr. MacDonell," Paine said, and sat down.

Kenner changed the subject. "Doctor, how quickly could you train your officers to use tranquilizer guns?"

MacDonell explained it would take more technically qualified officers. It involved a modest knowledge of pharmacology and the ability to estimate a dose of tranquilizer, on an animal of unknown weight and body mass at a distance. The physical condition of the animal was important. And to top it off, he pointed out, the animal is seldom standing still. There was also the question of who could legally purchase tranquilizers if a licensed veterinarian was not actually involved. "And the darts, fully loaded, cost the city fifteen bucks each. To compare," he said, "a bullet costs just a few cents…"

"Dr. MacDonell," Simpson asked. "Are you saying that it's preferable to shoot an animal than to dart it because of the cost?"

MacDonell shook his head. "No, just that it's cheaper. 'Preferable' is a value judgment." He glanced around the table. "In either case, I'd need better officers if I were to start letting all my people carry firearms and dart guns."

"Better how?"

"Better trained, sir, and better qualified in the first place. Applicants for our jobs are frequently unemployable in most other situations. Some are barely literate and most have no aptitude for animal work. You ask for a dogcatcher, pay dogcatcher wages, you'll get a dogcatcher. Personally, I feel a psychiatric screening, like you give police candidates wouldn't be a bad idea."

Kenner laughed.

"Laugh all you want, Mr. Kenner. Giving an illiterate, poorly-motivated person a gun or an expensive, complicated, and often dangerous tranquilizer system isn't acceptable to me. Not at all." He hesitated. "Maybe I ought to have my head examined," he muttered under his breath.

"Address the committee with your comments," Kenner snapped.

Holding up her hand for calm, Mooney smiled sourly at Kenner. "Please…gentlemen."

MacDonell shook his head wearily and stared at the wall.

And so it went. The meeting lasted another half hour, until someone asked if MacDonell couldn't squeeze out a few more patrols in the Rice University area.

MacDonell shook his head, side to side. "In the past nine years I've trimmed, pared, cut the fat, cut out some muscle. Now I'm getting bone." MacDonell couldn't hide his feelings on the subject. "And I've just pointed out the cost of darts. When money's no object I can do anything."

Mooney nodded in agreement. "Doctor, the council has to establish priorities," she said. "The taxpayers expect us to improve or at to least maintain services without raising taxes. We have hard choices to make."

"But what about our kids' 4-H projects!" Soames burst out from the back.

There was a crackling silence. Mooney stood up, signaling the end of the meeting.

"Doctor, what about it?" Kenner said as they all stood.

"I'll see what I can do," MacDonell murmured.

The room began to clear. "Any thoughts about this meeting?" Ryder asked, extending her Channel 12 microphone.

MacDonell didn't look at her. "No comment, Red," he replied, looking into the camera lens.

"What are you going to do about the committee requests?" a print reporter asked.

MacDonell wanted to avoid confrontations and he also wanted to get home.

"I'll see what I can do," he replied, slipping through the jumble of reporters and stragglers.

In the hall one of the TV cameraman pulled MacDonell aside. "Doc, a suggestion. Mooney and her crowd used the term 'we:' What are *we* doing here, what are *we* doing there. You kept sáying, 'I:' *I* have this, *I* do that. You take on all the responsibility." He smiled. "For what it's worth."

MacDonell returned the smile. "I'll remember that."

By the time the crowd dispersed it was dark outside. A light, steady rain pelted MacDonell as he ran across McKinney Street. He made it down the ramp into the parking garage below the library. The little car groaned as it climbed up from the bowels of the old building.

On the street the rain strengthened. He checked with his dispatcher and headed west on McKinney to San Jacinto, then north under the gleaming Houston Center. He passed the old Harris County Courthouse with its heavy stone steps and dripping oaks. Across Congress Street the overhang of the glass-bottomed Family Law Center sheltered a few protesters. One, with a droopy sign, paced in the downpour.

MacDonell crossed Buffalo Bayou, passed the new city jail. The place was only a few years old and already the city needed another. He made it past two burned out warehouse shells. Plywood ramps and covered walks indicated renovations in progress. Through the concrete canyon to I-10, MacDonell connected with the Eastex. As he merged with heavy traffic cars hydroplaned, roostertails spouted. In less than a mile traffic clotted and stopped altogether. On the freeway the rain surged and roared in his ears. The drops were as big as balloons. Wipers failed and progress ceased.

MacDonell had time to think about the meeting. Mooney was ineffectual, Dockery and Reed were both absent. Kenner was a pain. Everybody wanted more, but of what? None of them really knew. By the time he got home it was 8:30. His back ached from gripping the wheel. Rain pounded the driveway, filled the gutters, and clogged the downspouts.

Jeannie met him in the garage. She told him Lil had started to gurgle, and when she coughed up a half-cup of pink fluid Jeannie had taken her to Dr. Summerfield. "She'll be there at least through the night."

"What did he have to say?" MacDonell asked as he slumped at the table and looked at his meal.

"She's old, Duncan. Worn out."

"Tell me about it."

Jeannie laid down her fork and wiped her lips with her napkin. "He says you'll have to make up your mind sooner rather than later."

"Summerfield's never hunted over a good dog."

Jeannie nodded. "I don't think he hunts."

"Hemingway thought a man ought to die standing up, with a gun in one hand and a shot of whiskey in the other."

"She's not a man, Duncan, she's a dog. A dear old dog."

He tried to focus on his plate. "Don't tell me how to kill dogs," he said. "I know all about killing dogs." Dinner was a small green salad, warmed up spaghetti and garlic bread, and a flat Lambrusco. He hardly touched the food. Picking up the wine, he took a small sip. "Where's the bubbles?"

Her shoulders drooped. "I'm afraid I'm just out of bubbles," she whispered. A tear appeared in the corner of her eye, but she quickly wiped it away.

Jeannie had little else to say and her husband didn't ask much more. Even the cat prowled the kitchen, looking for a fight.

MacDonell went to bed early and missed the news. Tomorrow would be soon enough to see the media report on what they thought had happened at this evening's meeting.

CHAPTER ELEVEN

"*D*OGS KILL KIDS' 4-H PROJECTS!" was the Chronicle's Wednesday headline. The first three words, DOGS KILL KIDS,' were at the top of the column and the rest was just below the fold. Robin Paine and Mercy Smith, spokesperson for the HCSPCA, were quoted in the article attesting to the city's unwarranted practice of releasing animals to homeless derelicts. Soames was quoted as saying he recommended shooting strays, *"just like they did in the old days."* He suggested the death of a child would be the outcome if animal control officers were not trained and equipped with tranquilizers and firearms.

A second section headline read, "COALITION REBUFFED!" This article was a catch-all featuring opinions, but little worthwhile information on the meeting of the previous evening. Prominent, however, was a quotation attributed to the director of the city's animal control bureau: *"Some (animal control) applicants are barely literate and most of them have no aptitude for animal work."*

The call came as MacDonell poured hot water in his cup. Trimble didn't waste time with any howdy-do. "Duncan, do you have a thinking problem? I can't believe your off-the-wall comments about our illiterate city employees!" he shouted.

MacDonell kept his head. "You've been misinformed, Dr. Trimble," he said, showing just the right amount of respect.

"Inform me then. I want to make sure I have a totally accurate picture."

"Well, sir, if you'd been there you'd know I made just two comments to the press. I said, 'No comment,' and, 'I'll see what I can do.'" MacDonell took a deep breath. "Other than that, I was asked questions for almost two hours. My answers were honest and accurate."

"Is that right? Didn't you tell Mr. Dockery your employees were illiterate and not cut out to work with animals?"

"No, I didn't. Dockery wasn't there. His boy Lonnie Kenner was. I told Kenner most *applicants* are illiterate...and unfortunately, that's the case."

"Doctor MacDonell, you have no political sense whatsoever. In the future, and I'll put this in writing if I have to, you're to refrain from making public statements of any kind! Do you understand me? ANY!"

MacDonell had to pull the receiver away from his ear on the last word. "Yes, sir," he said.

"Now…" Trimble continued, calming. "Can you tell me how many of your people are trained to handle tranquilizers?"

"I can. My field chief and my chief bite investigator."

"Two? That's it? What about equipment?"

"We ordered four sets last year, but if you remember, you cut the purchase order in half."

Trimble was silent, mulling it over.

"Perhaps," he said after a long silence, "…perhaps you didn't do a good enough job selling me on your requirements."

"That must be it," MacDonell replied. He was steaming but he realized Trimble had no concept of animal operations in a big city. He would give the physician the benefit of the doubt. "I don't think you understand, sir. The tranquilizer is not some kind of magic bullet. There's a lot more to it than bang—zap! There's dosage estimation. With street dogs you have to get close, which isn't always easy."

MacDonell was looking for the words. "Some of these animals don't react the way you might expect."

"I'm familiar with how tranquilizers work," Trimble said. "This is the 90's, Doctor. Marlin Perkins doesn't seem to have any trouble. Get with the program!"

MacDonell sensed heat along with frustration. The tops of his ears burned. Trimble knew nothing about the effect of tranquilizers in animals. No doubt he'd never had one of his patients bolt and run under a house, carrying a $15 syringe in his brisket. And, of course, MacDonell didn't have an editing room to slice out all the unphotogenic death scenes. He remained quiet. After a long tension-filled moment, Trimble reopened the conversation.

"Doctor, I want you to develop an extensive training program. I want you to qualify every one of your officers to handle tranquilizers. Equip them and train them. Is that clear?"

"Clear as a bell."

"I'll authorize you to fill one empty slot for a trainer, but you already have a budget. With re-prioritization I don't see why you can't come up with the equipment. The city hasn't gotten any bigger. You're a manager, so manage."

"What's your position on firearms?"

"What's our current policy?"

"We've never had a written policy your predecessor would approve of. I have a few old weapons, but I only authorize their use if it's a last resort, and then it has to be under strict control. More than one officer must be present."

Trimble was quiet for a while.

MacDonell nudged him, "Sir?"

"I'm pretty much against them, I guess."

"Good," MacDonell agreed. "So am I."

Trimble made a funny noise. "Well…one of the council members favors the idea, doesn't he?"

"Yes, Mr. Dockery, I believe."

Trimble hesitated. "Let me get back to you on that," he said, and hung up the phone.

Through the process of annexation Houston maintained its status as the third largest city in the country, according to measured land area. Almost six hundred square miles. And in backyards, in garages, in boxes under beds, twice, sometimes three times a year—the *miracle of birth*.

Faster than the public and private agencies could put them to sleep, or the eighteen-wheelers could squash them, animals were replicating. Dogs fornicated on street corners, in school yards, in parks and parking lots. Cats did it while balancing on fences and rooftops. And to top it off, some yahoo Houston newscaster recently celebrated the fact that a seventeen year-old cat had found its way into the Guiness Book of World Records by giving birth to its 484th kitten.

MacDonell searched his desk and came up with a handful of shotgun shells. They were old and the brass had started to turn green. He took up his pacing.

Veterinarians offered what physicians would call an ovarohysterectomy for a mere thirty dollars. The price hadn't changed in thirty years. But in many neighborhoods where cost made the difference, residents couldn't afford dog and cat surgery anyway. Groceries were their pressing problem. And a growing number had yet to solve the mystery of how they, themselves, got pregnant.

MacDonell fumed, paced, stewed, and talked to himself.

At 2:00 p.m. he called Connie Oaks into his office. They wrestled with the operational budget. By this time in the fiscal year it was pretty well committed. At 4:00 p.m. MacDonell canceled one of the three new trucks on the capital equipment list. Instead, they would buy fifteen new sets of Telinject equipment. It was decided. If the prices remained as advertised there might even be $2000 left over. MacDonell paced while Oaks went over the cost. The guns parts came out of Germany to a distributor in California. There was a waiting list. With considerable misgiving, they drafted a requisition. One-meter tubes, half-meter tubes, hand-pieces, air-pumps, darts, needles with hubs, needles without hubs.

While Oaks gathered the documents and slogged his way through the catalogs, MacDonell did a different kind of research. He collected personnel records and looked at test scores from the last certification exam. He still needed a training officer.

Late in the afternoon he'd narrowed it down to the two investigators: the male was the poorer shot and had the beginnings of an attendance problem, the other was very pregnant and soon to go on maternity leave. That evening MacDonell and Oaks parted, with but half the problem solved.

***

"What's for dinner?"

"*Rippchen mit kraut,*" Jeannie sang out.

MacDonell let out a troubled sigh.

"I thought you'd like it."

"Oh, I do. I've just got to come up with a shooting instructor. You want a job."

"Not on your tintype."

While changing his clothes, MacDonell caught sight of his body in the mirrored closet door. His legs looked white, his eyes gaunt. After a quiet moment he decided he'd keep the embarrassment of Trimble's chewing-out to himself. He put on red shorts, took a deep breath, and headed for the kitchen.

Everything smelled good, Jeannie was bubbling, and Lil was back home, looking perky for a fourteen year-old matron with a bad pump. As soon as she arrived, Jeannie reported, she had quarreled with the cat. God was in his heaven.

The pork chop was thick, sweet, and tender. The kraut was Bavarian, sweet with bits of apple and caraway seeds to add flavor. Home fries on the side.

"Because of this one pork chop, you get the privilege of eating bran flakes and carrot sticks for the next week," she observed with a twinkle.

"It's worth it," he tried to say with his mouth full.

After dinner, MacDonell filled his bird feeders. Much to his delight, Lil followed him around the yard like a pup.

***

MacDonell arrived at his office early Thursday morning. Coming through the door he kicked the cactus and spent five minutes scooping up dirt and debris, and cramming it back in the pot. He made coffee and washed up a couple of cups. As soon as Oaks got in the two men went over the previous day's plan to redirect capital funds. The phone buzzed and MacDonell picked it up.

"Answering your own phones now?" said a female voice. It was J.D. Longley.

"Willie's not in yet," he said. "What's up these days?"

"I've been reading about you in the papers."

"Oh Lord."

"Sounds like you're up to your neck."

"I'm well past that."

"I got to thinking about you last night," she said. "I suppose, as a return on past favors, I could give that job offer of yours a little consideration. Is it still open?"

The rest of the morning MacDonell floated. Being a retired master sergeant himself, Oaks was easy to convince. In his aggressive style, he reviewed the personnel manual and established the quickest way to ship the paperwork. By 9:30 a.m. his clerk was typing the hiring order. At

10:00, MacDonell signed it and called the department budget officer. After a brief conversation MacDonell filled his chest with air. This was almost too easy.

Longley showed up at 11:45. MacDonell wanted to introduce her to Bragg and Oaks, and maybe take them all to lunch. "Where's Frank?" he asked Willie on the intercom.

In a second she buzzed back. "They say he in the field, Doctor Mac. Way out on the south side."

"Oh well," said MacDonell. He grabbed Oaks and the three drove to a rare restaurant lunch. MacDonell thought Longley might squeal to Jeannie, so he suffered through a small salad and iced tea. Oaks had the same. Longley, on the other hand, wolfed down two chili-burgers, a large order of fries, and a milkshake. She was a big girl.

MacDonell formalized the job offer.

"I can use the extra cash right now," she said. "Besides, its an opportunity to see how the city works."

Oaks went into unnecessary detail telling her about the dart gun order and explaining the purchase order system, and how it differed from military supply. Longley offered to come in on Saturday and ride with the weekend officers so she could evaluate the training they would need.

After a quick drive back, Longley gave both men a strong handshake and left them standing in the parking lot. By the end of the first week, she had met all the day shift officers, borrowed a dart gun and MacDonell's text, *Chemical Immobilization of North American Wildlife,* and begun drafting lesson plans.

Chapter Twelve

---

*S*uddenly it turned cold in Texas. Blue-northers lined up outside Amarillo and took turns raking the state. The Bayou City caught the leading edge of a new front every four days, and an all-time low temperature was recorded during the third week in February. Homeless men and women queued up at area shelters. In the back pages of the Chronicle, Jeannie found the pitiful story of one man who had succumbed to the cold. Boys had found him by a shipping container near some railroad tracks. The paper said he had tried to escape the cold, but died of exposure. The coroner said identification would be difficult since animals had eaten portions of the body.

A county-wide call went out for blankets, winter coats, gloves, and other warm apparel. Sheltering the homeless became the all-consuming project of three of the area's biggest charitable organizations. Channel 12 collected more than a thousand blankets in a one-day campaign.

North, in The Woodlands, frozen pipes were a gold mine for area plumbers. Kingwood residents got a reprieve, but MacDonell took precautions to wrap some pipes, anyway.

Monday, February 21st, Willie buzzed in to her boss. Lieutenant Sam Goodson, HPD, was on the phone.

"Doctor Mac, how the hell you are?" Goodson began.

"Fine as frog's hair," MacDonell said, laying down his pen and pushing back his chair. "And yourself, Lieutenant?"

Goodson, HPD Homicide, was a recent acquaintance. Two years earlier Goodson, as a sergeant, had uncovered an odd case of animal sacrifice in the city. As a result he had learned some interesting lessons in public health, and MacDonell had become familiar with the inner workings of HPD. Since then Goodson had been promoted to lieutenant.

The banter was lively and harmless.

"What can I do for you?" asked MacDonell after a time.

"There's something I need to talk to you about," Goodson said. MacDonell detected a somber note in Goodson's tone. "I'd like to drop over with a couple of my sergeants and let you look at some pictures. I think we've got a little case you could help us with."

Before they arrived MacDonell scrubbed out some real china mugs. A steaming pot of coffee was set out, along with envelopes of sugar and a small jar of non-dairy creamer. A plastic spoon rounded out the guest service.

"Looks like we get the good silver," Goodson said, as he eased over and closed the office door. The granite-jawed Goodson was in his typical work outfit, gray golf slacks, gray turtle-neck, gray belt, gray socks, and gray patent-leather shoes. A small ivory-handled automatic, high at the waist, completed the ensemble. To MacDonell he looked like a character out of a black and white movie.

The lieutenant's dark gray sport coat came off and was thrown over a chair. One sergeant wore a hound's-tooth sport coat, the other a tan tweed with a meerschaum pipe stuck in the pocket. Each had a small gold badge affixed to his belt which peeked out at intervals. After mixing coffee and cream, and a minute or two of small talk, Goodson came to the point.

"Drink up, Doc," he said. "We've got some nasty pictures for you to look at and we don't want you to lose your breakfast."

MacDonell sipped his coffee and looked around at the officers hovering over his desk. "Let's go ahead and look, folks," he said. "Vets have strong stomachs. It's a course we take."

The tweed pipe smoker produced a brown envelope and slid out the contents. Ten 8 x 10 color photos were laid across MacDonell's desk, two rows of five. At first it was difficult to determine what he was looking at. The majority were close-ups. As MacDonell went over them, the image he registered was that of a scattered collection of human remains surrounding a wooden shipping container. A torso, part of a lower leg, and a skull were visible. Smaller bones and body parts had been scattered over a wider area.

A wide-angle shot showed the breadth of the carnage and displayed the assembled personal effects of the victim. They included a near-full bottle of wine—the seal had been broken—a cook pot, and some odds and ends of paper and trash. There was more clothing than actual body parts. Most of the thorax was intact, but the abdomen had been pretty well disemboweled. The man—it appeared to be a man—had been wearing a heavy military-style field jacket. There was also one hightop sneaker with the remains of a tibia and fibula jutting out. In the top row, one photograph showed that the skin of the left side of the face had been peeled off. The soft tissue of the throat was gone and the cervical vertebrae had been disarticulated. What was there, and it wasn't much, appeared to be the remains of a black male.

MacDonell scratched his head, rubbed his nose, and stifled a sneeze. "This body was found awhile ago out along the Hempstead Highway?" He was reiterating part of Goodson's monologue, offered while the prints were being laid out.

"That's it," Goodson replied.

"Then I remember something in the Chronicle about it. The report was a little off, I guess. This guy's been dead longer than a week."

"Pretty good, Mac." Goodson said. "The Medical Examiner says it could have been late December or the first part of January."

"Any identification?"

"A wedding band with an inscription," Goodson revealed. "M.E. loves L.E."

MacDonell put his elbows on his desk, rested his chin on his left hand, and studied the pictures again.

"How far out?" asked MacDonell.

"West Little York, just inside the Toll Road, near Cole Creek. Sixty yards from the SP right-of-way."

The officer in the hound's-tooth jacket cocked his head. "You think it was dogs?"

MacDonell gave him a look. "What? Do I think dogs killed him, or do I think dogs chewed the bones?"

Hound's-tooth selected one photo and slid it across the desk. "Take a look at this," he said. It was a footprint, large, long, and narrow. "That's not a dog or a coyote print, is it? See, isn't that a coon print beside it?"

MacDonell nodded, got out a magnifier, and studied it for several minutes. "I see what you're getting at," he said. He pulled at his beard.

"Could it be a wolf?" Goodson asked.

"Did you measure it? I mean, there's nothing to indicate its size except the prints of the other animals." MacDonell twisted his mustache between his thumb and forefinger. "It's an awfully clear print for such an old kill."

Goodson explained. "We found it under this piece of corrugated iron sheeting you see here in this other shot. We figure the metal protected it from the weather."

"The report in the paper said he died of exposure. I imagine stray dogs and other animals could have done this to the body. I don't think it's too unusual."

"This print may have been there when the man died," Sam explained.

"Could be," MacDonell agreed, "...or even before."

The tweed collected his photographs and stuffed them back in the envelope. Producing a second envelope he proceeded to lay out another batch of equally graphic photos. Three rows of seven, and one row of six. They covered the desk. "Do you see any similarities between these and the first ones?"

MacDonell closed his eyes for a second. "Damn. That would gag a maggot," he muttered.

This time the corpse was fresh.

"When did this one happen?" he asked, picking up one of the pictures and turning it ninety degrees.

"Last night," Goodson answered. "Sometime after midnight, so the lab boys say."

Goodson paced up and down. MacDonell watched him. He was holding back and MacDonell knew it. After a minute Goodson slumped onto the couch. The sergeants stood.

"Doc, we think the guy was alive when this happened."

"Jeez, Louise" MacDonell said. "I thought all we had to worry about was being raped, robbed, or murdered. You're telling me we've got dogs picking off the stragglers."

"That's what we think," Goodson said.

"Or wolves," hound's-tooth added.

MacDonell shook his head. "Nah, not wolves…but I see where you're coming from."

Goodson smiled. "You'll help us then?"

"Help you do what?"

"Help us figure out if this was done by a wolf."

"That print is big, but I doubt it's a wolf."

"There's a lot of similarities between these two bodies, Mac," Goodson said. "Some of the teeth marks indicate a very large animal was involved."

"I can see that."

"The liver and stomach are gone in this last guy and of course in the first one, too."

"Anything else?"

"The ME says the first guy had a broken ankle. He thinks it occurred at the time of death. Possibly a struggle."

"Were there any prints with this last one?"

"The body was on concrete, and it was raining when the first officer got there. He said there were big prints, but they got washed away while the lab boys were setting up."

"Let me do some digging," MacDonell said. "I'll get back with you. To be quite honest, I've never seen a dog print that big, yet narrow. But a wolf? It's not likely, Sam."

They talked a little more and MacDonell gave them a few other suggestions. Then all four men stepped outside. The pipe smoker buttonholed MacDonell at the door.

"Can I ask you a question, Doc?"

"Sure."

"My wife wants to know. What's the difference between this place and the humane society?"

MacDonell smiled. "Tell her humane societies protect animals from people, and we do just the opposite."

He pulled at his lower lip. "Another question. What would you do if you come up on a real wolf?"

MacDonell didn't hesitate. "I'd either head for the tall timber, *or* stand perfectly still and hope the wolf had a short attention span."

***

MacDonell spent the rest of the morning with Oaks, but the photographs had reached in and taken hold. At lunch he took out his sandwich and a diet drink, and sat with his feet on his desk. After several minutes of chewing he went to the tiny library behind Willie's desk. Selecting a text entitled *Prevention and Control of Wildlife Damage,* he returned, closed the door, sat down and flipped to the section on

Canis

Carnivores, Pages C-93 through C-97: Wolves. He studied the book for several minutes.

Willie arrived back from lunch and he heard her tapping on his door. "Robin Paine called several times," she said.

The last person MacDonell wanted to talk to was Robin Paine. "Ask Carol to come over, please? And Frank, if you can find him."

Clemmons arrived in three minutes, Bragg was in the field. The dispatcher said he was inspecting a guard dog kennel on the Gulf Freeway. It would take him an hour.

"Carol, what do you know about wolves?"

"Red or gray?" she asked.

"Red."

She sat on the vinyl couch and pulled one leg up under her. "Canis rufus," she said. She thought for a second before continuing. "They're smaller than the gray. They're also supposed to be extinct, but Texas Fish and Wildlife made an effort to reestablish them some years back."

"What's their range?" he asked

"Historically it was as far east as Tennessee and extended as far west as New Mexico or Arizona? Why?"

"Remember the vagrant's body those kids found a few days back? The paper said the guy froze to death over by US-290. They figured dogs chewed on him."

"Yeah."

"Well…"

"Somebody thinks it was wolves?"

"That's what HPD Homicide seems to think."

"That's fucking ridiculous," she said, closing her eyes. "What are they smoking down there?"

MacDonell ignored her profanity and twisted his chin whiskers. Gazing straight ahead, he looked past her and on through the walls. "They've got pictures," he said. "Body parts scattered from hell to breakfast. Exactly what you'd expect at a canine kill site." He was remembering the little boy up in Dallas, attacked by four pit bulls; the baby in the crib at College Station; the old lady killed in Memphis. And of course twenty month-old David McKay came to mind. It was December, 1982, when the infant had been half-eaten by two guard dogs right here in Houston. David lived for forty-five days in total, screaming agony.

Clemmons leaned back on the couch and put her long hands behind her head. "What do they want, dental impressions?"

MacDonell remained serious. "They had one photo, a tight shot of a footprint. They didn't have a mold of it or any measurements. It was just in one of the pictures."

"Yeah...so?"

MacDonell thought for a minute. "I've never seen the footprint of a wolf, red or gray but, this one was similar to all the pictures I've seen."

"Like how?"

"You know, narrow. Like a coyote print, but bigger. I told them to show it around over at Parks and Wildlife."

She pondered a moment. "You know very well we get coyotes in the city," she grinned. It was an old joke. They'd darted one on a local golf course a few years back and the animal rights people went ballistic. "Maybe it was one hellacious big coyote."

"You're right. A coyote is more likely. I'd like to have seen a cast of that print." He stretched. "They didn't have any reference point in the photo. It just looked big." He twisted his mustache some more. "There were some raccoon prints too, and by comparison it was enormous."

"Raccoons vary in size all over the place," she said, shrugging.

Suddenly, Bragg's booming voice could be heard in Willie's office. He poked his head around the corner and checked to see who was in. "Hi, Doc. You looking for me?"

"Yes, I am. Come in. Close the door. I've got a project for you."

Bragg sighed, giving the impression he was worn out. "Oh God, Doc..."

MacDonell ignored it. He handed Bragg a note pad. "Write this down. I want a count on guard dog companies in the area. That should be easy. How many in the City, how many out in the County." He waved at the wall. "Put pins on my map. Then go through the phone book. See how many pet stores sell exotics, tigers, wolves, big carnivores."

MacDonell turned to Clemmons. "Stop over at the bite case office, will you, Carol. Ask how many guard dogs have been involved in attacks."

"Sure".

MacDonell turned back to Bragg. "Frank, ask your sergeants to go through the complaint files for the past year. Find out how wild animals have been reported in the city. Leave out reptiles, monkeys, possums, escaped ferrets. I'm interested in large flesh-eaters like wolves, coyotes, and bobcats. There must be quite a few. I want dates and locations."

"Isn't that stuff in your computer?"

"Only successful pick-ups. I want complaints."

"What's this all about?"

"At roll call, ask Sergeant Clark to find out if anyone can recall any cases where an animal was found with a corpse. You know, owner has a heart attack, dog is starving. I want to talk to any officer involved in that kind of thing."

"Is that all?" Bragg asked ironically. He appeared to see a few long days coming up.

"One last thing. Remember when I asked you to pick up Pitkin's dogs?"

"Yeah."

"And I said look for an eleventh dog?"

"Yeah."

"Tell the district officer to check Pitkin's van two or three times a week. If he sees the dog, tell him to call me immediately."

"What's this all about?"

"I'll tell you after tomorrow's staff meeting. Right now I need to talk to Carol."

Bragg stomped out and MacDonell heard him throw the note pad across Willie's office.

When they were alone MacDonell spoke quietly. "Goodson said they found a second body last night. It was torn apart, a lot like the first one. Trouble is, he wasn't out in the tules. This was a downtown derelict. They him found under the Pierce Elevated, close to St. Joseph's Hospital."

Clemmons' jaw dropped. "You're kidding? Same footprints?"

"Yeah, but the rain swept in under the elevated and washed them away before they could get a good photo."

"God, that's horrible." Clemmons scrunched up her shoulders and shuddered. "I don't think coyotes wander that far downtown."

"Goodson says the man may have been sick or drunk, but they think he was alive. They think he was attacked and killed..." he paused, "...and then partly eaten by one or more large dogs, or wolves. His entire liver, spleen, and most of the other viscera were gone, and apparently it didn't take very long."

"Good God, the Pierce Elevated?"

"Couple hundred street people sleep there every night," MacDonell said.

"And nobody heard anything?"

MacDonell shrugged.

Clemmons looked at him carefully. "Shit!" she said.

***

The following morning the Chronicle's police-beat writer, an elfin little man named Eldon Grimes, hinted there might be more to the death of a homeless man than the police were willing to talk about. The article was graphic. Everything was there except photos, and Grimes speculated wildly about a body "shredded by dogs."

Canis

MacDonell asked Oaks and Clemmons to stick around after the staff meeting. The others got in the way when he was fishing for ideas, and they leaked like washerless faucets. He asked Willie to screen his calls. Reluctantly, he called Bragg back into the room and added him to the circle.

The meeting took about ten minutes. MacDonell briefed them on everything he had learned so far. He rearranged the districts from twelve to ten, and reassigned the two extra officers to the area around the Pierce Elevated.

"This is bullshit," Bragg whispered to Oaks.

MacDonell aimed his last remark at the captain. "As it turns out," he said, "the police are pretty sure the second man was very much alive when he was attacked and dismembered. Just remember, every time someone gets shot in a convenience store the cops take the heat. When some poor devil freezes to death on the street because he didn't have any shelter, that's the city council's fault. But if a pack of dogs kills somebody, it's our neck."

***

As MacDonell expected the evening paper had some speculative commentary. The Chronicle's lead article in the Metro section showed a picture of three bug-eyed spaniels behind a chain link gate. The article included an interview with councilman Dockery. The headline was "ANIMALS IN THE CITY, A GROWING PROBLEM."

Strangely, the Chronicle focused on the rising problem of dog bites and strays. It was a balanced piece, accompanied by another old file photo of a little girl with over a hundred stitches in her face. There was a small, oblique reference to the two bodies dismembered by strays.

Dockery, in his statement, said he had been receiving increasing complaints about animals running at large in his district. His constituents griped that the response from the city was always, *"you'll have to pick up the dog yourself.*" The councilman tangentially suggested that dogcatchers should concentrate on picking up strays. They should de-emphasize the issuance of court citations, get out of their trucks and chase the animals. He wanted old-fashioned dogcatchers, and his constituents wanted the same.

One of the smaller papers had a similar article. Its headline, "PUT TEETH IN DOG ORDINANCE," was a bit more imaginative, and it took a different slant, quoting criticism of the city and the animal control director by a prominent humane group. They wanted Chapter 6 of the city ordinance to be amended to require that all pets owned by what they called 'non-breeders' be rendered sterile. They proposed a special new license for people they called 'responsible dog breeders.' None of the terms used were defined and the article declared that, *"Dr. Duncan MacDonell should get out on the streets and spay the unlicensed dogs to reduce the number running loose."* There was also the usual comment about what was called, *"the city's practice of selling animals for research."* This practice, it said, discouraged people from turning animals over to the city for adoption or disposal. It ended with a comparison of their group's high adoption percentage against what it called the bureau's *"dismal placement record."* The solution: find more people to adopt the strays.

Trimble's reaction to all this was to have his PIO call MacDonell the next morning. She explained that her boss was getting very tired of reading negative articles about animal control. She asked MacDonell what he thought the problem might be.

He told her.

She made skeptical little squeaks.

"My officers are not a bunch of cartoon characters," he said. "Chasing dogs down the street is stupid, unscientific, and a waste of manpower. When my officers run around after strays they bring in one or two a day. When they go where a citizen has confined an animal, the trucks come in loaded down." The problem was not how to pick up more. "Every cage, on every ward, is full—every damn day."

She said Trimble wasn't interested in that and hung up.

At 2:00 p.m. interoffice mail produced fourteen letters protesting the sale of animals for research. They came over from Trimble's office. Two were thoughtful letters from grade school teachers. Twelve were copies of something composed by Robin Paine, and were dated prior to the newspaper articles. The PIO's instructions were for MacDonell to draft a one-page response for Trimble's signature. "Remember," a handwritten note said, "Dr. T. really cares about animals!!"

MacDonell put his head on his desk. Trimble was on the adjunct faculty of the Baylor College of Medicine. Baylor was a big purchaser of research animals, second only to the UT med school. Pulling out a yellow legal pad he started to draft a reply. After half a page he tore it off and pitched it. He started anew, but couldn't concentrate. The wall map loomed. He turned and stared at it, then at his dead cactus, then out the window, then at his watch.

Willie stuck her head in the door. "Don't forget to turn out the lights," she said.

Chapter Thirteen

---

*I*n Kingwood, dinner was ethnic. Jeannie prepared a chicken-enchilada casserole, with a tart and limey green sauce, not too spicy, lots of melted jack cheese, a hint of fresh cilantro. For color there were sliced avocados and corn relish. She baked hot jalapeño cornbread and found a six-pack of dos Equis at Randall's. The conversation moved to state politics and he found it hard to keep up.

By 10:00 p.m. he had fallen asleep twice. He woke up to watch the news, but it was a rehash. He went to the garage, got his map book from the car, and studied the area around the Midtown district where Pitkin had his digs. When the book slid off his lap around 1:00 a.m., it woke him up. He drank cold milk, padded around the house in his bare feet, checked the locks, and set the alarms.

***

At 3:00 a.m. downtown Houston is silent. Under the elevated freeways it is dark. Alexander Pitkin didn't mind the dark. It was the damp and decay that made his bones ache.

Traffic is nonexistent at this hour. Pitkin cracked his eyes and listened. His friends were silent. They had argued among themselves until after 11:00, and were awake until after midnight, but after awhile, they too, drifted off. He could hear them breathing and an occasional lump, lump, lump, lump, lump, as they scratched in their sleep.

His wrist itched around the watch band. Reaching under the thin blanket, he scratched, digging with his fingernails. His wrist burned. He had made it bleed. Turning his wrist over, he held the watch close to his eyes. A blade of light pierced the crack in the van wall and he could see the face of the watch. It was a modern digital that told time in impudent flashes. The plastic band was starting to come apart. There was a large scratch across the face. The time flashed over and over, 3:01, 3:01, 3:01, 3:02, 3:02.

Rolling to his left side, he fished deep into his pocket for his father's watch. Now this was a fine, round, Swiss timepiece, complete with a heavy gold chain, an excellent example of European craftsmanship. The back was carved with an auerhahn, a Bavarian black grouse, surrounded with oak leaves and acorns. And it truly was an auerhahn, not a capercaillie as an American jeweler had once tried to tell him. On the cover a magnificent stag, gold and silver. It was exquisite. The stag was strong, bold, in the rut, but the workmanship was delicate, not at all like things produced in the United States.

Pitkin rubbed his thumb across the carvings. Although the figures were burnished from years of handling, they were still sharp and clear. The amber street light provided illumination. He could see his mother's picture if he opened the lid. She had given him the watch before he and his sister got on the train. That was in 1934. He was four years old then, but in all these years he had never lost the watch—and he never would. He had buried it once, in a sealed box. It had lain under the ground for more than a year. When he took it out, there was a dark stain under the crystal. It crossed the number eleven and discolored the upper one third of the face. It was damaged, and that was his shame, but he loved the watch. After a hundred years it still kept perfect time. The shiny black hands counted the hours and minutes and seconds of his life, as they had his father's, and he knew they would continue with satisfying accuracy.

Pitkin had taken it in for repairs once, when he was seventeen. The repairman was an Oriental technician, not an Uhrmacher, and he would not let Pitkin oversee the work. He remembered he had snatched the watch away and found another man, a man named Schwann, Carl Schwann, a jeweler from Prague, who agreed to let him view the entire procedure. It had cost a little more, but the extra cost paid a handsome dividend. He had learned all he needed to know to clean and maintain the watch himself.

Pitkin kept a leather pouch with small compartments. His watch-maker's tools fit into separate pockets where they waited to perform the ritual of opening the watch.

He wound the watch and counted twelve full turns: left and right, left and right, left and right. Pressing on the thumb release, he snapped the lid open and was pleased by the solid sound of quality. The time he knew to be exact: three minutes and thirty-one seconds after three in the morning. His mother smiled at him. The men with the dark boots and the steel pots on their heads would not take him.

Now the dogs were starting to stir. Soon it would be time to get his breakfast. He lay for a few minutes more. The dogs were scratching. He scratched, too, his wrist and his ribs on the left side, then his ankles.

In another minute he was up. He put on his shoes and his jacket. He folded his blanket into a small square, then into a roll and pushed it under the front seat. Next he crawled backward, on his hands and knees. He kicked at the metal doors and they opened. He stepped down and stretched his arms in the moist air. He bent, kneaded his thighs with his hands, then he bent further and massaged his calves. The stiff-ness would disappear when he began to move around. A half-bucket of gray water stood near his feet. It was for the dogs. He bent, picked out an insect, wet his hands, straightened, then rubbed his hands through his thin wispy hair, then over his face. Looking around, he wiped his hands on his pants.

He studied the street and the areas beyond. Everything looked right. Then he studied his immediate surroundings. Nothing missing. Nothing out of place.

Pitkin began to walk north. Two of the dogs followed for about twenty yards. At some invisible point they turned back, circled restlessly, then watched him. He went between the large concrete columns for about a hundred yards, then crossed the access road and returned along the opposite side. Pitkin stood and watched his dogs from across the concrete expanse. They appeared not to see him and instead busied themselves, nosing around and finding their places. Some had more than one resting place, but each dog had at least one. After previous episodes of fighting, they had decided all this for themselves. The ranking between dogs was now stable.

Pitkin passed his rooms at about fifty yards distance, then doubled back to the south. By following his pre-planned routes, he could avoid any connection between himself and his rooms. That's what he called them, "his rooms."

Eight blocks away behind a bakery, a paper bag had been left for him on a window ledge. He peered in the bag. There were two loaves of brown bread and one of white. He picked up the bag and went next to the metal dumpster. It was open and on top of the jumble of paper and boxes was a large pile of sugared donuts. He picked out twenty of the cleanest. Coffee grounds had been thrown on top of some and these he avoided.

It would be a mile back to his rooms by the route he had chosen. That would take awhile, so Pitkin set the bag on the sidewalk and entered an all-night grocery. He took a cup from the dispenser. The man behind the counter eyed him as he filled the cup with steaming coffee. It was fifty cents and he paid for it with a quarter, a nickel, and twenty pennies. The man said, "four cents tax." Pitkin stared at him, then sipped the coffee deliberately and moved to the door.

"Four cents tax," the man repeated.

"I do not pay tax," Pitkin said. These were his first words of the day. Then he spit in the cup and walked out the door.

The sky was turning a soft pink. Pitkin made his way back to his rooms over a more circuitous route. It would take more than half an hour longer. Twice he put the cup of coffee on the fender of a parked car, reached in the bag, took out a donut, and continued his journey.

By 8:00 a.m. Pitkin had fed his dogs the donuts and bread. He cleaned himself with the water from a five gallon jerry can. He took off his shirt and washed under his arms, his chest, and struggled to wash his back. Tomorrow he would wash below his waist.

By 9:00 he had organized his rooms and inventoried his aluminum, copper tubing, lead battery plates, and other cash equivalents. Then he left. By 11:30 he returned and sorted through the collections from his eastern route. He slept for an hour. At 1:30 in the afternoon, he went out and gathered aluminum scraps and a few more cans. Later he walked to a place where he could trade them. Twice during the day he took the bus. He didn't like riding the bus and he stood or sat near the door when he did ride.

The clock at the Texas Commerce Bank said 2:30. He waited until he was sure no one was looking and then he confirmed the exact time with his pocket watch. He always wore a coat and a hat to do his banking business. He deposited two hundred and twenty-five dollars. The lady at the teller's window made a sour face as he signed the deposit slip. She allowed the bills to lie on the counter while she talked to another employee. Then she laid a sheet of paper over the small stack of currency and picked it up without touching it. She looked at his signature for a long time before completing the transaction. He had kept nine dollars and fifty-five cents in his pocket, but that was none of her business.

Next, Pitkin went to the Black Angus Meat Market and purchased eight dollars' worth of meat, separated into two packages. One was the cheapest hamburger with the largest percentage of fat and trimmings; the other contained a fine cut of flank steak. The butcher gave him several large rib bones wrapped in two more packages. There was no charge for the bones.

By the time he arrived at the warehouse it was two minutes to 6:00 p.m. He stood on the broken sidewalk for twenty minutes before the street was empty of people and passing cars. Then Pitkin pushed the meat packages through the gap in the splintered plywood sheet that covered a street level window. A car came around the corner and slowed past him. Five more minutes passed before the street was again clear. Quickly, he squeezed through the gap and disappeared inside.

Pitkin stumbled over a pile of pipes and worked his way to the second floor. Somewhere a dog barked. Near the back of the building he found the tall door with the padlock, and reaching into his pocket he produced a small change purse. Extracting a key he unlocked the door. Before entering he selected two of the meat packages, the flank steak and one of bones. He pushed them both through ahead of him.

"Fleisch," he said, "fleisch, fleisch." It was the second time he had spoken that day.

A great dark shadow yanked the packages away and began tearing at the wrappings. Pitkin stood with drooping shoulders and watched as the ravenous animal ate. It tore the end off each package and ate meat, bone, paper, and string. When the beast finished, it came to Pitkin and licked his hands and smelled him all over. Pitkin held up one finger and clucked with his tongue against the roof of his mouth. The animal sat immediately, then moved its front feet forward, laid flat on its belly, and began to clean itself. Pitkin stroked the fine animal and crooned to it softly. Before he left, he filled the animal's water bucket from a leaking pipe and drank some water himself.

On the return trip Pitkin stopped in front of a small Vietnamese grocery and looked at his wristwatch. It flashed 7:10, 7:10, 7:10. Looking up and down the street, he saw no one. He reached deep into his pocket and pulled out his father's watch. He pressed the small thumb release and the lid popped open. He found it to be twelve minutes and twenty-five seconds past 7:00—the correct time. His mother was still smiling at him. He closed the lid and put the watch in his pocket. Then he looked at the storefront.

Two men were lounging behind the glass. They were dark-complected men. Maybe Syrians, or worse, Turks. A chill ran through Pitkin's body. This was not good. He knew them; he had seen them with others under the elevated. These were wicked men. He knew they had seen him and they had coveted his watch.

This worried Pitkin but he knew what to do.

By the time he walked back to his rooms under the Eastex, it was late, after 9:00. He had taken a well-planned route, doubling back several times, and was certain the two men could not have followed him. His feet hurt, but he set to work and laid a fire in a small metal pot. Then he opened the two remaining packages and cooked himself half of the fatty hamburger. The rest he saved. The dogs that guarded his rooms fought over the remaining package of rib bones.

For awhile, Pitkin decided, he would tie one or two of the dogs a short distance away from his rooms. They would watch and bark and this would give him added protection from the wicked Turks, if they came in the night.

CHAPTER FOURTEEN

*I*t was 9:30 a.m. when Willie Fish poked her head around the door and spoke in a clear, soft voice. "Doctor Mac, you remember that TV reporter from Channel 12? She's on your private line. She says it's personal."

MacDonell grumbled to himself, but picked up the phone. "What can I do for you, Red?" he asked, trying to inject some genuine warmth into his voice.

Ryder started off fast. "Look, Doctor, you know Robin Paine. Right?"

"I know him," MacDonell said. He was unable to keep the sour tone out of his reply. It was Robin Paine again. Robin Paine still. Robin Paine-in-the-ass.

"Well, go along with me for a minute, will you? I'm trying to negotiate a little truce. You know Robin has this animal park project he's been working on down in Brazoria County. He calls it Pollyanna Park."

"I've heard about it," MacDonell answered.

"Channel 12 sponsors it, you know. And we were wondering if we could ask you to come down for a visit. Maybe we could do a piece with you in it. You know, a segment on the park's good works and the cooperation between the city and the park in caring for animals that are hard to find homes for."

How smooth, he thought.

"We could make you look very good," she said.

"Come on, Red, I *am* very good."

"I know you are, Doctor. However, sometimes even the best of us can use a little PR."

No argument there, MacDonell thought. "What's in it for you?" he asked.

"Cooperation, that's all. Cooperation and good will."

It's a little late for that, he thought. "I'd have to clear it with my director, and the department's PIO. But, of course, you already know that."

"We've already talked to Dr. Trimble and he loved the idea," Ryder replied.

There was an uncomfortable silence while he tried to figure out how to answer. Talk to the press—don't talk to the press. He ground his teeth. One thing he could always count on was consistency. "Let me get back to you on it? Give me your number," he said, with resignation in his voice.

MacDonell hung up the phone and looked at the papers on his desk. There was plenty of work to do. He put his head in his hands and squeezed his temples. He wondered how long he was going to have this particular headache.

To be safe he called Trimble's office. The man wasn't in. Neither was the PIO. However, the secretary confirmed what he suspected. Ryder and Paine had been in Trimble's office a day or so ago, and talked to the man himself. "They seemed to agree on whatever it was they talked about," the secretary told him. "Everybody was smiling." MacDonell was convinced that someone other than himself was running the bureau.

He made the appointment with Ryder for late in the afternoon. Then he chewed his liverwurst and onion sandwich and hoped for bad breath. By 3:00 p.m. he was on the road. Pollyanna Park was south, in Brazoria County, and at 3:45 he rolled through a set of tall, rickety pole gates and across an oyster shell parking lot. He could smell the gulf.

Except for Channel 12's Chevy Blazer, MacDonell saw no other vehicles. He parked close to the building. It was a dry, pleasant place. The original building was small, and it had been amended several times in a haphazard way. There was a generous sprinkling of cedar bushes throughout the property and one large live oak next to the sprawling building.

A pole-fence corral on the left of the building contained three horses: a dark bay, a dun, and a chestnut. A boy of about twelve was brushing the chestnut. A big pasture at the rear held a variety of scrawny cattle. One exception was a monstrous longhorn steer. The rest looked underfed and at least one limped when it moved. There was little shade, and the cows gathered in a muddy corner by a large metal watering trough and an empty feed bunker. Two goats with droopy ears ran up to MacDonell's car, bleated a few times, then wandered off. MacDonell sat with the windows rolled down, enjoying the sweet odor of farm animals.

The screen door opened and a stony-faced young woman in jeans and a light cotton shirt leaned out the door. "Come on in," she yelled. "Have a look around."

MacDonell steeled himself. "God," he thought, "I hope they haven't planned any TV stunts for this afternoon." He put on his old hat, walked to the door and stepped inside.

Inside a dried-out saddle, some tack, two gray metal desks, and two barrels labeled Rolled Oats constituted the furnishings. Two hipless, braless cowgirls in faded jeans, boots, and striped shirts tilted back on metal folding chairs. Both were grim, sun-bleached palominos, no lips. Their legs stretched long in front of them and they each squeezed a diet coke. An artist's rendering of a much fancier gate decorated one wall. A faded panel door behind the women looked as if it went to the back of the building. Another door with a window and dusty chintz curtains opened into the corral. A third door led to a closet or an inner office.

"You are Doctor MacDonell, aren't you?" one of the girls asked when he had closed the door.

"Yes ma'am," he said.

One girl smirked. "Robin's going to be a little late," she said. "We expect him in a few minutes."

"No problem," MacDonell said. He took his hat off and looked for a place to sit.

The taller of the two girls avoided his eyes and spoke to the wall behind him. "He says we should make you comfortable. Want a soft drink or something?"

"That's nice, no thanks."

"We've got to go put some liniment on one of the mares. You can wait in his office if you like." The shorter woman clomped across the room. She put a key in the closet door, pushed it open, and motioned him to have a seat. "It's the only air-conditioned room in the building," she said.

MacDonell stepped in and shifted his hat under his arm. He looked around the small windowless office. He listened a minute, then moved to the door and opened it wide. Peering out into the tack room, he found the two women had slipped out to go doctor the horse. He let the door stand open.

Turning around, MacDonell scanned the cluttered office. In spite of it being February, the air-conditioner chugged away turning the room into an icebox. The place smelled of mouse urine. On the wall behind a desk was a blow-up of an old photograph of a monkey tied into a test apparatus. Bleak and grainy, the picture showed intravenous tubes and wires running from the animal to various measuring devices in the background. He had seen it dozens of times. Taken at Brooks AFB in the 80's, it was used by the People for the Ethical Treatment of Animals to inflame the passions of old activists and stir the blood of new converts. Every so often it was mailed to animal fanciers, humane organizations, and other potential financial supporters.

Pinned to the wall beside the monkey photo were ten Polaroids in a neat row. MacDonell walked closer, bent at the waist, and squinted through his bifocals. Two pictures were of a ruddy barrel-chested man in blue bib overalls. The strap on one side was down, and the man's hairy chest stuck out. Standing to one side was a stumpy-looking bear on a heavy chain. MacDonell recognized the man and the setting. It was rednecking at its best. A third picture showed a figure in black, a ninja— Robin Paine. MacDonell recalled an uproar a couple years back over a roadhouse featuring bear wrestling, and Paine's group demanding the BARC file cruelty charges. By the time Bragg determined the location to be in the city limits, the act had headed south.

The other photos were of spread-eagled mud wrestlers, hard looking women in neon bikinis, awash in a watery brown gruel. They were groveling and writhing in a plastic lined pit. Leering men with longnecked bottles of beer provided the raucous background for the pictures. MacDonell surmised that Paine had been out checking on the wrestling bear and had stuck around to catch a few of the other attractions.

He looked at his watch. Outside he could hear sounds of a horse cantering. He looked at the desk and the wall with its sad collection of pictures. On a small shelf under the pictures was a large red three-ring binder. He looked at his watch a second time and then nosed around for a magazine to read. He stepped to the shelf and lifted the cover of the binder. It contained slotted plastic dividers with more Polaroids. The pictures were of neglected animals, skinny, sick horses, and sad dogs. MacDonell flipped a few more pages. Between the last two pages was a gummy stack of dark, unfocused Polaroids, people in surgical greens, steel cages, green oxygen tanks, and a surgery table with overhead lights. He recognized the University of Texas cardiac research lab.

A commotion in the parking lot signaled that he should be minding his own business. He closed the binder and walked to the office door.

Robin Paine held the outer door open and Rhonda Ryder stepped in. She was followed by her cameraman. She appeared out of place in the dusty surroundings dressed in a short, tight-fitting, black outfit with a wide cream-colored belt and matching spike heels. There was cream piping around the lapels and at least one too many buttons were undone at the collar. Her makeup was a little heavy, but it looked like the standard TV cover-up.

Paine made an excuse about being late and introduced the cameraman. MacDonell knew the man, and they exchanged nods. Everyone was pleasant, but Paine seemed to be anticipating hostility or at least sharp words. MacDonell picked up a folding chair, turned it around, and straddled it cowboy style. "Mind if I sit?"

"Did the girls offer you a cold drink?" Paine asked.

"Sure did. Showed me your inner sanctum and asked me to make myself comfortable."

Paine glanced at the open door. "Good," he said.

MacDonell thought the young man looked undone. "What can I do for you folks?" he asked. He wanted to end the visit as soon as he could and get out.

"Doctor Mac," Ryder began, "thanks for coming. As I mentioned on the phone, we're planning an extensive publicity campaign centered here on Pollyanna Park. We'd like to get some cooperation from the city in…"

"Before we get specific, Rhonda," Paine interrupted, "I think we ought to show him our successes."

"If you like."

"Show me what?" MacDonell asked.

Paine, in the manner of a small rooster, swaggered to the heavy door at the far side of the room and said, "Let's look." Behind the door, a short hallway led to a second door. Behind it, several chain-link gates defined small indoor kennels. A variety of good-looking dogs stood at the front of each kennel and vied for a pat or a scratch. The odor was sharp. A few wiggled at their gates, but most jumped up on the chain-link. The barking was boisterous, but non-threatening. MacDonell put his knuckles up to the noses of several and they sniffed, shivered, and licked at his fingers.

"You sure have a way with animals," Ryder said.

"Yup," MacDonell replied. He looked into the woman's eyes, thinking it was time to turn on the bullshit detector and watch where he stepped.

At the far end, a large single kennel the size of a small bedroom filled the back one-third of the building. Rebar had been welded in a vertical pattern behind the original chain-link, which appeared well-chewed. MacDonell sensed that Paine was trying to make the whole thing appear casual, but as if drawn by a magnet, the group shuffled on toward the reinforced chain-link. Paine was effusive, giving small details on each animal as they passed. He explained how he had acquired each one, what it looked like before he got it, and the vast improvement in its appearance and temperament.

When Paine got to the big kennel, he paused. "And here," he said with a flourish, "is what I do best."

In the cell were two veteran pit bulls. One was an enormous, fawn-colored male. Both ears were torn and the cheeks and flews were covered with battle scars. MacDonell estimated its weight at ninety pounds. The other was a gray-brindle male with a wide white blaze on the face, neck, and chest. It weighed eighty-five pounds. Both were far too big for typical backwoods contests and, in spite of the raucous noise, both were sleeping.

"Notice how they get along," Paine said.

MacDonell knelt and studied the two dogs. One had been dragged in. Watermarks on the floor were tell-tale. "Big feet on that one," was MacDonell's only comment. He suspected the two behemoths had been zonked.

"When I got these two, I had to hammer them apart with a breaking stick. Took four of us. They were locked up like two semi's in a head-on collision." Paine showed his teeth in a wide smile.

"Thrilling," said MacDonell.

"But now after lots of love, good nutrition, and plenty of behavioral conditioning, I'm able to control their natural instinct to fight."

MacDonell looked up and frowned. "I wouldn't have guessed you'd admit that fighting was a natural instinct for this breed."

Paine gave him a challenging look, but couldn't seem to organize his thoughts.

Reaching, MacDonell retrieved a small piece of green plastic from the floor. It was the plastic sleeve used to protect a sterile needle. He stuck it in his pocket and stood up, marveling at the stupidity of these people. "Amazing," he remarked.

"Isn't it?" Ryder agreed. "We were there with a camera when the constables busted that bunch of Neanderthals."

They turned and headed back the way they had come, Paine and Ryder leading the way. It struck MacDonell that there were no small breeds in any of the cages. "I'm impressed," he said. "But what's all this got to do with me?"

"Doctor Mac," Ryder began, showing all her TV teeth, "to be quite candid, the park needs more public participation, more contributions. We want to develop the idea that the city and Pollyanna Park and Channel 12 can work together to bring about accomplishments like the ones you've seen here today." She gestured back at the snoring pit bulls. "To make a meaningful improvement in the lives of animals in Houston we need money. Channel 12 has already programmed a number of thirty-second spots, and a few sixty-second spots, in the next two months to inform the public of Robin's work. If the city could find a way to participate in some of our programs, then potential donors will know there's a solid underpinning in the organization." She put a hand on Paine's shoulder. "Robin has big plans," she said, smiling at him and then back at MacDonell.

"In other words, you're developing your credibility."

"I suppose you could put it that way."

"Do the wheels at Channel 12 know about all this?" MacDonell asked.

Ryder tried to disguise a dark look, then forced a smile. "Of course they do," she said. "I speak for the station."

MacDonell wondered if Channel 12 knew what they were getting into. "How do you see the city fitting into this project?"

"For one thing, it won't cost you. We know for a fact you pick up lots of animals that are hard to place," Paine said. "Tigers, lions, small exotics, livestock, undesirable canines." They reached the big tack room and Ryder and her cameraman sat down. Paine reached out with his foot and closed the door to the kennel. Ryder crossed her legs, exposing a yard of thigh. Paine watched MacDonell's eyes and kept on talking. "We'd like you to donate a few animals so we can get them into rehabilitation. Maybe a big cat."

So would lots of people, MacDonell thought.

"With animals like that I can develop this place into a money making proposition." Paine hesitated, realizing his remark must have sounded wrong. "Of course, it would become a haven for mistreated animals," he said, hurrying on.

"I prefer to see wild animals in the wild," MacDonell said. "Short of that, in a properly managed zoo."

"But you'll admit most zoos won't take the kinds of animals you get in," Paine argued.

Sadly, MacDonell couldn't disagree. He stood for a moment, considering everything he'd seen and heard, and he didn't find much to be impressed with. A menagerie was a bunch of animals collected by an amateur, and Paine qualified. MacDonell had seen plenty of well-meaning people exhibiting animals in slapdash roadside cages, hoping for funds to flood in. It never worked. And rehabilitating killer dogs—it was like paroling rapists.

"If you want a personal observation," MacDonell said, "if every pit bull on the face of the earth would evaporate tomorrow morning, I wouldn't mourn their passing."

"You're against pit bulldogs, I take it," Ryder said.

"They're not one of God's creatures, darlin'. The damn things are man's handiwork. To tell you the truth, I'd trade a million of them for one scrawny pair of passenger pigeons or a dozen Attwater's prairie chickens. I think recycling a fighting dog is a waste of money that could be put to better use. And I sure don't agree that agencies supported by tax dollars should be a part of it. Other than that, I don't have any strong opinions." He stepped to the door. "I've got to go, but I'll tell you what I will do. I'll share all this with Dr. Trimble. I'll let you know how he feels. Is that fair?"

"You don't support our project, then?"

"I represent a public health agency, Robin. I don't see how any of this improves the public health. From what I've seen you don't have the facilities for the big cats we get in, and frankly, rehabilitating pit bull-dogs?…please."

In the parking lot, Ryder launched a parting shot. "You have an awfully one-sided view of what's good for animals."

MacDonell leaned against his car. "Not long ago," he said, "a council-man called me and reported a woman keeping a pig in a residential neighborhood. He knew we had ordinances against certain livestock and he wanted action. The lady argued the pig was related to an even more famous pig. She said her pig was an attraction. It helped feed the homeless. So she called her state representative. He, of course, jumped on it like the proverbial duck on a June bug. I had to go to Austin, stand before a committee and be raked over the coals by this pip-squeak about a law I didn't write. He implied I was a racist and used the term 'selective enforcement,' saying pigs, as a race of animals, were being dis-criminated against. He got a lot of laughs, but what he wanted was to exempt this one stinking pig, selective enforcement in his constituent's favor. It was all designed to get both men a little media attention, and it did. The councilman's now a state senator, and the other idiot got reelected."

MacDonell got in his car, rolled down the glass and started the engine. "They're doing great things with genetic engineering up at A & M," MacDonell said, trying to sound casual. "Last year the animal science department crossed abalone DNA with crocodile DNA. Strange looking thing."

Ryder looked at him, puzzled.

"They called it an *ab-o-dile.*"

The cameraman smirked and Paine started to walk away.

"Couldn't call it a *croc-o-baloney.* Could they?"

Chapter Fifteen

*T*he phone rang three times before MacDonell could get to it. He had told the kids three rings was it. Somebody better answer the darn thing or heads would roll. Now the kids were gone and here he was stumbling in the dark trying to find the stupid thing himself. He squinted at the clock, then fumbled to find his glasses. He picked up the clock and held it close to his eyes. It was 2:07 a.m.

"Mac," the voice said. "Sorry to bother you so late, but can you come to the city tonight?" It was Sam Goodson.

"Tonight? It's two in the morning."

"I wouldn't call if it wasn't important."

"What's up?" MacDonell said, feeling for his glasses.

"We've found another body, Doc. It's like the others. There's not much left, but we'd like you to come take a look. This time there's footprints."

***

MacDonell could see red and blue strobes from blocks away. A chill ran up his back. The scene between LaBranch and Crawford was well lit. It was in a forgotten park across from a small federal building. Floods on tripods illuminated the area. Along the curb, knee-high thistles had sprouted and gone to seed, bright green winter rye had taken over. Near the intersection of Crawford and Webster, uniformed officers were holding the media behind yellow tape.

Goodson spotted MacDonell and escorted him through a cluster of lab men to the muddy foot impressions. Weeds were trampled, chunks of grass torn out. The nearby body bag was half full. Trying to ignore the gore, MacDonell got on one knee and took a close look at several well-defined tracks. "Get pictures of these?" he asked.

"Our guys know what they're doing, Doc."

"Got a tape?" MacDonell continued.

"We measured them already," Goodson answered. "They're five and three quarter inches."

"You include the tip of the nails?"

"Just a minute," Goodson said. "Hey, Gordie," he yelled, and trotted over to one of the lab men.

MacDonell rose, crossed the ruptured sidewalk, stepped off the curb, and walked several yards. He slowed, hunkered down again. Bloody animal tracks disappeared south. Raising his head, he looked down the block, then got up and walked along Crawford. Shreds of clothing, blood, and general nastiness were everywhere. In a minute Goodson was puffing alongside holding a flashlight. "He says he measured the length of this part right here, Doc." Goodson handed MacDonell a rolled-up tape and used his palm to indicate the pad and toes from the front toe to the back of the heel pad. MacDonell and Goodson walked back to the prints.

"Let me explain this. You've got to add another three quarters of an inch for the front toe nail. If you do that, it makes a grand total of six and a half inches." MacDonell gave him a sober look. "Your wolf theory grows and grows."

"That's what we thought," Goodson said, squinting into the lights. "Some mess, huh?"

They drifted to the street again. "Still, this is a lot of damage for only one animal. It would take several dogs and more than an hour to tear a guy apart like that." MacDonell paused, pulled out a note pad and continued walking. "Adult gray wolves have a print between four and a half and six inches, measured from the heel pad to the end of the longest claw. Red wolves are about an inch shorter. That's what the books say." MacDonell stopped walking and looked back up the street. "What impresses me most is the stride. Look here," he pointed, "and here." He walked five steps, "and here."

Goodson puzzled along. "What do you think?"

MacDonell looked at him. "Another three-fourths of an inch for the claw and you've got a world record Canadian gray wolf."

The two men sauntered back up Crawford to where MacDonell had parked his car. They talked a little more and Goodson revealed there would be a meeting at the 61 Riesner headquarters in the morning. "Can you make it?"

"I'd take it as a compliment," MacDonell answered. "And here's a suggestion."

"Yeah, what?"

"If I were you, I'd wash those tracks off the sidewalk before you let the media in here. Before you know it, one of the papers is going to run a werewolf story."

***

It was too late to drive home so MacDonell went to his office. He picked up the paper, unlocked the outer door, laid his hat on the credenza, and hung up his coat. He unlocked Willie's office and turned on the lights. There was a hollow quality to the empty administrative area. Willie's desk was neat, tidy, and locked. As expected, she had put everything away except a modest package that stood in the middle of her desk. The paperwork showed it had been delivered from a local gun shop. Connie Oaks had initialed the purchase order.

MacDonell cut the tape with a letter opener, unfolded the flaps, and inventoried the contents. The box contained one hundred rounds of .410 ammunition—rifled slugs, five hundred rounds of .22 ammunition—long rifle, hollow points, and one twenty-round box of .30-.30 ammo. MacDonell closed the lid and laid the shipping documents on top of the box.

He looked around the silent office. Two yellow call slips were stuck on his message board. They had come while he was in Brazoria County visiting Pollyanna Park. The first note was in Willie's handsome script. It said, "Doctor T. say no guns!" It had the PIO's phone number on it. MacDonell glanced at the package. Time was when he could purchase weapons, but had no way to buy ammunition.

The second note was from Oaks. It let him know of a meeting at 11:00 in the director's office; the long range planners group. MacDonell could send a representative. He took out his pen, circled the word 'representative,' scribbled an OK over it, and stuck it in Oaks' slot. Goodson's meeting wouldn't be a sleeper.

MacDonell smiled to himself. The bureau had always used firearms to some extent. Officers hadn't carried sidearms since the transfer from the police to the health department, but issuing .410's had been done for years. That was until a break-in emptied the bureau's armory of twenty-six shotguns in 1975. Except for the sawed-off recovered from a pawn shop in '79, only two remained. MacDonell's predecessor added the .22's and .30-.30's in the event a cattle truck or horse trailer tipped over and a veterinarian was unavailable. It was rare.

The city's original animal ordinance, with an effective date of August 1st 1865, stated that unlicensed dogs would be destroyed (shot) by the sheriff after a certain grace period. Today tranquilizers offered other choices.

MacDonell favored the air-driven dart, and in past years had provided training for a handful of his best officers. His big problem would be keeping the ones Longley taught. The officers MacDonell had trained had already been lured to smaller cities. Even Harris County offered better salaries. Giving a fast burner the expensive training just to see Dallas or San Antonio reap the benefit was frustrating.

The question of putting firearms back into the hands of animal control officers had been debated five years ago, after MacDonell requested a firearms policy. He never received a reply. And when Trimble arrived, MacDonell even drafted a policy. Trimble had lost it.

MacDonell studied the classified section of the paper, snipped out a small section, and then put on water for coffee. He had already started on his second cup when his staff began trickling in. When Willie arrived he had her store the ammunition in the safe. At 8:30 HPD called and MacDonell was told the meeting at Riesner would be at 10:30. He used the intervening time to catch up on his paperwork. At 9:00 he called Trimble's PIO. She wasn't in. He tried Trimble directly. No luck. At 10:00 he called again; neither were in. He put Trimble's note and the newspaper clipping in his shirt pocket and headed downtown.

The meeting was on the third floor at 61 Riesner. The building looked like an old warehouse that had been wedged in as an after-thought behind the municipal courts building. Blue and white cruisers parked in small clusters, like horses at hitching rails. MacDonell found parking in two inches of standing water under an I-45 overpass.

Every chair was filled with impressive-looking policemen. MacDonell stood just inside the door, feeling conspicuous among the uniforms and big gold shields. He kept his health department badge tucked in his coat pocket.

After several inside jokes and dog wisecracks the meeting got down to serious business. MacDonell noted that in spite of the lighthearted bantering, the officers seemed tense. In any other city, three deaths with the same M.O. would be called serial killings.

Since there were visitors present, Sam Goodson received an intro-duction from his captain and was identified as the prime investigator. Sam stood up, made an opening statement, then presented thirty minutes of facts and evidence. In essence, the deaths were to be treated as three separate, but related, incidents. Nonetheless, as MacDonell listened he noted several bits of information that, in his mind, connected the deaths to each other closer than ever.

All three victims had been males, one black, two white, all homeless. Each man had been savaged in the same ferocious manner. In all cases it appeared some parts of the internal organs of the victims had been ripped out and eaten by the attacking animal or animals. In the last two cases the ME suspected the victims were alive at the time the animals got hold of them, but that information was being withheld from the media. The first death hadn't been discovered soon enough to make a determination certain, but the man did have a machete-like ankle wound which had cracked the bone. One complicating factor was the first death. It had occurred more than fifteen miles from the vicinity of the last two.

The clearest and most convincing link between the first and third deaths was the footprints, or photos of footprints. These were on display at the front of the room on a small easel. An officer from the Texas Department of Parks and Wildlife sat near the head of the table. He was reluctant to confirm Goodson's theory, but he did agree that both prints were 'wolf-like.' He qualified everything by remarking that wolves were thought to be extinct in this area. Efforts to reintroduce the red wolf into its historic habitat several years ago had been a relative failure. Relative, in that new generations had not been produced in the wild, as far as the wildlife people could tell. The officer mentioned the range of an adult red wolf was between 25 and 30 square miles, an area with a diameter of about five miles.

At this point, MacDonell cleared his throat and raised his hand. Goodson nodded and introduced him as the chief of the city's Bureau of Animal Regulation and Care.

"Do you have a question, Doctor?" Goodson asked.

Turning to the Wildlife officer, MacDonell asked, "Red wolves hybridize with other canine species, don't they?"

"I'm not a wolf biologist, Doctor, but that is my impression."

"Would you guess that they hybridize more or less easily than the gray wolf?" MacDonell continued.

"I'm not sure. I don't know enough about them to say."

"You'd agree that this 25 to 30 mile range is based on the normal diet of a wolf in a wilderness area, wouldn't you?"

The wildlife man nodded his head.

"What's your point, Doc?" Goodson asked.

"Well," MacDonell said, "from what I've read, the red wolf feeds on rodents: mice, rabbits, muskrats, cotton rats, and an occasional nutria."

The wildlife officer shrugged. "Like I said, I'm not a wolf biologist. That sounds reasonable, though."

"My point is that the last known red wolf in Texas was trapped in 1970 and released. Today that wolf would be twenty-five years old, if it was still alive." MacDonell shoved his hands deeper in his pockets and leaned against the wall. "Even if we have the hybrid descendant of a red wolf, it's calving season. I can't understand why, with all the food available, it would suddenly start killing and eating something as large as a human."

The police captain turned in his chair. "I thought wolves hunted things as large as an elk."

"That's the Canadian gray wolf, Captain," MacDonell answered. "Not a red wolf."

"What are you saying, Doc?" the captain asked.

MacDonell looked at the floor for a second and then looked at the man asking the question. "You may think I'm nuts, but judging from the footprints and all the damage, my bet is that we've got an imported Canadian gray wolf out there. Or even worse, a wolf/dog hybrid."

The room filled with buzzing voices. Goodson held up his hand for quiet and MacDonell began again. "Gentlemen, I don't think a gray wolf could have trotted all the way down here from Canada. Somebody would have had to import it. But my money's on the other possibility—that it's a hybrid."

"A what?" the captain asked.

"In the United States today, the wolf/dog hybrid is getting to be a real problem, Captain. The wolf and the dog are both members of the same species, Canis. *Canis lupus* is the gray wolf and *Canis rufus* is the red. *Canis familiaris* is the domesticated dog. All three variants can interbreed. For that matter, you can include *Canis latrans*, the common coyote. Right now it just happens that wolf/dog hybrids are popular among certain macho animal lovers."

"Wouldn't breeding a wolf with a dog give you something in between? A half-wolf, half-poodle doesn't sound too dangerous to me," the captain said with a grin.

"In the first place, it's seldom a poodle," MacDonell countered. "When you intentionally breed two animals like this, you choose large robust specimens and you often get what the cattle breeders call first-cross or hybrid vigor, a large healthy specimen, frequently bigger than either parent. The numb-nuts who do this kind of thing expect it to look like a wolf, but act like a dog. The problems start when it doesn't read the plan. The animal sometimes looks like a Malamute, or a Husky, but, sad to say, it often acts like a wolf."

"People raise these things?" a sergeant asked.

"Yes," MacDonell answered, pulling a piece of folded newsprint from his jacket pocket. "It's an ego thing. The Chronicle lists one for sale this morning. A twelve week old pup. It's in the pet section."

There was a low buzz of exclamation and amazed curses. One or two officers seemed mesmerized by what they were hearing.

"The real problem, as I see it, is pretty soon these monsters start aggravating their owners. A friend or family member gets nipped, the critter outgrows its cage, or actually eats the cage, or the owner just plain gets tired of feeding it. The next thing you know it's sold or otherwise passed on to someone else. The situation repeats itself, person to person, family to family, until a major tragedy occurs. Back in 1988 a wolf/dog hybrid in Florida went from one family to another until it got turned over to a humane society. They didn't realize what they had either, and since it was such an impressive beast, they couldn't resist finding it a good home. They adopted it out to a couple that put it behind a four foot fence. Within a few hours it went over that fence. A few streets away it killed a four year old boy."

The captain saw what MacDonell was driving at. "You're telling us this isn't some wild animal that's moved into the city. It was brought in and it's now living with some family and being let out to roam at night?"

MacDonell nodded. "That's a possibility."

"Can you be sure about this, Doc?" a sergeant asked.

"Damn, Sarg, I'm doing the best I can…this is what I call 'MacDonell's first theory.'"

A rumble of laughter passed around the room.

"But…" MacDonell continued, "I think the notion is every bit as good as the theory that a native Texas red wolf ran short of rabbits out on 290 and moved into the city."

Goodson had a question. "How would your theory account for the death out on 290 and then two more twenty miles away?"

MacDonell aimed a thumb out the window. "I see people going down the Eastex every day with a dog tied—or in some cases not tied—in the back of a pickup." MacDonell looked around at the assembled officers. "You guys see them too. When you see a big Rottweiler, you don't give it a second thought." He looked around the room. "Next time you see a Husky or a Malamute, I bet you'll think twice."

"I sure as hell will," the sergeant said.

There was a hum of agreement around the table. A few officers tried to crack little jokes, but the effort died.

Goodson spoke again. "I think the next order of business is a plan of action." He looked at the assembled officers.

There was a general silence, though a few officers whispered among themselves. Someone quipped about cutting a requisition for silver bullets. A ripple of laughter relieved some of the tension.

"Regular bullets ought to work," MacDonell said. "However, if I'm right, the solution is going to be a lot harder than the revelation."

"I figure we ought to turn this problem over to your organization," the captain muttered. "We're not dogcatchers."

Two policemen stood up.

"Wait a minute, guys," MacDonell said over the bustle. "I can talk to the owner of the pup in the paper, but if it doesn't pan out, I'm about at the end of my investigative rope. I've got a total field force of eighteen officers and on the day shift and only two or three people on the two night shifts. I've got six firearms in my entire arsenal, and two of those are .22's, and my training officer is brand new and still working out the kinks."

A sergeant raised his hand. "No handguns?"

MacDonell shook his head. "We're more concerned with accuracy than firepower. Remember, what we go after seldom returns fire. And none of my people are certified peace officers, anyway. All of which means I'm not equipped to take this on. Remember, the city covers six hundred square miles. HPD is going to have to take the lead."

That obvious bit of logic brought nods, and those officers who were standing sat down.

MacDonell went on. "My little bureau can run a computer check to see if anyone has been stupid enough to registered a wolf/dog hybrid. I can ask Harris County to do the same. These animals are illegal in Houston, but I'm not sure about the county. It'll be a short list, I can tell you that."

"How about Crimestoppers?" somebody asked. "We could ask people to call us if they've seen one of these hybrids."

MacDonell shook his head. "People are poor at identifying dogs. Most think every black dog is a Lab and every attack is a pit bull. When the media reports a child being bitten, we get calls reporting pits everywhere. They turn out to be everything from Boxers to Boston Terriers."

"We got a footprint, Doc." the captain remembered.

"What's the admissibility of dog prints in court?" MacDonell asked.

Goodson shrugged.

Human footprints were one thing, but MacDonell suspected no one in the room had presented animal tracks as evidence in a court of law.

Soon everybody was talking again.

"Suppose the owner just up and hauls ass." someone said.

"How you gonna move anything as big as a wolf without being seen?" someone else asked.

The discussion went on until noon without agreement. Goodson decided on a minimal course of action. As a start, a small force of police officers would patrol in the area downtown under the elevated. MacDonell agreed to furnish one officer with a T-gun each evening to provide back-up. The meeting broke at 12:15 and MacDonell went with Goodson to his office to work out the details.

"Tell me something, Sam," MacDonell said when the door was closed. "What would you guys be doing different if this was a regular serial killing?"

Goodson studied MacDonell's face. "Regular?"

"You know what I mean!"

"I guess I'd be running prints through the FBI computer, looking for a weapon, checking ballistics, fiber analysis, patterns of wounding, blood spatter patterns, doing psychological profiles, and running up a big phone bill with the FBI's Violent Crimes people out in Quantico."

"Uh huh."

"You see my problem?" Goodson said.

Goodson treated MacDonell to an indigestible police lunch. After consuming a peppery Boudain on a bun, MacDonell went back to BARC. He wondered what firemen ate.

***

Sitting backward on a chair in front of Willie's desk, MacDonell listened as she brought him up to speed on the day's events. Lots of calls expressing opinions on shooting strays in the city. Four to three against, she said.

"And...?"

"And I tell 'em, 'call up 8000 Stadium.'"

"By the way, did Connie make it to that meeting?"

"Mr. Oaks, he stay home, sick. Cap'n Bragg, he go."

"Hmff..." MacDonell muttered. "Is he back yet?"

"Not yet. And you ain't gonna b'lieve. He say Doc Trimble done emceed the meeting."

"No way."

"I ain't pulling your leg, Doc. That's what the man say."

Later MacDonell found Bragg and explained about helping Goodson with an officer on the evening shift. "Keep it low key," he told the captain. "See to it he has a few darts and a good radio."

The day ended with rainstorms prowling the edges of Houston. MacDonell slogged home with a tail-wind, sprinkles, and scattered hail.

Chapter Sixteen

*I*n the cold-blooded north, winter was rock solid. Across the Great Lakes, blizzards brought traffic to a halt. From Duluth to Detroit cities were digging out. Except for those who drove the snowplows nobody moved. By noon Houston was forecast in the mid to low seventies. Galveston beaches would be sprinkled with aimless strollers and a few sunbathers.

As the hibernal season continued, late migrators began their circular approach. Larger and more numerous than the stark white whooping crane, the sandy brown Winnebago, and the lesser motor homes began their annual appearance on gulf coast freeways. Flocks of Minnesota and Michigan snowbirds wheeled and turned, looking for an early opening golf course.

For the permanent resident, Houston is an unzoned anachronism. Within the length of a single street, people of glaringly dissimilar means live side by side. On fashionable River Oaks Boulevard the mansions of Houston's royalty, with their expanses of St. Augustine grass, stretch endlessly. Majestic iron gates and ivy-covered walls keep the riffraff out and the occasional Vietnamese potbellied pig in.

One Key-Map page away, in the old Midtown area, men sleep in their clothes under the elevateds. At the turn of the century this enclave was the classiest place in Houston, preceding River Oaks in sophisticated living. Soon, however, small home businesses began to chip away at the edges of the old silk-stocking district. The next sign was auto repair in the driveway or goats in the backyard, or worse, a print shop in a converted garage. And more recently Asians moved in to establish ethnic food markets.

Frank Bragg left his house early, his radio and map book under his arm. He tossed the sun-bleached volume on the dash, turned on the 2-way and let it warm, then took a heading on the towers of the big city. Bragg didn't drive a truck with frosty white cages like the rest of the fleet. As BARC's one and only captain, he felt the need to disguise his dogcatcher image. The better to monitor his officers, he said. A small airline crate behind the forest green cab was the single clue that he dealt in animals.

On the seat beside him, the Motorola chattered as officers reported themselves 10-8 (ready for duty) in their districts. As usual, calls were coming fast to beat Bragg's forty-five minute time limit.

Bragg was anxious to get to the office and he kept a heavy foot. His first task would be to draft the week's shift changes. Assignments for the late shift had been posted, but tonight Bragg intended to supplement it. The smooth walnut stock of one of the bureau's two Winchesters gleamed on the seat beside him.

Farther to the north, MacDonell was headed in the same direction. He was half an hour behind schedule. Before leaving, he gave Jeannie detailed instructions on taking Lil to see Dr. Summerfield. She was ailing again and they discussed several options, including the looming question of euthanasia. "If it comes to it," he'd said, "I'll do it. I'll be damned if I'll let some other sob do it while I'm at work—not after fourteen years." They hadn't disagreed, but he wanted to make sure Jeannie was clear on whose responsibility it was.

In the city, on Rosalie Place, Sharon Westergaard was late for work, too. Her alarm hadn't gone off and she was rushing around, trying to do her hair and find the right skirt. Breakfast was coffee only, and she left the paper in its plastic bag. She would also have to pass on her jogging for just this one morning. Callie, her big German Shepherd, would spend the day in the backyard. Since it was clear, and the fence had been repaired, it was a reasonable alternative, and Callie could always get in on the screened porch.

Sharon patted Callie on her big head and let her out the back door. Then, digging for car keys she hurried to the garage. She waved at the man next door as she backed out.

For once in a coon's age, BARC anticipated an uneventful day. Starting off, the fleet was operational when the morning shift began checking out. Connie Oaks had a truck deadlined, but it was an older model. A ton and a half of dog food had been delivered and stored on the third level of the domed animal shelter. A personnel space had cleared and he was interviewing a clerk-typist.

Late in the morning Bragg found the lady in Montgomery County selling the wolf/dog pup, and from her he had gotten the name and address of the buyer, a person in Alvin, Texas. The seller didn't own either parent and had imported two pups from someone in Washington State. She had kept one and sold the other to the Alvin lady for $350.

According to Bragg's research, there were six guard dog companies in the Houston/Galveston area. Two were inside the city limits. He had been to all six and talked to the owners. One place had twenty-one animals. The rest had fewer than ten and only one used pit bulls exclusively. The popular breeds were Dobermans, Rottweilers and German Shepherds. There was one trio of large Akitas.

Most of the dogs Bragg had seen were not high quality, but many were AKC-registrable. The operator using pit bulls boasted of putting his dogs through Schutzhund training.

While pinning MacDonell's map, Bragg reminded him of a time when officers destroyed a pair of pits that escaped an industrial park and headed to a grade school. It stirred up a yellow jacket's nest. The dog's owner threatened to sue the city. MacDonell deplored the shooting, even though it had been justified, but what bothered him most was the fact city prosecutors and some members of council waffled when it came to backing up his officers. The city successfully dodged the suit, as MacDonell remembered, and the company had since gone out of business. Nevertheless, he made it clear to the entire field force that he wanted to avoid similar confrontations.

The phone lit up and Willie buzzed in. MacDonell nodded into the phone and dismissed Bragg. In seconds he realized that history would be made. Trimble was coming out to BARC for a look around, and MacDonell received the courtesy of a two hour notice. It was the first announced visit in his recollection, and the first he would be present to participate in. It would be a bother to keep the good doctor entertained, but because it was so rare, he wanted to take full advantage of the opportunity.

Trimble arrived with his driver, his PIO, and a health department photographer. MacDonell started in his office by explaining the twelve districts and the manpower distribution required to cover the city. Trimble's eyes glazed over. MacDonell went on to the daily animal population and the turn-over rate. He could see it didn't register. Hurriedly, he outlined his new training effort and his attempt to provide assistance to HPD. He mentioned the police concern that a dangerous animal had attacked street people in the old Midtown area. To MacDonell's surprise the twitchy physician bolted out, knocking over the in-basket and sending papers flying. The three retainers scurried along behind.

"The police haven't developed a method of narrowing this thing down..." MacDonell called after him. He was at a quick pace to keep up, and talking to the man's back. "...but."

Outside, Trimble turned around and interrupted. "Dr. MacDonell, I don't want to hear about your urge to play war games with the police department. You're not a soldier anymore. You're a health officer. Remember that." The photographer popped a flare.

MacDonell boiled inside. "Two homeless men, maybe three, have been attacked, killed, and dismembered by an unidentified animal. HPD asked for assistance."

Trimble stopped, turned, looked MacDonell level in the eyes and shrugged his shoulders. "I don't want to talk about it anymore," he said. "Let the police take care of it. If they call you again, tell them to have Chief Brisco contact me directly. Now let's get on with it. I need to be seen by a few of your employees."

Okay, MacDonell thought…if that's the way you want it. "I'd like you to visit the euthanasia room and meet Dr. Clemmons. We're unloading just now, and we have some stopped up drains."

"Let's keep this up-beat, Duncan. I don't have a lot of time."

As they toured the front, Trimble elaborated on a visit he'd had from Robin Paine. The PIO took notes. MacDonell tried to give Trimble his opinion of the young man and his plan to involve the city in his projects.

"You went there, then?" Trimble asked.

"I did."

"What did you think of it?"

MacDonell shook his head and described the place. Trimble was pre-occupied and even MacDonell's vivid description of the two chemically mellowed dogs failed to dampen his enthusiasm.

"No, no, no," Trimble chattered. "PR, that's the ticket. Good PR. It'll increase our adoptions. It's surefire." He shook hands with clerks, kennel help, visitors, even the security guard, stopping to wash his hands at least twice. The wet floors and the animal odors were a particular problem for him. He avoided walls, countertops, doorknobs, and puddles. In a surprise move, however, he stopped to get his picture taken poking his finger through the bars at a puppy. When it licked at him, he asked for a paper towel.

MacDonell tried to get to a topic of substance but the farce continued. Trimble was preoccupied with one compelling objective: getting back to 8000 Stadium Drive.

MacDonell tried a question. "Have you come to any conclusions about firearms, sir?"

"Firearms," Trimble snapped. "Didn't you get my note. I don't foresee any animal situation that can't be handled with tranquilizers. Your woman *is* working, isn't she?"

When Trimble's car cleared the gate, MacDonell went to his office, ripped off his tie and threw down his coat. In a fury he attacked the mountain of paperwork that had fallen out of his in-basket and littered his floor. For three solid hours he explained to disgruntled citizens, in writing, why the laws of the city were so aggravating. He waxed eloquent about why the rights of animal lovers clashed with the rights of animal haters.

At 6:00 MacDonell put it away and headed up the Eastex. Jeannie had made reservations for dinner at Pappas with J.D. Longley, and he was late. He was still churning when he got to the restaurant. The women had already ordered.

MacDonell tasted his wife's fish and mumbled something.

"That's salmon, darling," Jeannie told him. "When I get you home I'm taking your temperature."

Longley smiled.

He sampled Jeannie's wine and slumped in his chair.

"You like?"

"Mmmm."

"Sit up straight."

The crowd was sparse. MacDonell ordered a second bottle of wine. When it came he pushed back his chair and indicated that he would pour.

Longley extended her glass.

"How are you finding things?" he said.

Longley said she'd finished her lesson plans a few days before, and the first shipment of new Telinject equipment was in. She bubbled, and MacDonell envied her enthusiasm.

She put down her wine and closed her eyes. "Your captain knows a lot less about animals than he should, Doctor Mac, and it carries over to the entire field force. Half of them can't tell one breed of dog or cat from another. And some of them just don't seem to care."

"Tell me about it. Animal work like this doesn't always attract the best minds."

"We need to teach these officers that dogs and cats are more than just nuisances," she said. "Give them a chance to experience the positive side. I've set up an obedience demonstration for next Saturday and everybody is invited."

"You doing this by yourself?"

"I've asked one of your field officers, Ron Reyes, to help me. He says he's in a Schutzhund club and might be able to persuade a buddy to put on some protection dog work."

"Schutzhund?"

She gave him a skeptical look. "I'm not sure how good they are."

MacDonell stroked his chin.

"With your permission, I'd like to acquaint your officers with a larger variety of animal experiences, dog shows, field trials, bomb and drug detection work, rescue dogs, that kind of stuff. Some of your older officers would ticket a seeing-eye dog just for the hell of it."

"I hate to disappoint you, but if you want any kind of turnout, I'll have to authorize paid overtime."

Her eyes narrowed. "And…?"

MacDonell looked at Jeannie then at Longley. "I can swing it," he said.

Jeannie turned to her husband. "You're so busy now you can't handle it all. Willie told me you had forty letters to answer today."

"Willie talks too much."

"And you're taking on too much," Jeannie snapped back. "What about Carol taking up some of the slack?"

MacDonell looked at his wife in astonishment. "Are you kidding? If I had her job, I'd probably be hitting the sauce or I'd shoot myself."

Jeannie lowered her voice. "Don't talk like that."

"Trimble says I need to concentrate on PR."

Longley wiped her lips and took a sip of wine. "Would the department fund an officer to train a therapy dog and take it around to nursing homes?" she asked. "I'm sure your boss would see that as a valuable public health project."

MacDonell closed his eyes and propped his chin on his fist. It was a good idea. He thought about Trimble. "I'll give it a good think," he said.

Jeannie ran a cool hand over his bald head. "Tired, Honey? It's that stupid wolf business, piled on top of everything else."

"Wolf business?" Longley said. She looked back and forth. "What wolf business?"

MacDonell looked at her wide eyes. She'd had too much wine and he wondered if he should let her drive. "We're keeping it quiet," he said. "The police, or at least one policeman, think a wolf has moved into the city and is preying on derelicts. Or, as I suggested to him, a hybrid."

Longley drained her glass. "Wolves?

"Or a couple big pits. Whatever the hell, at least one animal with a big print has attacked and—get this—*eaten* large parts of several street people."

"Several?"

"Three at the most."

"What about these cheap excuses for guard dogs you see running around junkyards?" she asked, pouring another glass.

"I've thought about that too. I've given it to Bragg."

She swirled the wine in her glass. "Can I help out?"

"Don't you think you've got enough to keep busy?"

"Probably."

MacDonell gave her a tired smile. "I'll let you know."

Jeannie put in an oar. "Tell J.D. about Pitkin's dogs, Duncan," she said.

"She's read about it," he said. He turned to J.D. "The old man's crazy enough."

Longley gave a low whistle and looked back and forth between MacDonell and Jeannie. She was getting tipsy. She laughed. "Maybe he's trying to solve the housing problem."

"Now you sound just like Duncan." Jeannie said.

MacDonell grimaced, but laughed at the bad joke and made one of his own. "She's right. Maybe I should write up a proposal…"

"Duncan!" Jeannie said, with mild outrage. "People will take you seriously."

MacDonell and Longley grinned at each other, and he turned to his pet peeve. "Wouldn't it be wonderful," he said, "if owners actually obeyed the law and every dog had a tag? We could run a computer check and find all these pit bulls, Rottweilers, wolves, hybrids, and look-alikes.

"Yeah," Longley agreed. "You could find the nasty ones and zap them before they had a chance."

"That's cold, J.D.," MacDonell observed. "The city must be getting to you. You okay to drive?"

"I'm okay. It was supposed to be irony." She sipped her wine. "I have to admit," she said, "this is the last time in my life I'll work at a place that puts perfectly healthy animals to sleep." She took another sip and looked out the window at the traffic. "Dr. Clemmons says you've calculated the weekly turn-over in tons."

"Not me," MacDonell said, holding up his hands. "It was my predecessor. He figured seven to ten tons of dogs and cats go from our place to the landfill every week. Gives you a jolt, doesn't it?" MacDonell emptied the wine into his glass and set the bottle on the next table. "I think his intention was to jar the city council into realizing the enormous waste of it all."

"Did it?"

"No. They pretty much ignored him."

MacDonell held up his wine. "The Germans have a good idea," he said. "They tax and tattoo every pooch in the republic. And I mean every last one, each with his own unique number, just like a car. As a result they have no large scale pet destruction problem. Put down the Germans for efficiency, but at least they've figured out how not to kill their own pets."

"Clever Germans," she said, "Maybe we should tag people," Longley said. Her eyes shone. "Hitler tattooed people."

The wine's getting to her, MacDonell thought. "We do tattoo all the biters," he said, then he shook his head and looked into his glass. The conversation was getting silly. He took out a credit card and touched the sleeve of a passing waiter.

"I've got another idea," Longley announced. "You're familiar with the internet?"

"I've heard of it…but I won't say I'm familiar with it."

"Well, suppose you took a picture of every animal your officers brought in? You could put their snapshot up on the net like a rogues gallery. Then people could search for their lost dogs and cats from the comfort of their own home."

The neglected Australian dog tags flashed briefly through MacDonell's mind. "It's a neat idea," he admitted, "but it won't happen in my life time."

They folded their napkins, stood up and moved to the exit.

"BARC got its first computer about five years after the council members got theirs." MacDonell growled. "Of course their need was much more pressing. They had to keep track of their big money contributors."

"My aren't we bitter," Jeannie remarked.

In the parking lot Longley paced up and down, walked a straight line, and insisted she could drive safely. She asked again about scheduling more animal activities.

"Use your imagination," he agreed. "I'm game for anything that'll stimulate the officer's interest."

***

MacDonell was checking on the dog and locking the garage. When Jeannie got into the kitchen the phone was ringing. It was after midnight. She picked it up and talked to Sam Goodson, while MacDonell was still saying goodnight to Lil.

"Lieutenant Goodson," she said, stepping out to the garage and handing over the cordless. "Sounds a little up-tight."

A feeling of dread rushed to combine with the dullness MacDonell felt from the wine. "Don't tell me," he said.

Goodson's voice was loud. "Doc, I've got some bad news, but it's not what you're thinking. We shot something. We got a big, *big* dog." He paused. "Actually, your guy got it."

"My guy?"

"Yeah. Your Captain Bragg. He shot it about forty-five minutes ago. Trouble is, I don't think it's the one that killed our three trolls."

"Darted it?"

"No, Doc. He *shot* it."

MacDonell cursed under his breath. "Where are you?"

CHAPTER SEVENTEEN

Sharon Westergaard was over the crying part of her rage when MacDonell got there. At this point she was talking lawsuit in a high, clear voice. Callie, her enormous German Shepherd, lay a few yards away wrapped in a lilac-flowered bedspread.

"I don't believe this, Frank. Go over it again." MacDonell was resisting the strong urge to put his foot in the bigger man's lower GI tract.

Bragg started into his whiny explanation, but halfway through MacDonell turned away in disgust.

"My officer agrees, that's about the way it went down, Doc," Goodson said. "He was watching this big German Shepherd come trotting down the street. He drew his weapon, too, if it's any consolation."

"Yeah, Sam," MacDonell replied in dark anger, "but he didn't blow it away."

Goodson nodded. "Your guy just pulls up out of the blue, rolls down his window, lays this rifle on his arm, and blasts the dog right there in the street. The lady was jogging about fifteen yards back. Nobody noticed her, not even my man."

"Listen, Doc," Bragg began. "After that meeting, Trimble told me he wanted something done about this killer dog situation before we got anymore bad publicity. So I…"

"Trimble authorized you to come out here?" MacDonell flashed. "I don't believe it! Who in hell do you work for, anyway?!"

Bragg cringed at that. "He said we should take decisive action and if it took more firepower it was okay by him. He thought the situation was getting out of hand."

"The situation's out of hand all right!"

"Doc, it was a natural mistake," Bragg cried.

"You're a fool," MacDonell muttered.

"What do you think will happen?" Bragg asked.

"I'll tell you what'll happen, Frank. After all this wonderful PR, the lady will file suit. About five thousand for the dog, I expect. Another twenty for pain and suffering."

"That's not so bad, then," Bragg said, and looked relieved.

MacDonell looked into Bragg's eyes. "You idiot! City Legal will drag its heels for a year and then send the claim over for my opinion." He took a deep breath. "And I'm going to recommend they settle."

"Twenty-five thousand...for a dog?"

MacDonell got into his car. "If she asked me I'd tell her to go for fifty. Be in my office first thing in the morning." He slammed the door and keyed the ignition.

A half-block away MacDonell ran into a Chevy Blazer with Channel 12 printed in big red letters on the door. A tall man stepped into the middle of the street. MacDonell eased up and rolled down his window. A cameraman stood nearby fumbling with his cables and battery pack.

"Doctor MacDonell, can you tell us who shot the lady's dog?" He shoved the microphone in the car window. This was Dan France, Channel 12's night-beat reporter.

MacDonell hesitated, recalling Trimble's admonition to stay away from the press.

"That's what we're trying to determine," MacDonell answered.

"Doesn't this guy work for you?"

"Tell you what, Dan. Have Ryder call me tomorrow. I'll talk to her about this." MacDonell rolled up his window and accelerated up the street and onto the Eastex.

***

It was 1:30 a.m. when MacDonell got home. He couldn't sleep. He was being jerked around by Trimble and he knew it. Exhausted, he sat in the kitchen and explained it all to Jeannie. The health director had all but insisted he get out of the gun business. "Apparently he told Frank just the opposite. Frank shot the dog, but now I'll have to take the heat."

"Why you?" Jeannie asked.

"Who else?"

"You need to have a showdown about this."

MacDonell stared at his hands for a long time. "Look, Honey," he said. "I learned a long time ago, you take care of your boss. Make him look good, even if he's a jerk. If you bite somebody's butt, make sure it's not the man who pays your salary."

She shook her head. "These birds? They're looking out for their own fannies and to heck with yours." Her brown eyes flashed.

"I can't diddle my boss," MacDonell said. "It's not in me." Then he smiled at her. "But it's good to see that I've got Tinkerbell all pissed off."

Jeannie slid her chair back from the kitchen table, stood, and put her fists on her hips. "Duncan, you have to make a statement. Have you talked to any reporters?"

"Not yet."

"Well, do it!" she said. "Tell them Trimble authorized that stupid jackass to shoot the dog." Jeannie raised her voice. "Do it! And if they don't like it, quit! We can live on our savings. I'll sell my grandmother's rings. You know I will." Her voice was quivering.

"Yeah, I know you will. Come on, let's go to bed."

***

MacDonell made it to the office before 8:00. His mouth tasted like vinegar and his head felt like hardwood. At one minute after 8:00 his phone rang. He was in the office alone. Willie was Xeroxing in the next building. He hesitated, then picked it up. It was Ryder.

"Doctor Mac, hi! Dan France told me you'd give me an exclusive if I called you at home. I called, but your wife said you had already left for the office."

There was a moment of indecision while he chewed the inside of his lip, then he whispered into the mouthpiece. "Look Red, I've changed my mind. For now, I'll just answer the question Dan asked me last night. He wanted to know who shot the lady's dog."

"What lady's dog?" she said.

"Don't play games, Red. The answer is: my officer shot it. Name withheld, pending investigation. The dog was loose in the street when my officer saw it, no collar, no license. My officer alleges it was at large. At that time of night he didn't expect to see anything quite that size. The officer was out there with departmental authority. It was accidental and I know he regrets it. So do I."

"Who's responsible?"

"For now, I am."

"Was the dog threatening anyone?"

"No comment until we can complete our investigation."

"Doctor, what was your officer doing out that late?"

"It was a routine night patrol in support of HPD," he said, then immediately regretted it.

"HPD?" she said.

MacDonell cursed himself for the slip of his tongue. "If you want any information, you'll have to ask them."

At 9:00 a.m. MacDonell called the director's office. He asked for an appointment with Trimble. He was told the man was out of town. An unscheduled trip. Next he called the PIO. Her secretary said she had taken a one day vacation.

MacDonell called Goodson and let him know the content of the interview with Ryder and warned him she might be calling. "I didn't mention your name, Sam. With 4500 police officers, it may take her awhile to find you."

"I'll handle it," he said. "Don't worry, pal."

"One other thing," MacDonell said.

"What?"

"Remember the prints we looked at on Crawford Street? Wolf tracks, we said. Well, something occurred to me the other night."

Goodson waited.

"Did you notice how they stopped, suddenly?"

"What do you mean?" Goodson asked.

"Well, they didn't just fade off in the distance. One stride they were heavy and well-formed. Then they just flat disappeared. You'd think they would have gotten fainter and fainter as the blood wore off the animal's feet. Instead, they went up in smoke." There was silence on the phone. "Are you still there, Sam?"

"Yeah, Doc, I'm still here. But I don't get it."

"I've got some ideas I want to bounce off you, Sam. Can you come over today?"

"Absolutely."

"I'd like to look at your photographs again, too. If you don't mind."

***

The afternoon talk shows picked up the topic of shooting dogs in a modern city. Connie Oaks had his radio on and called MacDonell in. "Listen to this," he said.

"City dogcatchers, late last night, shot and killed a local woman's pet dog. The woman, 27 year old Sharon Westergaard, living in the 2300 Block of Rosalie Place, was jogging behind her dog, Callie, when gunfire *erupted, narrowly missing her."* He gave the number. *"Let's hear what you have to say."*

The program was hosted by a popular radio personality known as Randy Ruff. It wasn't his real name, but it sounded good in the promos. Ruff Talk. Today the talk was all negative and Ruff was milking it like a cow.

MacDonell went back to his office. He didn't care for solicited opinions. In half an hour, Oaks came in and sat down. "We're taking some heavy hits, Chief" he said.

"I imagine we are," MacDonell said dryly.

"One guy said we should wipe out all the dogs on the street before one of them kills a little child. Sounded like that pig farmer."

MacDonell nodded.

"Ten other people called the pig farmer a fascist." Oaks waved a hand. "Then Paine calls and says you gave the order to 'shoot to kill.' I got so pissed I broke the knob off my radio."

MacDonell managed a weak smile.

Oaks started out the door.

"Connie, you're tight with the clerks up at 8000 Stadium Drive. Think you could get me Trimble's home phone number?"

Oaks puzzled a moment, then smiled. "Did an' did."

CHAPTER EIGHTEEN

*P*itkin heard a rock slam against the side of his "rooms." He sat up straight.

The outside dogs set up a convincing commotion. One barked and the other two joined in. The pups sleeping inside barked, then were quiet—listening. One woofed, stopped, cocked an ear, and woofed again. Pitkin reached out and thumped it on the head.

A second rock clanged against the side of the van. The entire chorus cursed the night. An outside dog yelped and fell silent.

Pitkin tolerated this kind of harassment. Kids did it. They would peg a rock or a clod, then run like hell. He knew they would get tired soon and leave him alone. He waited…half an hour, then fell asleep sitting up.

At 2:00 a.m. Pitkin sensed a familiar pressure in his bladder. He sat listening for several minutes, then scooted to the double doors and kicked them open. It was quiet except for an occasional truck skimming along above him. He slipped out. His feet were bare and he stepped in a pile of moist dog feces. He scuffed his feet, wiping the pasty goo from the left, then the right. He went about thirty feet to where a concrete column rose up in support of the highway. He looked around, wiped his bare feet on the cold cement, again, then unzipped his fly and began watering the pillar.

Pitkin heard something moving fast. The air hissed. Then he felt an exploding pain and saw a red and yellow star burst in front of his eyes.

When he regained a little consciousness he felt first warm, and then cold. His cheekbone on the left side began to throb, sending a liquid signal to his brain. For ten minutes, or maybe it was just one minute, he tried to move his left arm up and touch his face. The arm wouldn't move. He felt something warm and wet on his face. He blinked and blinked and focused. The wet on his face he recognized. It was one of the pups. It licked and licked and licked. When the numb feeling left and he managed to move his arm, he pushed the pup away. It came back and continued to lick the side of his face.

Pitkin tried to sit up but couldn't. He rolled over on his stomach and tried to orient himself with the ground. In another half hour he moved again. The pillar was close enough to touch. The part of his brain that calculated his position on the earth began to function and he tried to sit up again. In a minute he had his knees under him, but his shoulders and arms and head were still on the surface of the earth. He extended his left arm and touched something. It was dry and had sharp corners. His brain said it was a wooden object, a two-by-four about five feet long. Pitkin grasped it and pulled it toward him. It made a scraping sound on the concrete. He hugged the two-by-four for almost an hour. By then he had figured out where he was and what had happened.

Pitkin pushed up with the two-by-four and found himself on his knees. His head felt like it was swimming in a warm pool of dishwater. He tried to stand but couldn't. Putting his head in the crook of his right elbow, he squeezed his face. The pain throbbed, but when he dropped his arm he could see. Pitkin crawled a little. He realized if he tried, and made slow deliberate movements, he could stand up. He walked several feet and then checked his progress. He was closer to his rooms, but needed to make a course correction. He noticed that his pants were still unzipped. Lacking the hand/eye coordination necessary to close them, he dismissed it as a minor detail. In awhile he was back at the van. He crawled inside to gather his strength.

Pitkin didn't remember how long he slept, but when he opened his eyes the sun was well overhead. He looked at his left wrist and scratched it with his finger. The watch said 10:29, 10:29, 10:29. He rolled over and fished into his deep pocket for his father's watch. He searched the crevices and the seams. There was no watch. He rolled over on the other side, and the act of rolling made his head throb. Feeling the depths of the other pocket, he could find a spoon with a sharp pointed handle, a ball point pen, and some paper money, but no watch. He tried to search his sleeping room. It was small and filled with objects he had collected. There was a warm wet dog, a thin blanket and some clothing, a metal bucket, and several plastic buckets. There was his collection of books and a shoe box with papers. The watch wasn't in the box. He searched again, then rubbed his forehead and looked at the dried blood that came off on his hand. He had a large cut on the left side of his head.

Pitkin went outside and looked at the streets. The sun was high. Two of the pups were lying over by the concrete pillar. Their heads were smashed.

He put one of the dead pups in his large plastic bucket and carried it half a block to a dumpster. Then he rinsed the bucket at a filling station on the way back and returned with half a bucket of tepid water and took a bath.

Alexander Pitkin was not an ignorant man. He concluded it had been the Turks who had rolled him for his father's watch. The more he thought, the more certain he became. For the two Turks it had been a mistake. A bad mistake. Maybe their last mistake.

***

"You bring the pictures?"

Goodson produced a brown envelope and MacDonell examined each photograph carefully. "This one," he said, selecting the wide shot of the site on highway 290. "What's all this junk?"

"Mostly it's his personal effects. Otherwise, just junk. Paper and trash."

"What's that, right there?"

Goodson squinted. "Beats me, a piece of cardboard, I guess."

"The shape of it. I've seen it before."

Goodson shook his head.

MacDonell took out his magnifier and studied it, but said nothing more.

Sam jumped in. "Okay, what about the footprints?"

MacDonell glanced at the detective. "Well," he said, "I've got two ideas. First, I've got this guy. He lives in the area. Been in the papers lately. His name is Alexander Pitkin. Surrounds himself with a bunch of curs."

Goodson listened. MacDonell started at the beginning and explained about Flannery's cats and Pitkin's history of screwy behavior. Then he related the incident when the enormous dog had tried to open his car.

"This guy has a wolf/dog whatchamacallit?"

"I didn't give it a physical, but it had the size. The important thing is, you could draw a circle around where the last two victim's bodies were found, and Pitkin lives smack in the middle. Of course the body out on 290—that's another matter. He could never get that far. Pitkin's van is kaput. He's afoot."

"What did the dog look like?"

"You'll have to remember, Sam, I only saw it for a few seconds. It was more like a Mastiff than a wolf."

MacDonell reached into a drawer and lifted out his 900 page dog atlas. He showed Sam several examples of Mastiffs and other related breeds. There were thirty-six different breeds in the mastiff group. They included three subgroups: familiar breeds like the Great Dane, the Rottweiler, and the American Staffordshire Terrier, along with some not-so-common breeds like the Aryan Molossus, the Landseer, the Tosa Inu, the Fila Brasileiro, and the Danish Broholmer.

"How many you got in this book, anyway?"

"A little over four hundred."

"And your guys pulled in Pitkin and all his dogs, but you couldn't find no Mastiff?"

"Nope. Never did find it. It just disappeared and the old man never produced it. Denied it existed. My district officers drive by his shack two or three times a day, but no one's ever seen it again."

"You want us to check it out?" Sam suggested. "Put a stake-out on it?"

"That's a little overkill, isn't it?"

"Not if it gets results. I've got three stiffs to explain. If Pitkin has a killer dog, we need to get it. And lock his ass up." Goodson steepled his fingers. "What's your other idea?"

"The tracks. The ones on Crawford. They just stop. I think maybe the creature jumped into a car or on the back of a truck, or something?"

"You mean someone carted it off?" Goodson asked.

"Sure."

"I guess that would explain why the tracks quit like that." Goodson thought a minute. "Has Pitkin got a truck?"

"As far as I know, all he's got is that old van with all the tires flat. Of course, he might have a car stashed somewhere."

"We could run a license check. If he has anything registered in his name, we could find out."

***

Pitkin spotted the two Turks warming themselves over a flaming steel drum under the elevated. They were much younger than he was. Both men, he estimated, were in their forties. One was a little taller than the other, but both were solid. They were too solid for him to go after with his sharpened spoon, his pig-sticker. Besides, there were two of them. He would need help.

After watching the two men all day, he knew he couldn't do what needed to be done in daylight. There were too many people under the elevated and it would be easier after dark. He followed them twice, keeping his distance, and was certain they hadn't seen him. The men hadn't pawned the watch either. Earlier, he saw the tall one pull it out and look at it.

They were holed up in an old house on Jackson, between Drew and Tuam. After standing on the curb for several minutes they had slipped between houses. From a block away, Pitkin saw them go in the back door.

When it got dark they were still in the house. He looked at his wrist-watch and it flashed 9:04, 9:04, 9:04. He agonized about the correct time. Because of these two, the wrist watch was all he had, and for now he would have to trust it. His father's watch was now measuring the lives of the Turks, not his.

He went to the nearby Black Angus Meat Market. It was closed, but he went around back and found a small piece of red meat in one of the cans; not much, a small shriveled piece. It was black and smelled strong, but it would do.

It was a long walk and cold at this time of night.

He had forgotten his jacket so he walked fast and rubbed his arms to keep warm. After awhile, he began to cough and could see his breath floating before him. He would see theirs float away, too, he promised himself.

When Pitkin got to the warehouse, he found that someone had nailed the plywood shut. For a moment he feared that his secret place had been discovered. Struggling, he prized open the sheet of plywood. Then, bending the nails over with his thumb, he snaked his body through the crack.

He had been in this place late at night. Always the darkness was stifling. He sat and waited until his vision improved, then he climbed over the pipes and made his way to the second floor. He could hear the animal whining when he got to the door.

First he searched in the boxes piled by the door. The leather strap was still rolled in a neat spiral and wedged in the bottom of one of the boxes. He pushed the rotting meat through a crack in the door and then fumbled with the lock. It wasn't a meal for the dog; that would come later. He wanted to whet its appetite, get the juices to flow. Pitkin knew dogs. Anticipation was the key. After the dog swallowed the meat, he slipped the strap in place around its neck.

Together they made their way down the stairs and over the pipes. He kept the strap wrapped around his wrist to keep it short and to hold the dog's head up. The animal had great power. If it got out on the end of the lead, he could be pulled along and lose control.

Pitkin and the dog took a well-planned route. It was longer, but safer. By the time they got to the old house it was late, well after midnight. He looked at the wrist watch. It said, 12:51, 12:52, 12:52. He took up a place straight across from the narrow alleyway between the houses where the two men had gone in.

He had the advantage of the shadows cast by the old building behind him. Pitkin pondered whether or not they were still inside, and he listened for a sign. The clink of a pot or a pan would be enough to confirm his hopes. Maybe one of them would cough. A good many of the men living on the streets coughed at night.

They waited, Pitkin and the dog. Pitkin had plenty of time, he wasn't hungry, and he didn't mind waiting. He'd been waiting all his life. Waiting for a new life to start. Waiting for an old life to end.

There wasn't much of a moon. Thankfully, the street light at the end of the block cast a helpful shadow across the alley. The giant dog was restless. It quivered beside him. The man put his hand on the dog's head and it quivered even more. It looked up at him in anticipation.

The street light cast a cold glare at the foot of the alley. The shadow of the house on the right framed a long spike of light all the way to the back of the house. The spike narrowed as it sliced the space between the houses. If they came out, he would see them. First their heads, the tall one, and then the other. As they came out, the light would be in their faces. Maybe he should release the dog when the first sound came. Then the dog would not be exposed so much to the street light. And what if they went the other way, beside the garage, and out the back? There wouldn't be much time to decide then, he would have to decide now.

There was a soft squeak, like the lid of a coffin, as the back door opened. Pitkin was certain of it. His lips were dry. He couldn't see, but something was there. The dog whined. The strap was already off. Pitkin's hand quivered. He touched the dog's ribs and said something, something low and subdued. An old command in his native tongue. The dog bolted across the street and into the blackness.

Now the sounds came, the sounds he longed to hear. He heard a muted cry of fear, a struggle, and then several low worrying, snarling sounds. The dog had found something soft and yielding and was tearing at it.

Pitkin remembered the watch. He hurried across the street. He didn't run, but he wanted to avoid the light and get into the safe shadows of the house. Get the watch, he thought. Get his father's watch.

He tripped over something and fell to his knees. He extended his hands and crawled forward on all fours. He was now engulfed in the shadow, too. The dog was beside him, ripping and tearing. "Fleisch, fleisch!" the old man hissed.

He heard a deep growl, and reached his hand toward the sound.

***

MacDonell couldn't sleep. Jeannie had talked him into a visit to The Olive Garden. He regretted it. Lasagna and spaghetti rumbled and sloshed in the Chianti. He rolled on his side and it was worse. The most comfortable position was on his back and he thought about people drowning in their own vomit. He put a pillow under his shoulders. It didn't help.

At 3:15 the phone rang. I should get an unlisted number like the other department weenies, he thought.

"Doc, it's me again. We've got *two* more bodies. You've got to see this to believe it. Can you come?"

In a froggy voice, MacDonell told Goodson it would take forty minutes. Jeannie mumbled something about a day job.

Thirty minutes later MacDonell pulled off the Eastex at the Tuam exit. This was Pitkin's territory. He might suggest they pick up the old man. He crossed Chenevert, then plugged a red flasher into his cigarette lighter and stuck it on the roof. It was only the second time he had used it, and it made him feel self-conscious.

Goodson met him at the yellow tape. The lieutenant lifted it up high enough to drive under and waved him on. MacDonell parked by the crime lab truck and got out.

"You're going to love this one," Goodson said. "Both bodies are back between these two houses."

A technician was setting up the tripods and working with the lights. Sam got a flashlight. "It'll be a few more minutes before they set up the floods," he said. "Come around here."

The first body was lying face down in some tall grass. It was about ten feet from the sidewalk, and all MacDonell could see were legs. Goodson walked around the body, being careful not to mess up any obvious evidence.

"We've got two witnesses who knew him," Goodson said. "They call him Himie...no last name, just Himie."

"Shine the light on his head, Sam," MacDonell said. There was something familiar about the pants and shoes.

MacDonell looked at the tattered remains, the thin tufts of white hair, the fragile splotchy skin. "I know him, too," MacDonell said.

"Yeah?" Goodson didn't seem surprised.

"His name is Alexander Pitkin."

The two men stood for a moment and looked at each other. Goodson turned to the narrow space between the houses. "The photographer has already finished this area," he said. "Come back here, but be careful where you step. I want you to see the other body." Near the far end of the space between the houses, in front of a small shed, Goodson waved his light around in the grass. "What's this look like?"

MacDonell borrowed the light and went over the body carefully. He sucked in air and shook his head. The body was that of a huge dog. "It's pretty chopped up," he answered. "But it looks like a Mastiff to me. I'd say it's missed a few meals, but it'll still go over 125 pounds—maybe more"

"This the one that attacked your car?"

"Got to be."

MacDonell palpated the area behind the dog's skull. The skin and muscle were still intact on the dorsal surface of the neck. The soft under-parts of the throat were crushed and torn, exposing the esophagus and trachea. "Whatever killed it ripped out the throat and broke its neck," he said.

"Himie isn't much different," Goodson muttered.

MacDonell felt the front legs, then the hind legs. "A broken femur, too. The last time I saw a dog mutilated this bad it had been hit by a train."

A three or four foot trail of intestine and a large chunk of liver protruded from a massive rip in the abdominal wall. After going over the two bodies again, and looking at the scene under the glare of the floodlights, MacDonell went and sat in the open door of his car.

In a few minutes Goodson showed up with two rather subdued men in shabby clothes. The tall one did the talking. The short man looked like he might vomit if he thought too much about what had happened.

The tall one didn't reveal much new information, but repeated what he did have to say several times.

"Himie, he sic'd his dog on us!" he said over and over. "Himie, he sic'd his dog on us!"

"Why do you think he did that?" Goodson asked.

"How the hell do I know? He's crazy."

"What else happened?"

"I don't know. Me and Eddie, we run like hell."

"How many dogs did you see?"

"I didn't actually see no dogs. You, Eddie?"

Eddie shook his head indicating that he didn't see or couldn't remember. MacDonell couldn't recall when he'd ever seen a man look as pale as Eddie. As he stepped in a little closer, he detected a tell-tale sour odor. The man had already vomited.

"What did you hear?" MacDonell asked.

"We just hear his dog, man. Then a scream."

"Did it bark at you, growl, what?" MacDonell pumped them.

"Naw, it was quiet like…it just sound like it…well, you know…it sound like it's eatin' on something. I thought it done had a holt on Eddie, then I look up an' Eddie, he was out ahead a' me, smokin'. We run between the house and the garage and made it to the street. Somebody yell to git the hell out, man, and we got. I was scared as shit, man."

"Who yelled?" MacDonell asked.

"Beats hell outta me, man. Musta been ol' Himie, I guess," the tall man said. "Out…out…that's all I hear, man."

MacDonell gave the men a curious look and rubbed his head. A sprinkling of tiny hairs were standing on end in the cold air.

"When did you realize the dog wasn't chasing you?" Goodson asked.

"Well, shit, I guess when it yelped was when I stopped running. A block and a half, mebbe more."

The questioning went round and round for about thirty minutes. How long have you known Himie? Where do you live? How long have you been in Houston? That kind of thing. It was the name, rank, and serial number game and MacDonell knew it well. The two men were tired, scared, and didn't have a lot to contribute after the first time through it.

"The question is," MacDonell thought out loud, "who or what killed Himie's…uh, Pitkin's dog?"

"I think ol' Himie got some of his own damn medicine," the tall one said.

"Did you see any cars or trucks?"

"I didn't see nothin!" the tall one replied.

"I give up," MacDonell told Goodson. "This is a lot more complicated than I thought. Have you found any clear prints?"

"No real good ones," a uniformed officer confirmed. "We're gonna keep looking."

"I don't know what else to suggest, Sam. The only thing I know for sure is, this shoots a gaping hole in my idea that it was Pitkin's dog."

"Yeah," Goodson said, "and whatever it is, it's still out there."

"And it's a helluva lot more dog than the old man's."

"If it truly is a dog. What time you got, Mac?"

"It's Saturday morning."

Chapter Nineteen

***

Saturday morning. Saturday morning? MacDonell's subconscious was telling him something. Saturday morning? He'd made it home and to bed by 5:00 a.m., but now he lay there, breathing slow and deep. Saturday Morning!

"Huh!" He sat up in bed. It was 7:30 a.m. "I've got to go in this morning, Honey," he said, nudging Jeannie.

From deep in the quilts, her voice whispered, "It's Saturday…go back to sleep."

"No, I've got to go in," he repeated. "J.D.'s putting on her obedience demonstration this morning and I've got to make it. It's costing me a fortune in overtime."

"Ohhh nooo," came the tiny voice, again.

"I'm sorry. I'm the boss. I've got to show the flag."

The best thing about the Eastex on a Saturday was the light traffic. MacDonell was surprised and pleased when he rolled in and found a fair number of employees. What didn't surprise him was the pitiful few field officers. Thirteen members of the office staff and seven from the kennel had showed up. Besides Longley and ACO Ron Reyes, who was showing off his Rottweiler, only four field officers made it in. Longley had set up an obedience course. MacDonell squeezed past the people standing at the gate by the dispatcher's office.

Willie Fish was sitting in a folding chair and visiting with the clerks and cashiers. She smiled and handed him a paper sack filled with pastry. He crouched beside her.

"Only one," she said. "Your better half had me to promise."

He gave the crowd a furtive glance. "Her spies are everywhere," he said.

Five minutes after MacDonell arrived, Bragg drove in, parked his truck inside the old tin barn, and walked over to stand with the four field officers. MacDonell studied him with passing interest. He was the only field officer authorized to wear civvies, and he still had on yesterday's shirt. His hair was uncombed and he hadn't shaved. With reluctance he acknowledged his boss, then ambled across to where MacDonell was standing.

Up close Bragg looked like a shredded wheat breakfast. MacDonell knew the man was still smarting from the shooting incident. Since MacDonell had yet to decided on a punishment, he avoided the subject. Instead, he broke the news of Pitkin's fatal mutilation. Mild surprise crossed Bragg's face.

"We found his big dog last night, too, Frank. The mastiff I told you about."

Bragg was silent.

"What's left of it is in the postmortem room."

"What happened to it?"

"That's what HPD is trying to figure out."

Bragg shook his head, hunched his shoulders, and blew on a hot cup of coffee he held lightly between his fingertips. There was a bandage on his left hand and the smell of stale beer lingered. The conversation was brief and it was obvious Bragg was not his usual self.

"Hurt yourself?" MacDonell asked.

"Fixing a lamp for my wife last night. Shoved a screwdriver in my hand," he replied.

"Painful?"

"Nah."

"See a doctor?"

"It ain't that bad."

After an uncomfortable minute Bragg walked back to his field officers. He huddled up with Reyes and the others, and they whispered back and forth.

MacDonell turned and began visiting with the clerical staff.

"All ready to go, Doctor Mac?" It was Longley. She stood tall and straight in military fatigue trousers, boots, and a sky-blue shirt. "I thought you might miss it."

"Not a chance," he said. "Want me to give you an introduction?"

"I was hoping you would," she said, flashing her straight white teeth.

MacDonell was determined to make this educational as well as entertaining. He shook off his desire to sleep, fixed a smile on his face, and gave Longley a brief but glowing introduction, citing her extensive experience in handling and training military working dogs. Finally, he announced this would not be the last opportunity for the staff to learn about animal training. Then he turned the gathering over to Master Sergeant J.D. Longley, USAF, 'Retired.'

Longley had backed her Bronco up to the gate and dropped the tailgate. It was shiny red with a narrow white stripe, and he could tell she was proud of it. No one was ready for what happened next. Longley walked to the center of the grassy area and whistled sharply. Exploding from a Sky-Kennel in the back of the Bronco, a tri-color blur leaped from the tailgate. Bursting through the gate, it flashed through the crowd. The spectators were dumbfounded.

Within seconds a mostly-white Jack Russell Terrier, with black and tan markings on its back and head, crouched at Longley's feet, its eyes riveted on hers.

"This is Blitzen," Longley said, and the crowd clapped.

MacDonell found the dog to be more than spirited, it was exuberant. And Longley seemed to have a special knack for this too. She demonstrated the simple stuff first, explaining each step in an obedience dog's training. The invisible link between her and the happy terrier could not have been more obvious. The twelve pound dog dashed about, eagerly showing off its skill in heeling off leash, the long sit, and the long down. When she demonstrated the drop on recall, Blitzen slid to a scorching stop in the grass and generated a spontaneous round of applause. It was not a typical AKC performance.

Next, Longley explained the various AKC obedience degrees the dog had earned, and how they were earned. While she talked, Blitzen stretched out on her belly in the grass and extended her legs front and back. Afterward, Longley showed off a few more complex stunts. The broad jump and high jump were impressive for such a small dog. Longley had set the obstacles higher than MacDonell expected, but Blitzen roared up to the wooden jumps and sailed over with room to spare. The way the dog performed everything, at a dead run, it wouldn't have surprised him if the dog could do cartwheels.

Longley's demonstration of several scent discrimination tests got an undeservedly weak spattering of applause. Also, the subtlety of the directed jumping seemed to go over a few people's heads.

The terrier responded instantly to even the slightest hand signals. A few back flips done behind Longley's back appeared to be spontaneous and got everyone to laughing; however, MacDonell and one or two others recognized the discrete signals she was giving behind her back.

When she finished, Blitzen leaped into Longley's arms and licked her face. To a warm round of applause, she relinquished the spotlight and turned the remainder of the demonstration over to ACO Ron Reyes and his Rottweiler, Turk.

Reyes lowered his voice and asked everyone to step outside the fence to observe his dog's work from the safety of the parking lot. Some of it was macho posturing, but MacDonell agreed it was a good idea.

MacDonell slipped a second donut from the bag as he helped Willie move her chair. Longley walked Blitzen through the crowd and, after some visiting, found her way over to where MacDonell was leaning with his fingers inserted in the chain link. Bending low, she picked up the dog and held it squirming in her arms. It didn't take long before most of the crowd, and even one of the field officers, had come over and scratched the dog's ears and made a complimentary remark.

"We got a breakthrough today," he remarked as he patted Blitzen on the head. "I didn't expect this big of a turnout, even though we're paying most of them."

"Maybe," she said. "However, I think you've got a little problem you ought to know about," Longley whispered without looking at him.

He leaned forward and she whispered again. "You may need to counsel a few of your younger kennel staff and at least two of the cashiers."

"Huh. Why?"

"At least five of your folks are carrying," she whispered again.

He didn't react at first. "Carrying?"

Longley nodded to her right. "The lady in the loose fitting brown dress, the one with corn rows."

MacDonell looked over at Argentina Patterson. Argentina smiled at them, revealing a large gold tooth.

"She's got a little weed. It's in the shopping bag."

MacDonell smiled at Argentina and leaned forward again.

"You're kidding," he whispered. "She's a grandmother."

"The two kennel officers and the cashier over against the truck, and the field officer talking to the captain," she indicated with her eyes.

"Yes?" he said.

"Marijuana," she said without judgment.

"How…?"

"Blitzen," she said. "She alerted on all five of them. The older lady twice."

MacDonell shook his head and looked at the chattering crowd.

"Also, someone was carrying a gun."

"Was?"

"I think it was an officer that left already. He said something to Bragg and Reyes, then took off."

"How do you know it wasn't one of our weapons?"

"It was concealed. Had to be a handgun."

"Was he driving one of my trucks?"

"No, a little tan Toyota."

MacDonell tried to remember which officer he had seen drive off. Too late to confront the man now, he thought.

Reyes had convinced a member of his Schutzhund club to come out and give him a hand. MacDonell saw the man as Latin, about twenty-five, over six feet tall, with heavily muscled shoulders and forearms. He sported a well-trimmed goatee and dark, wraparound sunglasses. He kept to himself, sat in the shade, smoked one dark brown cigarette after another, and flipped the butts through the fence. To MacDonell the man appeared unaccustomed to daylight. It wasn't the shades, it was the way he moved. He soon dubbed the man 'the Snake.'

While the crowd was rearranging itself and slipping off for cold drinks, the Snake donned an olive drab padded suit, pants, and jacket. The right sleeve was long and had extra padding. It was well chewed.

Reyes muzzled his Rottweiler and tied it to the fence. The dog was far from being a show quality animal. It was cow-hocked and its head was too narrow for MacDonell's liking. Still, it was a reasonable representative of the breed.

Reyes first tried to explain the various attributes of the Schutzhund-trained dog. He was no speaker, but he made it clear the German word "Schutzhund" translated into "protection dog" in English. What he failed to explain was that the dog must provide a variety of other functions, including obedience and tracking. These were in addition to the pure aggression so many people wanted these days. Reyes put the dog on a heavy leather leash and trotted it along the inside of the fence so everyone could get a good look at it. It was soon obvious to MacDonell that the man needed the dog to gain the respect he could not otherwise command.

"Keep your fingers out of the fence, girls," Reyes said. "He's a helluva-dog, a helluva-dog."

Reyes began by demonstrating some of the same basic commands Longley had already been through. MacDonell, and everyone else, could see the animal needed more work. It sat only after the third command and was reluctant to do that. He was also rusty on the long down and eased down after a half-minute of coaxing. Reyes' method of discipline involved jerking the animal with the leash and swinging it off the ground. The dog had a neck like a tree trunk and took the punishment without complaint. Even the most uneducated observer could tell the two animals were products of different training methods. Blitzen had performed for the sheer joy of it, Turk was being put through his paces on threat of pain.

"I didn't think he would be so crude about it," Longley said. "This isn't traditional Schutzhund work."

MacDonell nodded. "Negative reinforcement at its worst. I wonder how he'd do if I kicked *his* fanny around like that."

"I'm not sure he realizes how bad it looks," she said.

"It's a great study in contrasts. I'm sure everyone can see it."

Reyes glossed over the obedience work and excused the tracking because the enclosure was not expansive enough for a good demonstration. He quickly got to what most thought was 'the good part.' The Snake would agitate the dog, and Turk would roar with questionable conviction and display a full set of teeth. Turk's reward was to be allowed to grab the sleeve and give it a good shake.

"The poor thing isn't into this," Longley said.

"You're right," MacDonell agreed. "He hesitates before taking the sleeve and releases before Reyes gives the 'out' command."

"He's not liking what he's doing, at all," she added. "This should be a joy. If the dog were mine, I'd go back to the more basic obedience work."

"It's a good example of someone wanting to get to the macho protection work too fast and bypasses the duller stuff," MacDonell said. "Pretty typical."

The attack runs were inconsistent. The first one was extremely violent, with the dog leaving the ground and flying at his target. The Snake was knocked off his feet, but Reyes was able to drag the dog off. On the second run, Turk flared to the side and only feinted an attack. For that, he was whipped across the back four or five times with the leather strap. The ladies in the crowd winced.

"Maybe we should call this off," Longley whispered.

MacDonell motioned with his hand. "Let's see what he does now."

The first off-leash attack was also not well-executed. Turk took off before the command, "Get Him," was given. He got under the sleeve and nailed the Snake high in the hip and got clubbed on the head for his effort. By the time the two men got their act together the dog was tiring. After that the attacks began to lack the level of aggression real Schutzhund trainers want.

Longley gave MacDonell an apologetic look, shook her head, and turned away.

After a brief rest and exchange of animals, the Snake brought out a large UKC version of an American Staffordshire Terrier. The dog was a tiger-striped dark brindle with an off-center blaze of white. It was heavy boned, muscular and colorful, with one white front foot.

"What is it horsemen say about one white foot?" MacDonell asked, jokingly.

"Buy 'em," Longley responded.

Now Reyes put on the sweaty suit. After a lingering session between the two men, Reyes went to the far end of the compound. He took up a questionable position with his back to the dog. This ninety pound animal was far better behaved, and went through the few obligatory obedience commands in flawless style. MacDonell noticed, though, that the dog would sneak a peek at Reyes between commands.

After the preliminaries the Snake placed his dog in the down position, off leash, and commanded it to stay. The dog raised himself to a half-crouch position and looked toward Reyes. The handler had already turned away and walked three or four exaggerated paces from the dog. As he started to turn back, the animal launched itself like a bottle rocket. Reyes was just reaching through the fence for an offered can of pop when the dog closed in. It had crossed the forty foot gap in no time, its belly close to the ground. No sound, no warning.

"No! Dammit, NOOO!" the Snake yelled.

The dog didn't stop. MacDonell stood, transfixed as the big pit bull streaked in from about ten feet and drove Reyes into the wire. Reyes didn't go down immediately, but hung onto the fence. The crowd gasped as the dog hit Reyes, chest high, slashing into the flaring coat which had fallen open. It got a large chunk of coat between its teeth. MacDonell raced to the gate as the dog swung its body, jerking the officer off his feet. In microseconds, the dog was shaking the front of the coat with such violence Reyes' head began banging the bottom of the fence in a rapid-fire series of jolts.

Snake got hold of the dog's collar just as MacDonell arrived. Reyes' uniform shirt was pulled out through the disintegrating coat. The handler reached into his belt and produced an old-time dogfighter's breaking wedge. He forced the stick between the molars on the left side and slammed it with his fist.

In a minute, the Snake led his dog to the opposite side of the yard with a large part of Reyes' shirt hanging from his mouth. Meanwhile, Longley had made it through the crowd and around to the gate. She raced across the grass toward Reyes, reaching him as MacDonell opened the shirt. She had her first-aid kit from the Bronco.

There was dog slobber and two angry red welts on Reyes' chest. The space between the marks was almost four inches wide and represented the upper canine teeth.

"You're lucky," MacDonell said.

"I'm through!" Reyes yelled, when he caught his breath. "I told him I didn't trust that dog."

"Not the first time, huh?" Longley asked.

"No! Shit no, lady! That dog takes this stuff too damn serious. It loses control."

"It could be corrected," Longley said to nobody in particular.

"Let's call it quits, Ron," MacDonell advised. "You guys have given everybody their money's worth, and besides it's getting too warm."

"I've got a couple announcements for everyone," Longley said. "I'm working on the possibility of getting a sheep dog demonstration. Maybe they'll be interested."

"Go ahead before they get away," MacDonell agreed and headed to his office. "Come see me when you get finished."

MacDonell went to his office, sat with his feet on his desk, and closed his eyes. What a night, he thought, and what a day. In about fifteen minutes Longley appeared at the outer door. She had Blitzen under her arm. She waved and came in.

"Mind if I bring the Blitz in here?" she asked. It's pretty warm in the car."

"No problem."

"I want to apologize for that sorry spectacle out there," she said.

"Not your fault," MacDonell said, leaning back and lacing his fingers behind his head. "I thought Ron knew more about Schutzhund than he does. He's like a lot of people in this business; he's interested in intimidation. I might be more supportive if I'd seen some tracking."

"That's what I was expecting, too. Neither dog has its Schutzhund-I degree."

"I'm not surprised."

Longley looked at her shoes. "Well, I'm still sorry."

"Not your fault at all. Have a seat."

Longley put Blitzen on the vinyl couch and sat down beside her. Blitzen watched MacDonell. When she was convinced nothing else would be asked of her she stretched her neck, put her chin on her forepaws, and settled in. Longley smiled and stroked the dog's ears.

"Give you a hundred bucks for her." MacDonell said.

"In your dreams."

"Drug detection dog, eh?" MacDonell asked.

"Among other things," was the answer. "Explosives, drugs, and less interesting things. That reminds me, another one of your field officers was also carrying a gun. I'm not sure which one."

"You're kidding?"

"No, it was one of the guys Bragg was talking to. Maybe it was Bragg himself. I didn't catch it quick enough when she gave the sign."

MacDonell started to get up.

"They're gone," she said. "Besides, it's none of my business. I shouldn't be so critical."

MacDonell shook his head in disgust and eased back down. He looked again at Blitzen. "Why a Jack Russell?"

"I don't know," she said. "Just because I like her. Most of my animals have been pretty unconventional."

"I'd say she's in a class by herself," MacDonell said. "Too bad I can't get my officers to perform like that."

"I hear that."

MacDonell folded his hands across his belly, "I wanted to talk to you about this problem with the street people getting chewed up."

Longley looked up. "I was thinking about that woman's German Shepherd," she said. "Could there be a connection?"

"I don't think her dog is much of a candidate," MacDonell exhaled. "The police think a couple of the victims were alive when they were attacked. Except last night. They're positive on that one."

"Another attack? Last night?" Longley asked, her eyes wide and curious. "What about—what's his name—the old guy under the freeway?"

"Pitkin, yes. Until about four o'clock this morning I thought he was a possible." MacDonell stared at the top of his desk. "Early this morning he and his dog were mauled to death, and it looks like the same animal, or pack of animals. I had Gallegos put the dog in the post-mortem room. Want to see it?"

Longley's mouth tightened. "Ugh, no," she said.

Blitzen looked up at her and yawned.

The three stared at each other for a long second.

"What does that leave you with?" Longley asked.

"I've come up with one or two other possibilities. First, it could be an animal, maybe hybrid, that gets out at night and runs the city. Three of the four kill sites are very close together. The other possibility is what you suggested at dinner the other night, some guard dog company's animals getting loose, marauding, then getting picked up in the morning."

Longley sat and looked out the window, apparently weighing the two ideas.

"Both sound reasonable," she said, "but I'm inclined to go for your second idea. Hybrids are pretty rare. On the other hand, I'll bet there are scads of so called guard dogs around Houston. And some of the nut cases don't have any real training at all. The owners just badger the animals and make them mean. Without a handler present that's pretty scary. You saw that AmStaff out in the yard? That dog was totally out of control."

"You may have something," he said.

Longley looked at him. "It's like you said the other night. It's too bad all the big dogs aren't registered. You could put a big red beacon on every bad actor, then maybe you could get a handle on this thing." She scooped up Blitzen and stood up. "I'll think about it." She paused again. "It sounds like you've got a tough problem."

They talked about her idea for a sheep dog trial as MacDonell saw her out to her Bronco, then went back to his office. It was a good idea. She had lots of good ideas. He sat behind his desk again, resting his eyes. A beacon? Thoughts began to percolate.

He opened the drawer on his credenza and rummaged through its contents. At the bottom was a large envelope and a manual. He carried it out and put it in his car.

CHAPTER TWENTY

*W*hen MacDonell got home, an HPD blue and white cruiser was parked in the driveway. He guessed that Sam Goodson was in the kitchen. No doubt he wanted to talk about last night. The neighbor raking leaves next door averted his eyes. MacDonell waited until he looked up, then, in a cautious voice, he said, "domestic dispute."

Inside, along with coffee, Jeannie was filling Sam with what she dubbed, 'English trifle.' "Don't you see enough of your veterinarian?" he asked. "Once a year is plenty." Then he saw Goodson's glum face. "Don't tell me the wolves ate another Houstonian?"

"Kind of…" Goodson replied, putting down his cup. "About six or eight weeks ago Galveston Homicide reported a man mutilated on the island in almost an identical manner to our victims. They're calling it an aggravated homicide."

"Isn't that just a nice name for murder?" MacDonell asked, pulling a chair up close. "And doesn't it require a motive?"

"Just listen, Doc. An informant told Galveston PD some joker, name of Constantine, was up here buying dogs."

"Up here? Up from where?"

"Colombia. The snitch says he was looking for as many as fifty. He put an advertisement in one of them mercenary-type magazines asking for trained dogs, and it looks like he had a few takers. The way this guy tells it, most of the people who answered the ad were in the local area, and Galveston thinks they held a dog auction. The snitch said the low bid was a thousand dollars a dog. You follow?"

"So far," MacDonell answered, "...but fifty dogs? All at once? That's impossible. Besides, why would Colombians buy dogs in Houston? Haven't they got enough in their country?"

"I guess not," Goodson said. "It sounded crazy to me, too. The way the snitch explained it, this Constantine picked up five dogs late Friday night. Kind of on a trial basis."

"That's a lot less than fifty."

"My guy says if the dogs work out, Constantine intends to come back and get five more."

MacDonell frowned and looked skeptical.

Goodson didn't understand it himself. "Supply and demand, I guess," he said, waving his hands. "Anyway, it gets worse. After the bidding, the turkey that got the low bid—his name was Fall, Erskin Fall—he disappears and the price jumps to three thousand per."

"You're saying what?"

"That's the interesting part." Goodson said. "Galveston thinks Fall won the bid but lost the war. They've given us copies of their lab photos." He handed MacDonell an envelope. "It looks like a wolf ate Erskin Fall's guts." He looked over at Jeannie. "So to speak."

"Gross," Jeannie muttered.

MacDonell scanned the photos. "I saw this on TV," he said. He stuffed the photos back in the envelope, then he cocked his head and looked across the patio at the pool. It reflected an iron sky. Dead leaves formed floating islands. Images of swarthy Colombian drug lords protecting themselves with monster dogs put him in a darker mood. He took off his glasses, rubbed his eyes, then looked back at the lieutenant.

Goodson was also in a mood. "The captain of the homicide division is all wrapped around the axle, and the big cheese is starting to lean on him."

MacDonell got up and went to the kitchen counter. "My boss wants me to stay out of it," he said, then picked up the coffee pot. "How about the informant? Can't you pick him up and do what cops do?"

"We'd like to, but he's Galveston's snitch, not ours. Besides, they let him and the Colombian get out on the same boat."

"That's nice," MacDonell said, refilling the cups. "And you think they took a shipment of five dogs with them?"

"Yeah, it looks that way," Goodson said.

"What about the other bidders? Any idea who they might be or how many there were?" MacDonell asked.

"No, but at least three or four," Goodson replied. "Which brings me to why I dropped by." He leaned back in his chair. "I'm wondering how anybody could assemble as many as fifty dogs? All at once?"

"You'd have to go to some place the size of Lackland Air Force Base to find that many."

"Yeah," Goodson agreed. He gave MacDonell a skeptical look.

"Say what you mean, Lieutenant"

Goodson looked at the floor. "Okay. How many large dogs do you figure you collect in a month?"

MacDonell bristled. "Nobody's going to pay three thousand dollars for the crummy mongrels we get in." He hesitated, realizing how he sounded. "Okay, okay, I expect someone occasionally claims an animal and resells it, but nothing worth that kind of money."

"But big dogs do come along, don't they? Given time, couldn't they be trained?"

"Are you investigating us?" MacDonell asked. His ears were starting to turn pink.

"Take it easy, Mac. One of my detectives knows this local humaniac, a guy named Paine. He talked to this guy about dog sources, and the guy suggested we find out how many big dogs you collect each month."

"ROBIN PAINE?!"

"Whoa, whoa. Take it easy. My detective don't know you. We're a big department."

"Paine's a jackass."

"That's what Clemmons told us."

"You've been talking to Carol?"

"Any objections?"

MacDonell was quiet for a second. "No, of course not," he said. He trailed off and stared at Jeannie. "To tell the truth, I suspect that every once in awhile dogs get shortstopped before they make it to our kennels. I don't think it's many, but I'm sure it happens."

"You got any suspects?"

Bragg came immediately to mind. He turned and looked at Jeannie. Her face reflected a mixture of discovery and skepticism. "Not anyone I can be sure of. Not yet, anyway."

"Ugh!" she said. She had been listening to the conversation. Now she shivered and left the kitchen. In a few seconds she returned and handed over the front section of yesterday's Chronicle. "Look at this. Shows you how crazy the world is."

It was part of a collection of fillers entitled WORLD BRIEFS. It was only five sentences long:

DRUG TESTING FOR FOOD; Rio de Janeiro, Brazil; Sources reported today that a large pharmaceutical importer has been testing experimental drugs on street children from the slums. The starving children were traded food for their services as human guinea pigs. Many have died as a result.

Apparently in the chaotic economic climate of Brazil it is considered quicker and cheaper to test drugs in this fashion than by conventional means. Rio is known for its hordes of poverty-stricken slum and street dwellers, and for its cultural violence.

MacDonell scanned the article, and stared at Goodson while the detective did the same.

MacDonell paced across the kitchen. He looked at Jeannie, then back at Goodson. "Some time ago the New Orleans police paid hobos five bucks apiece to let their dogs get, '*blooded*'."

"Blooded?" Goodson echoed.

"It was in the papers. The idea is to let the dogs get a bite. Gives them a chance to work out their frustrations, so to speak." MacDonell stood with his cup poised in his hand. "Now you tell me this Colombian bought five dogs. Link that to the fact that five people have also been torn to shreds. That's a strange coincidence. Suppose…suppose this dog buyer insists on a field trial? Think about it: five big killer dogs, five field trials. It might explain the distance between the attacks. Someone's moving these animals from place to place."

Goodson listened, his face showing his astonishment at what MacDonell was suggesting.

"Just like this Rio drug company testing on street kids?" Jeannie inserted.

"That's sick," Goodson said. He looked at Jeannie.

She shivered. "It's terrible if it's true."

"I know it sounds sick," MacDonell continued, "but think about it. The buyer becomes convinced he should pay three times the price per dog. Why should he? Maybe one of the bidders convinced him his product was superior. It's been field-tested."

"Holy Christ!" Goodson exclaimed. "That's cold-blooded."

"An attack dog, proven right before your eyes. It's not only a helluva sales gimmick, it's a motive."

Jeannie warmed up their coffee.

"The problem is, what can we do about it?" MacDonell asked between sips. "Assuming Jeannie's right?"

Goodson put down his coffee cup. "We look at all the sources of large nasty dogs. We get lists of breeders in the upper gulf area," Goodson suggested. "We stick to the big breeds. You could recommend the ones we need to look at. I imagine pit bulls and Rottweilers are at the top of the list."

MacDonell shook his head. "Sam, Sam, that sounds like the police way of doing things. Door-to-door flatfoot work. No offense, but I doubt if it would pan out. And it'll bring every dog breeder in Texas out of the woodwork. They're like the NRA. They have a constitutional right to own a killer dog, just like you have the right to own a machine gun. They'll eat your lunch. I've had sweet old ladies tell me, as soon as government outlaws pit bulls, the Doberman will be next, and before you know it, it'll be French Poodles."

Goodson swore under his breath.

"There are things we could do that wouldn't raise so much dust," MacDonell said. "These guard dog outfits, they gotta be involved. After all, they're in the nasty dog business."

"What do you suggest?" Goodson asked.

"This Erskin Fall character, he wasn't lily-white?"

"Small time, marijuana possession."

"Okay, look. I'm having guard dog companies checked out," MacDonell said. "Let me find out how many have night security contracts in the Midtown area, near where Pitkin and the others hung out."

"Who's looking into it?"

MacDonell looked into his cup. "I hate to tell you."

"Bragg?"

MacDonell nodded.

"We've got to come up with something a little less conservative, Mac. What about Paine? He's a dog trainer, couldn't he lend a hand?"

MacDonell looked at the lieutenant and thought about Paine's taste in dogs. "I've got a young lady who'll run circles around that jerk. I might have her go out and interview breeders. Let me think about it over the weekend. Maybe I can narrow things down a bit."

"If you're right, if this Constantine comes back, the whole business could repeat itself."

Heavy clouds moved in across Lake Houston during the conversation. Shadows darkened MacDonell's kitchen. On the pool, the reflections were inky black.

"Exactly what I was thinking," MacDonell agreed.

The two men eyed each other for several seconds. Goodson finished his coffee and stretched.

"It's Saturday, Mac. I'll call you Monday."

Goodson was pulling out of the driveway as the phone rang. MacDonell picked it up in the study. The conversation was brief. He hung up, took off his glasses, and held his head in his hands.

"Who was it?" Jeannie asked.

"Carol. She wanted to fill me in on a dog bite."

"She seldom calls on Saturdays. Who got bit?"

"Annabel Mooney's daughter."

"The councilwoman?"

"Pretty bad, too. She's in the hospital."

CHAPTER TWENTY-ONE

*O*n Monday morning MacDonell captured Bragg's attention early, before he could disappear. He began by assigning him the investigation of the Mooney girl's bite case.

Next he reminded Bragg of his earlier assignment to contact the guard dog companies. He closed the door and, in the privacy of his office, made sure Bragg understood his task. The language was clean, clear, and nonabusive.

In less than fifteen minutes the captain discovered Tejas Security Service, a small outfit out in the northwest. Just off the Tomball Parkway, highway 249.

Meanwhile, MacDonell got Longley to call the Harris County Kennel Club. Following instructions, she asked for lists of breeders. When she mentioned animal control, the club secretary became suspicious. She took down the number and told Longley she would call back. By noon, Longley had the phone number of the local AmStaff club. On his own, Bragg came up with the full client lists of two guard dog companies.

Longley spent two hours searching Bragg's lists and putting pins in MacDonell's wall map. There were forty-nine addresses. At entry number forty-three, she struck pay dirt. Tejas had a client in the Midtown area, a small film development company, in the 1500 block of Webster. It was five blocks from where the three men had been attacked. When

MacDonell came back from the candy machine she was sitting at his desk, a smug look on her face.

MacDonell called Sam Goodson. In half an hour Goodson called back. The film company was out of business.

At 2:45 a uniformed police officer showed up. He brought three more client lists and a complete list of the AmStaff Club members, the addresses of the Bay Area and the Houston Rottweiler Clubs. The officer smiled and said he would be more productive tomorrow when he could get an earlier start. Longley had to get more pins.

Late in the afternoon Bragg returned from Methodist Hospital. His interview with Annabel Mooney had not gone well. The councilmember was suffering from memory loss. The girl had been bitten in the face at an outdoor party, but no one could remember how the bite had occurred. The only thing she was certain of was the girl had not provoked the dog.

MacDonell sent him back with explicit instructions.

***

On Tuesday, MacDonell and Goodson decided to try a different approach. They would get out in the field themselves. Their first call was on CSI, Coastal Security Inc. It was out on Wallisville Road, in the county. Goodson asked a predetermined set of questions designed to get to the problem. A young woman in the office supplied a list of clients on the promise it would remain confidential. The casual question, "Is Mr. Constantine still looking for a few good dogs?" got a blank stare. The woman wasn't the owner and wasn't aware of any effort to solicit dogs for export, and she didn't have a good source of supply, anyway. She said they had nine dogs and were overbooked. The dogs, she said, worked at alternate businesses on randomly selected nights. She added that the owner was looking for a few good dogs himself.

Next they headed north on 290, past Jersey Village.

"That wife of yours is a very nice lady," Goodson said as the scenery rambled past.

MacDonell studied his map book.

"Looks like you robbed the cradle."

"Not really," MacDonell said, staring dreamily out the window.

"This is the closest place to where we found the first guy," Goodson remarked.

MacDonell looked at his map book again.

In a few minutes they turned off into a wide gravel lot. A low skulking building on the back of the property echoed of animals long-dead. Jimmy Larsen was in. He was a puffy fat man in a sleeveless orange jumpsuit, smelling of clipper spray and Pinesol. One of his dogs, a narrow-chested black and tan, lay on its side near the door. It raised its head and eyed the two visitors. When Larsen spoke to the dog, it put its head down and exhaled disappointedly into the dust.

Goodson showed his badge and got a casual response. MacDonell introduced himself and asked for a client list. The man squinted then searched the top of his desk, coming up with a copy of his shift schedules.

"What's up?" Larsen asked, keeping his eyes down.

Goodson began with simple questions. Larsen was evasive. He couldn't remember how long he had been in operation and he wasn't sure how many contracts he had. He confirmed the contract at 1500 Webster, but said it had expired.

"How many dogs do you have?" Goodson asked.

"Eight, twelve if you count the ones I'm training and the one I got loaned out."

"What breed?"

"AKC registered Rottweilers, that's all I run."

"Uh huh." Goodson replied. "Ever sell any?"

"Whatcha mean?"

"*Do you ever sell any?*"

"Once in awhile."

"You sell any to Constantine?"

The man shook his head and denied knowing or even hearing of a Colombian named Constantine. No matter how Goodson asked the questions, the fat man's story never varied.

MacDonell gave Goodson a quiet punch in the ribs. Then asked Larsen, "Ever *buy* any dogs?"

Larsen's eyes went back and forth between Goodson and MacDonell. "What?"

"I asked if you ever buy any?"

"Naw, I bred all the ones I got."

MacDonell looked at the dog by the door. "All registered with the AKC?"

"Huh?"

"Are they purebred?"

"Yeah, purebred…every one."

When the conversation ended they looked the place over, rubbed a finger in the dust, and studied the photos on the walls, then stepped around the sleeping dog and went out to the car.

"You did good, Mac. Caught him in a tight spot."

"How so?"

"He made you repeat your questions. You asked him, did he ever *buy* any. He says '*what?*' He was trying to think. His next answer was a lie."

"They teach you that stuff in cop school?"

Goodson slapped MacDonell on the shoulder.

"He looked a little green when I mentioned our Colombian friend, too," Goodson added as he got in the car. "I'll run a check on him, see if he's got a sheet."

"That's not all he lied about," MacDonell said. "If that dog is a purebred, I'm the King of England." MacDonell pulled the car door closed and looked at Goodson. "I'm sure Bragg knows him, too." MacDonell looked at the buildings as they pulled out of the lot. "I didn't like his looks to start with. But then, these people are a little strange."

The next trip was to the opposite side of Houston. At Griffon Industries, across the line in Brazoria County, the Constantine question got a quick and nasty reply.

"You can tell Constantine to go to hell!" the dark-complected man said as he reached inside a desk drawer. It was the first time since Vietnam that MacDonell had felt at risk. He held his breath. When the man pulled his hand out, he was holding a clipping from the Galveston paper.

"Here's what you get when you try to deal with Constantine," he snarled, and shoved the clipping across the desk. It was the obituary of kennel owner Erskin Fall.

"Were you one of the bidders?" Goodson asked.

"Not me."

"What about the man in this article?"

"Yeah."

"You know this man pretty well…this Erskin Fall?" Goodson asked.

"Skin, that's what we called him…Skin."

MacDonell had been observing this exchange with close attention after the hand went into the desk. Now he asked his own question. "That was a terrible accident. What happened to his dogs?"

"That weren't no accident," the man said, spitting on his own floor. "Skin got himself whacked."

"Probably," MacDonell agreed. "My question is, what happened to his dogs?"

"Constables and some of them fuckin' humaniacs went out and got 'em. Cleaned out his whole place."

"Who? County Sheriff, or Galveston Animal Control?" MacDonell asked.

"They all the same."

"No, they're not." MacDonell said, stepping forward and leaning his knuckles on the desk. "Which one, please?"

"Man, I already talked to the Galveston cops. They axed me all this stuff. Rode my ass for two, three hours."

"And I asked you which one!"

The man's eyes shifted around the room. He thought for a minute. "Poppycock Ranch, or something like that. One of them liberal outfits. Over between Pearland and Alvin. Usual bunch of fruits and nuts."

"Pollyanna Park?" MacDonell glanced at Goodson as he said the name. The detective raised his eyebrows.

"Yeah, that's probably it," the man said. "I didn't pay no attention at the time."

In the driveway, MacDonell said, "Paine strikes again."

"What about this Robin Paine?" Goodson asked. Is he…?"

"I'm prejudiced, Sam. I can't stand the little jerk."

"Should I put a tail on him?"

"You're the investigator. A lot of big mean dogs pass through his hands, I can tell you that."

"You think…?"

MacDonell shrugged. "Might be a good idea to keep an eye on him. He's pretty much out in the open. Works with Channel 12's Red Ryder."

Back in Houston, Goodson and MacDonell drove to the 1500 Block of Webster. MacDonell wanted to walk the fence-line of the film processing outfit, see if dogs could escape from the premises. After a brief survey there was no doubt. Dogs could go under, over, or in a few locations, even through the fence. The building itself appeared to be dog-proof.

Driving back to BARC, MacDonell noted the weather had warmed enough for the street population to be moving about. Under the Pierce Elevated, a cardboard city dotted the fenced-off parking areas.

"You asked about Jeannie," MacDonell muttered.

Goodson looked at him. "I was just making conversation."

"She was married when we met."

Goodson drove without comment.

"She came into my office one day with a little cat. It had a broken leg, and she had two black eyes."

The radio in Goodson's car sputtered. "What did you do?" he said in the uncomfortable silence.

"I had a talk with her husband. He was a fighter pilot."

"Oh yeah?"

They drove on, listening to the police dispatcher assign a family violence call.

Goodson pulled over and double parked. "I'm running out of options," he said. "My captain's yanked three of my people for shooting homicides."

"I thought there were five thousand cops in this city?"

"Not for dog bites. Besides, he thinks your theory about sic'n dogs on street bums is pretty far out."

MacDonell could read the frustration in Goodson's face. "What's next?" he asked.

Goodson lit a cigarette. "Since we're in the neighborhood," he said, nodding toward the sidewalk. Both men got out and approached a bulky man lying on a concrete bench. MacDonell noticed a threadbare blanket stenciled USMC. The man wore a Navy watch cap pulled down over his ears. Deep leathery creases started at the corners of his eyes and ran to his collar. In all the folds the man's eyes were a pair of blue pinpoints. They glowed like cutting torches and followed Goodson from the car all the way to the invisible line that marked his territory. The man's possessions sat beside him in an Iceberg Lettuce box. The man put out a scabby protective claw and hugged the box.

Goodson showed the man a small black leather folder with his gold badge and ID.

The man didn't move. "You vice?" his voice crackled.

"Homicide," Goodson replied.

The man sat up and rearranged the blanket over his lap. He hunched forward and gave the appearance he was freezing. Goodson had on a thin gray jacket and MacDonell was in shirtsleeves, rolled to the elbow. His tie fluttered.

"The TV says it's gonna rain tonight," Goodson remarked.

The man was ready with a wry answer. "Don't watch much teevy," he said.

"Where do you stay when it rains?" Goodson asked.

"Over there," the man said, indicating a spot a bit further under the elevated.

Two more street people shambled up and eavesdropped on the conversation. One wore a thin blue jacket with an Oiler insignia. The other had on a long black overcoat.

The man in the Oiler jacket touched MacDonell's sleeve. "Gimme a buck?" he demanded in a raspy growl.

MacDonell ignored him.

Goodson began to explore. "You see many dogs around here?" he asked, trying to sound conversational.

The man on the bench stared past at the concrete. "If you guys don't get that thing purty quick, some more of us is gonna die," he whispered.

"You think it's one dog or more than one?"

"Folks round here think it's like a lion, or something."

"What do you think?" asked Goodson.

"Me? I think it's a man." He gave Goodson a bleak stare. "Can't prove it."

"What makes you think it's a man?"

"This guy told me they all had their crotch ripped out," he whispered. "Maybe its some fancy queer with a leopard on a gold chain. I've heard about stuff like that."

"That's right," the spectator in the blue jacket agreed. He turned to MacDonell, "Gimme a buck?"

"Get a job," Goodson said.

"Gimme a buck."

"Beat it," said Goodson.

MacDonell handed the man a five, folded.

Goodson frowned. "You just bought some cheap wine."

MacDonell shrugged.

The man and his companion shambled off, muttering.

"It's a queer with a leopard," said the man on the bench.

They got back in the car. The rest of the way, Goodson was sullen. "We're not getting anywhere," he said.

"It's a big city," MacDonell replied.

"How many dogs do you think we got in Houston?"

MacDonell looked up at the visor. "Six or seven hundred thousand."

"How many you got registered?"

"Thirty-one thousand."

Goodson took both hands off the wheel and cracked his knuckles. "I'm going to need a miracle," he said.

***

It was after 5:30 when Goodson dropped MacDonell off at BARC. The evening shift trucks were all out. Except for the night dispatcher the place was deserted. He went to his office and stood before the map. After awhile he rummaged through his desk, found a yellow legal pad, and began listing the dates of the known mutilations. He added the approximate dates of the one off the Hempstead Highway and the one on the island. The last three were clustered in time as well as space, no more than ten days separating each event. The last two were only days apart.

Referring to his Key Map book he found the last three deaths were all on page 493. MacDonell turned to it and studied the streets and identified all three kill sites. He inked each spot with a green cross. They were all in one small cell, three quarters of a mile on a side, 493U. The film development company was in the same cell, 493U.

Even Sharon Westergaard's dog had been in that map cell when Bragg shot it. He thought about Bragg. The man was secretive and he was out of the office a lot. He was friendly with the guard dog people. Perhaps too friendly.

MacDonell looked at the grid and closed his eyes. He could still see the map image. The main feature of 493U was the intersection of Interstate 45 and US-59. The exact point where the two highways crossed was in the upper right hand corner of the cell. US-59 ran diagonally from upper right to lower left. The total area was a little over half a square mile. He clucked his tongue. In a city of six hundred square miles, three males, each one a derelict, were all killed in an identical manner in one half of a map square. Alexander Pitkin's van was in the next cell one row down and left one space, 493X.

The sun had gone down and the windows reflected the office in reverse. MacDonell looked at the reflection. His mind wandered to the derelicts he'd met today. By now, many were warming themselves beside flaming oil drums or sleeping on the heat-sucking concrete. He thought about human guinea pigs in Rio and the 'social cleansing squads' ridding cities of their human trash. He thought about the New Orleans police blooding their dogs.

MacDonell put on his jacket and locked the office. The sodium vapor lights had come on. Weary, he climbed into his car. A brown envelope and the Aussie dog tag paraphernalia were on the back seat. Working himself onto the Eastex, he tucked in behind a big red and blue bus. Looking at the rear of the Metro giant for several miles, he recalled something Louis Grizzard had written about sled dogs: 'If you ain't the lead dog the scenery never changes.' MacDonell changed lanes and passed the bus on the right. He watched it in his mirror for another mile before his idea took on form and substance.

As he crossed Will Clayton Parkway and headed into Humble he decided exactly how he could do it. Longley had given him the idea— she should get the credit. It was a long shot, he thought, as he passed over the San Jac bridge. Nevertheless, doing something was better than doing nothing.

Pulling into the driveway his attention was drawn to the tulip trees along the walk. Even in this evening gloom, the buds were glowing a rich fluorescent purple. The infrared sensor under the eaves picked him up and turned on the garage lights. To do what must be done, he too would have to see in the dark. Of this he was certain. As he opened the front door his mind was grinding out the details.

Jeannie was peeling onions at the sink. He crept up behind her and kissed her neck. "Have you kept any of those little key rings?" he asked.

She reached in a drawer next to the sink and handed him a plastic bag. "Whatever happened to 'hi, Honey, I'm home'?"

"You want to go bird-watching?" MacDonell asked.

"When?"

"Tomorrow night and maybe the next. Maybe the rest of the week."

"What are you up to?"

"Tell you while we eat. What's for dinner?"

While Jeannie served up 'apricot stuffed chicken breasts,' MacDonell went to his car, brought in the scanner and the envelope, and slid a pile of gray disks onto the dining room table: the Aussie dog tags. "Want to see how they work?"

"Magic, I'm sure."

The first twenty-five got a silver ring. Then Jeannie zipped over to a craft shop for three more packages. When she got back, she watched the kitchen TV while clipping rings onto the rest of the tags.

MacDonell sat, fiddling with his word processor. "Pick one," he said, showing her a variety of fonts.

Jeannie compared the pages with a copy of the city ordinance. "They look too draft-like, I guess."

"Willie can fix it." He cocked his head to one side and smiled at his wife. "They'll look convincing enough after being Xeroxed, especially crooked and underexposed."

"You clever rascal."
"It's the Australians."
"Now what?" she asked.
He shrugged. "Now we find someone to bell the cat."

CHAPTER TWENTY-TWO

*N*ext morning, briefcase in hand, MacDonell passed Bragg's office. Longley was in with Bragg and it dawned on him. His original thought had been to find a field officer to pull off his little ruse. It would take a badge, but Bragg's wouldn't do. He was too close to the guard dog people. She, however, had a badge and was probably the best candidate.

Inside the conversation was animated. Longley had her fists on her hips, chin jutted forward. She lifted her right hand, cocked her wrist, stuck a slim finger in Bragg's face.

MacDonell watched them for a second then rapped on the glass. Longley looked around first. He motioned toward his office with his thumb, tapped his watch, and held up five fingers. The two nodded their heads in unison.

After unlocking his office, MacDonell put the envelope of tags in the middle of his desk. Pulling some paperwork out of his briefcase he scanned it one last time, then called Willie.

"Xerox," he said. "Start by reducing it about twenty-five percent. If that doesn't work then experiment around. Make it look as close to the ordinance as possible."

"How many?" she asked.

"I'll need about twenty."

In five minutes, Bragg and Longley were standing in front of his desk.

"Who did you want?" asked Bragg.

MacDonell said, "Both."

It was easy to see Longley's hackles were still up. MacDonell wondered if his talk with Bragg was wearing off. He watched as they sat at opposite sides of the room.

"What's up, Doc?" Bragg asked.

"I have a high priority job for J.D.," MacDonell said, "but I need you to lend her your truck."

"I've got to run out to the north side in the next five minutes. Shaw in 12 called. He's relieving a lady of about thirty dogs and cats."

"He is? Tell me about it," MacDonell said.

"Neighbors noticed a stink. Adult Protective Services is out there. She's got live cats in the walls and under the floor boards. He found a bunch of dead ones, but he hasn't been able get a good count on the live ones."

"What about the Mooney bite case?"

"I'm working on it," he said. "Maybe Connie can find her a spare truck?"

"I already checked. He's got them all assigned."

The three sat looking at each other.

"I've got my Bronco," Longley said. "I don't mind, if it's important."

Connie Oaks passing by the door.

"I don't like people to use their own vehicles," MacDonell said.

"I really don't mind."

"Okay," he said. "Make sure you keep track of your mileage."

Bragg excused himself and disappeared.

"You're going to visit the guard dog companies," MacDonell told Longley. "All their dogs have to be tagged."

"Does Frank know about this?"

"He would if he'd stuck around," MacDonell said, smiling.

"Is it true?"

Canis

"The tags are free," he grinned. "Tell them it's new requirement. I'll give you a copy of the amended ordinance. Willie's making copies right now. If you get any guff, give them my private number."

"What's the scam?"

"None. I'm just shooting in the dark." He thought a second. "Tell you what. I'll get Connie to go, too. Between the two of you, it shouldn't take all day."

"Sounds like fun."

"Good," he said. "You can divert their attention with the dog tags while Connie locates their trucks."

He held up an Aussie tag.

"One of these little babies goes on each dog."

Longley turned a tag over in her hand.

MacDonell continued. "I'll give you enough for sixty dogs and a dozen vehicles. If you need a few more let me know." he looked at Longley. "Any questions?"

"Aren't most of these places out in the county?"

He nodded. "But they operate in the city."

"What'll keep them from taking the tag off?"

"Nothing," MacDonell answered.

"I could tell them any dog found running loose in the city without one could get shot by your captain."

MacDonell gave her a look, "What were you two arguing about?"

"He's a sexist pig. He wanted to know how I liked rough sex." She lowered her voice. "He messes with me I'll cripple him for life. Dumb bastard thinks he knows everything there is to know about women."

"Do me a favor. Put it in writing."

She waved her hand in the air. "Forget it."

MacDonell studied her for a moment, then called Oaks and gave him the same briefing.

Oaks couldn't wait.

"Make sure you hit CSI, Tejas, Larsen, and Griffon Industries first," MacDonell said. "And bring back any tags you don't use, Connie. They're ten bucks a whack."

Within minutes, Longley and Oaks were out the door.

MacDonell reserved a handful of tags for himself. At 10:00 Jeannie slipped in the side door. MacDonell collected his hat and checked out with Willie. "I'll be near the radio most of the day," he said.

By 10:45 MacDonell was pulling through the gates at Pollyanna Park. "I don't like this," Jeannie said.

"You stay here until I get inside," he told her.

The sky was high and blinding white. The lot was wide open, with no place to hide. He parked beside Paine's mint green Astrovan. On the other side of the van was the Chevy Blazer from Channel 12. Ryder must be here, he decided.

MacDonell looked around the grounds. Four or five people were in the corral. From a distance, one chubby female in a blue denim outfit and a black hat was saddling a mare.

MacDonell walked to the building. Through the screen he could see TV-12's camera sitting on a desk. Otherwise, the room was empty. He knocked, went in. and walked across the room counting: one thousand-one,…one thousand-two,…Jeannie would be out of the car by now. He went to the rear door and peered out at the corral. By now she would be at the rear of the van. He gave her five more seconds to attach a wire twist-tie around the bolt on the trailer hitch.

MacDonell came out. He saw Jeannie glance at the corral. The horse they were trying to saddle was acting up. Jeannie had finished the rear and struggled to get the wire over the front bumper strut. She twisted the tie three or four good turns with her left hand and braced herself against the bumper. MacDonell heard scuffling footsteps at the side of the building. He saw Jeannie straighten up.

"Who are you," a voice cracked. "What are you doing?"

"Is this a four-wheel drive?" Jeannie called back.

"Who wants to know?"

"My husband's the city veterinarian. He wants one of these in the worst way," Jeannie said, blinking. "You know him? Uh…Dr. MacDonell."

"YOU STILL REHABBING FIGHTING DOGS?" MacDonell boomed, as he came off the steps. The screen slammed behind him.

Paine whirled. "Oh, it's you."

Jeannie wilted like lettuce on a hot rock.

"You haven't met my wife?" MacDonell said with a wide Texas sweep of his arm. "This is Jeannie."

Jeannie put out a delicate hand but Paine made no effort to shake it.

"I came out here to show her some of them big dogs of yours. You still turning them into pussy cats?"

"When we get them."

"How about Schutzhund-trained guard dogs?" MacDonell asked. "Ever get any?"

Paine studied MacDonell's face. "I don't think so."

"What kind of a price would you put on a dog like that?" MacDonell asked, as if he were bidding on a carload of heifers.

"We don't price anything. We're non-profit."

"What did you give for Skin's dogs?" MacDonell asked abruptly.

"We seized those dogs. We don't buy…" Paine paused. "Who?" he said.

"Erskin Fall. The dog people called him Skin. You know him, don't you?" MacDonell pressed.

"No. I misunderstood you," Paine replied.

MacDonell changed the subject. "I understand Constantine is coming back," he said. He looked hard at Paine's eyes. If there was something there, he didn't see it. He wondered what Goodson would have seen.

Paine returned MacDonell's cool gaze. "I don't know who you're talking about," he said. The tone was emotionless and impossible to read.

"What are you doing out here?" Paine asked.

MacDonell had his story already worked out. "Like I said, I was in the neighborhood with my wife, and I figured I'd show her those two old pits you have. Where'd you say you picked them up?" He gave Paine a bland smile.

"I didn't say. Besides, they're not here anymore. We found homes for both of them."

"Oh, really?" MacDonell said. "I'm glad to hear it."

Jeannie leaned on the car. "This is a very nice place," she said, getting into the swing of things.

MacDonell agreed. "They've got a real menagerie, Honey."

Paine broke in. "Doctor, I hate to give the impression I'm too busy to visit, but I am. If you'd like another tour just give us a call."

MacDonell looked at Jeannie and got a slow nod of the head. "Okay," he said. "Can I bring my sweetheart?"

"Sure," Paine said, as MacDonell held the door for his wife.

MacDonell aimed the car at the gate, pressed down on the accelerator, and scratched a little gravel. Paine looked up. MacDonell slowed and watched in his rear view mirror as Paine now turned away from the van and headed toward the corral.

"So far, so good," MacDonell whispered.

"The guy's a creep," Jeannie observed.

At BARC MacDonell gave her a kiss and let her off in the main lot. He waited until she was out of sight, then he drove to the back and parked in his reserved space.

Connie Oaks was standing next to his car when MacDonell pulled up. He reached in, pulled out a legal pad, handed it to his boss, and reported on the day's progress. He and Longley had placed fifty-one tags on dogs, and he had tagged five vehicles himself. Oaks handed MacDonell the envelope with the remaining tags. The truck plate numbers and matching tag numbers were on the yellow pad. "We got all the dogs and both the trucks at Griffon Industries. The rest only had one truck each," he said. "We'll finish up tomorrow."

MacDonell slipped the remaining tags from his pocket into the envelope and put this and the lists in his car.

"I have to admit, J.D's pretty slick." Oaks said.

"How so?"

"Well, we worked out a routine. She'd take the tags in, talk a little smack, show them the ordinance, lay on the bullshit; I'd stay outside and put up the hood on their truck or kick the tires. It worked pretty good." Oaks laughed. "I saw a new side of the lady, though. She about nailed some poor trash on the way back."

"She what?"

"Oh, this wino was standing on the corner holding up a sign when we pulled up to a light. He tried to wash her windshield for a quarter. Smeared it up good. When he leaned on her Bronco, I thought she was going to run him over."

MacDonell scowled.

"New law says they got to stand eight feet from your car. She was so pissed she nearly couldn't drive."

"Where is she?"

"I told her to run it through the truck wash and go on home."

"You get all the tags where they're easily exposed?"

"No sweat, Doc," Oaks said. "They're kinda mud-colored anyway, and most of those trucks are junk. Tags sorta just blended right in."

"Good. Is Frank back?"

Oaks pointed to a pickup parked near the pumps. "I think he's in his office."

"Do me one more favor?"

"Name it".

"Put a couple tags on it before he comes out here. I'll go talk to him for awhile."

Oaks looked puzzled, but moved down the sidewalk and started across the lot. MacDonell wrote down some numbers and headed for Bragg's office. It was unlocked, but empty. He checked the dayroom, then went to his own office.

Willie was tidying up her desk.

"Heard from Frank?" MacDonell asked as he let himself in the door.

"He come in here 'bout a hour ago," she replied. She stopped and grinned at him broadly. "Guess whose dog done bit Miz Mooney's little girl?"

MacDonell rubbed his head and scratched his sideburns.

"Old Bull Frog Dockery, hisself," she chuckled.

MacDonell's jaw dropped. "Are you sure?"

"Dr. Clemmons tol' me Dockery done had hisself a barbecue in his backyard, an' the child was there with her mama."

"My God," MacDonell whispered.

"An' Dr. Clemmons, she talked over the whole thing with Miz Mooney's doctor. They decide the child gonna take all them shots if we don't figure out what dog done it. When Miz Mooney found that out, she went ahead an spilled the beans."

"Who knows about this," MacDonell asked.

"Just Dr. Clemmons, I 'spect."

MacDonell put a finger up to his lips. "I'll go find the captain. Meanwhile, let's keep this our little secret."

CHAPTER TWENTY-THREE

*M*acDonell sat with Jeannie in her black Honda and pointed the Aussie's UV light gun at passing trucks. If they worked as advertized he could scan a half-dozen vehicles in seconds. He could identify dog trucks from blocks away, even if they were lost in a sea of headlights or taillights.

Jeannie sat in the driver's seat trying to read. "You think it'll happen again, so soon?"

MacDonell thought a minute. "It's been two weeks since Pitkin was killed. It could be past due. That is, if they're contracting for more dogs."

"What does Sam think about this?"

"He's not getting as much support as he'd like."

"That's not what I'm asking. What does he think about this?"

"I haven't told him yet."

"I don't believe it! You didn't tell him?"

MacDonell looked at Jeannie, then past her to the street. "Nope," he said. "He's got his hands full, checking out dog breeders, doing door-to-door surveys in the neighborhoods, and running background checks on people in the guard dog business. Besides, this is not exactly legal."

Since this was their first night, MacDonell had selected Jackson between the St. Joseph's Hospital School of Nursing and the Cancer Lab. Down deep he wasn't certain it would work, or what he'd do if he found a security dog attacking someone. He had a dart gun between his feet, and a full vial of tranquilizer. The plan, such as it was, was to move west street by street. Thursday he would be on Crawford; Friday, LaBranch.

Student nurses were running back and forth across the street in their bathrobes. It didn't appear Jeannie would encounter any risk. It was nice to have her to talk to.

By 11:00 the traffic and the nurses had disappeared. When midnight came around the streets were deserted.

He faced south and let the traffic pass him on the right. Jeannie had fixed a small banquet. He ate, flashed the light, and ate some more. At 1:00 a.m. he caught himself nodding. Around 2:00, two shadowy figures crept down Webster and melted into the new shrubs put in recently by the Highway Department. Homelessness was spreading like an infection. It started to drizzle.

"It was right over there where the police found the second body," he said, pointing down the street to where the elevated fanned out above Chenevert.

Jeannie hugged herself and shuddered.

"It was pretty bad. Body parts were found ten or twelve feet away," he commented.

"Did I ask?" she said.

By 4:00 a.m. MacDonell's eyes closed and his head fell forward. Jeannie picked up the UV gun, but the streets were deserted. At 5:00 MacDonell called it off and they went to get a Denny's breakfast. While he was eating, he discovered his sensory organs were tangled. He could smell himself, but he couldn't taste maple syrup.

Jeannie drove home and insisted he take a shower before he went back down the Eastex. She turned the water on as hot as she could without scalding him and pushed him in. He put his head against the tiles, letting the hot needles play across his lower back. If I could lock my knees like a stork, he thought, I'd fall asleep standing up. A few more nights like this, he said to himself, and I'll be hanging upside down from the ceiling.

The Thursday day shift was routine at BARC. At 8:00 a.m. a truck was dispatched to a Harris County Constable's office. While MacDonell was playing detective, a sting on some north side sportsmen had netted six pit bulls and a chow. They were seized from a slow-footed dog fighter, nailed up inside a small mobile home for the night, and impounded this morning. Charges of cocaine trafficking, gambling, and illegal dog fighting were pending. A dozen dog fighters had gotten away.

Clemmons came to MacDonell's office at 10:00 and complained about lack of space in the prisoners ward. These cases often took months and the dogs would have to be held indefinitely. "They could die of old age," she bellyached.

Before the day was over, 104 dogs and cats were taken off the streets; an average day for the officers who were often accused of staying glued to their trucks, and never giving chase. In the quarantine ward twenty-nine biters were in residence. One victim, a five year old girl, had been bitten through the lip by at least one member of a three-dog gang. She was too young to identify the exact animal, and because of this each dog occupied a separate space in a ward with locks and heavy steel doors. The owners were furious and threatened suit. MacDonell listened, almost falling asleep. In the end, he sent them to the city attorney.

Four water moccasins were taken from a garage that had flooded, and a raccoon was removed from the roof of a school. Seventy-nine animals were destroyed from the Monday impounds. Four animals were reclaimed, and one lucky dog was adopted by a new owner. At 3:00 p.m., like countless other afternoons, a long-bed pickup left the back door of the freezer, headed for the landfill. It was heaped with plastic-wrapped packages, and for safety a large green tarp covered the load. The truck groaned and scraped bottom as it went over the hump in the asphalt by the back gate.

MacDonell stood on the deck outside his office and watched the truck leave. All of this because I wanted to go to vet school and help animals. He closed his eyes, listening for a minute to the clang of the steam hammer across the street.

Willie stuck her head out. "Information lady on the phone," she said. "I'm in the field."

After doing a few stretches and deep knee bends, he went back in and wrote and wrote and wrote until his eyes burned. At 5:00 he contemplated finding someone in the kennel to sell him a bennie. He reconsidered when he spied two of his kennel workers bopping past his window.

He fished the little zippered case out of his canvas briefcase and put the cuff around his left arm. He squeezed the bulb and watched the numbers flicker on the read-out. BP: 148/89. Not so bad. At 5:30 he left. Several letters were undone.

Because of the heavy traffic on the previous night MacDonell decided to start later, otherwise he'd never last till the weekend. He got home, ate, showered, and slept from 7:30 till around 11:00. At midnight he and Jeannie left the house, and by 1:00 a.m. they were hunkered down, this time at a new location. MacDonell junked his original plan and chose the corner of Gray and Fannin, across from the Trailways terminal. It was a good spot and they could see down both streets.

At 2:15 a.m. a truck came up Gray and turned south on Caroline. MacDonell picked it up three blocks away, when it crossed Austin. It was his first actual electronic response. The tags worked!

"I'll be switched" he whispered.

The scanner had given an audible click and the read-out showed 000,010,108. He read the number to Jeannie, who entered it in the notebook computer.

"Larsen's," she read, with palpable excitement.

"Hot damn," MacDonell said.

MacDonell motioned with his left hand. Jeannie slipped the computer in the door pocket and started the engine. A block south they caught a glimpse of the truck turning left on Hadley. He motioned again, she turned left and pulled to the curb. MacDonell watched as the driver got out, crossed the sidewalk, and disappeared through a gate in a chain-link fence. Jeannie read her husband's mind. She eased out and closed the distance.

The streets were wet and black, and reflections streaked the glittery surface. The driver was in the fence, or maybe inside the building itself. Jeannie moved closer, crossed the intersection, pulling within a car length of the truck.

There was no movement on the street. The nearest street light was two blocks ahead, and the back of the dog truck was bathed in thick shadows. A reflection from the street light caused a glare under the truck. It had four welded boxes on the back, two facing the rear. MacDonell wondered if any dogs were on board. Jeannie turned the engine off, but the hot motor pinged and popped. In a second the battery-driven fans came on. "Damn," he whispered.

"I forgot about the fans," she said.

MacDonell was wondering how he might turn them off when they went off by themselves. He opened his door and got out.

"Where are you going?"

He heard but didn't answer. He clicked his door and moved to the truck. Inside the Honda it had been toasty; out on the street it was flinty cold. The familiar smell of wet dogs confronted him. He looked at four round holes in the metal cage doors. They were solid quarter-inch sheet steel. He tried to imagine what kind of demon might be inside. Why had he chosen to bring his wife along to catch a killer dog? "I must be nuts," he thought.

He took a step forward. "Why didn't I bring a flashlight?" There was no sound from the truck. He looked at the kennel doors. The chains swung loose and the locks were open.

MacDonell remembered his experience with Pitkin's mastiff. He also remembered his last look at the old man's body. The ripped-out abdomen, the crushed and torn throat. He remembered the whopping strength of Pitkin's mastiff as it tried to peel the door off his car. Crouching, he searched the cracks around the kennel doors. The blackness wasn't sharp and shiny, it was dull and non-reflective. He couldn't see anything that would confirm or deny the presence of an animal. He listened, hoping to hear scratching or a yawn. Light rain spotted his bifocals. Straining to detect breathing, he noticed his own need to breathe. He sucked in air and held it. There was only the sound of his own heart pumping strong and loud. The dog smell grew stronger.

A prickling sensation crept up the back of his legs and a feeling of panic filled him. He was too far from his car if the heavy doors suddenly burst open.

The cage locks hung down. He moved, reached for the chain, slipped the left lock in the left door hasp. Then he reached for the right hand lock and repeated the process. Breathing easier, he stepped up and put an eye to the space between the bars at the top. In the car, Jeannie must have sensed his need for light. She flicked up the head lights. For an instant, the glare flooded the dark recesses of the cages. They were empty. He waved his hand and Jeannie cut the lights. Relaxing a little he circled the truck. He looked at the building. He could hear far-off pounding, and the frenzied response of at least two dogs inside. The handler was agitating his pooches.

"Whooee," MacDonell said, slipping in beside his wife. "It's colder than a turd in a dead Eskimo out there. Let's get out of here."

They moved up the street and waited in the dark. In five minutes the truck chugged past on the left and headed to the Eastex. It turned north, farted black smoke, and accelerated out onto the freeway.

"What do we do now?" Jeannie asked.

"Let him go. He's empty."

"It's 3:25."

Down the street two sets of headlights turned the corner and moved toward them. MacDonell gave a heavy sigh, reached back on the seat behind him and picked up the scanner. The headlights were more than three blocks away. He squeezed the trigger. The machine clicked and flashed a number. He looked it: 000,010,123. He read it out loud, but already knew who it was. Jeannie worked the computer. "Robin Paine," she whispered.

"Busy night?" MacDonell muttered.

He turned the machine off, then on, and flashed the invisible beam again. And again it identified, 000,010,123. As the two sets of lights got closer, they saw a mint green Astrovan followed by a white Chevy Blazer. The Blazer had a large red stripe. In the middle of the stripe, in ten inch black letters, it read, 'Channel 12 News.'

"What are they doing out here together?" Jeannie asked.

MacDonell wondered the same thing. After they passed he blipped the back of the van. The sweet little machine read 000,010,122.

"After they get down the street aways, go around the block. Let's see if we can find out what's going on."

Jeannie had the engine running before the van got to the next intersection. She turned the corner, snapped up the headlights and went back to Webster. The street was one-way in the wrong direction. Surging up to Gray, she went around and up two blocks. Returning on Fannin, she turned right on Hadley. Neither vehicle was on the street.

"Stop!" MacDonell snapped, and looked out the back. "Maybe we passed them."

There was no traffic. Nothing ahead, nothing behind. Jeannie moved to the next intersection. He scanned both ways with the UV. Nothing. The same at Travis. Again nothing. Jeannie whipped a sharp U-turn on Milam and returned down Hadley. They zipped up to every intersection, scanned both directions, and gunned ahead. In a few minutes, they were back to Crawford.

"Which way?" she asked.

MacDonell shook his head and pounded his fist on the dash. The animal rights activist and his entourage had given them the slip.

CHAPTER TWENTY-FOUR

*O*n Friday mornings MacDonell always scheduled a walk-through; today he was a few minutes behind. He emptied his in-basket, shuffled through its contents, and put a thin stack of employment applications in the middle of his desk. No real standouts. He headed across to the kennel.

Human/companion animal bond was a catchy term being tossed about by animal welfarists these days. It made them feel professional. MacDonell's shoulders sagged as he stepped into the building. He knew the tenuous bond was about to be slashed as many as three hundred times before the sun set on the Katy Prairie. At least eighty dogs and cats lay dead on the kennel floor and in the freezer carts here at the city's animal control bureau. That many were in the cooler at the HCSPCA and half that number at Harris County Animal Control. Far south at the Houston Humane League the number was smaller, but the result was equally irreversible. At Citizens for Animal Defense a small freezer was full. At more than two hundred locations throughout the city and county, veterinarians in private practice had accounted for another two or three each. Deer Park, Pasadena, and Bellaire were also handling their own euthanasia and disposal. So were Baytown and cities to the south and east.

MacDonell walked through the wards. The influx of newborns was starting. It would peak in April or May and repeat itself in September. At least three litters were in the red ward, all mixed breeds. A lonely yapper broke the silence.

The blue ward had one litter, but in it were ten coal-black puppies. The fuss-budget mother was a Shepherd mix and she was having a difficult time keeping her family inside the low cut cardboard box that had been added over the grated floor. Her worries would be over in 48 hours.

In the green ward, six bitches occupied the large kennels on the end of the row. Among them, the 'miracle of birth' had produced thirty-three unwanted pups.

It was after 9:00 a.m. and the yellow ward was no longer occupied by live animals. In almost every kennel there had been someone's companion. Forty-two individual kennels made up each ward. In a stroke of good fortune, two occupants from the yellow ward had been claimed during the allotted time. After the three-day holding period, one healthy pup had been selected for surgical sterilization and potential adoption. On the floor in front of the remaining thirty-nine kennels, thirty-nine black plastic bags now held the former occupants. Six of the bags included an additional seventeen newborns which had not lived long enough for their eyes to open. Fifty-six lives. In most cases the occupants had once been gentle and warm, with ready tongues long, wet and liberally applied. The sad-eyed guests waited, nervous, jittery, with a cocked ear each time the ward door opened. But what of all this waiting? MacDonell had ten years of reproducible records. In 94.7 percent of the cases the animals waited in vain. They had been trusting and noncritical, faithfully living up to their end of the human/companion animal bond.

MacDonell stepped over the bags and looked to see that the public door had been properly locked. A dull-eyed worker pushed a cart through the rear door. The floor would soon be cleared and the cleaning process would begin. Unloading would start at 2:00 p.m. Each new occupant would get its three days of food, water, warmth, then gentle, decent death. If the averages were accurate, and they always were, thirty would be put to sleep without ever reaching the yellow ward. They were the ones belonging to an owner who had opted for destruction rather than pay a fine or buy a license.

MacDonell circled the yellow ward and left the same way he had entered. Carol Clemmons sat in her glass enclosure sorting a tall stack of kennel cards. He trudged past the quarantine ward and the prisoner's ward and entered the triage area. In the exotic ward he knew there were a few chickens, a nutria, and a sloth-like Asian bintarong. He wasn't curious; they'd been there for days. He wondered what sad sight might be waiting on the dock, left over from the night shift.

To his surprise a Giant Schnauzer occupied the holding pen on the end. Its coat was heavy, matted, and dirty. Lupe Delgado was making an effort to cut a piece of wire from the animal's neck. The wire had grown into the dog's skin. It didn't try to bite, yet it wouldn't stand still either. Lupe wasn't getting the job done and Ron Reyes, who was standing outside the pen, wasn't offering any help. MacDonell watched the two men for several seconds. He thought about calling Clemmons. She was busy. After a second, he walked to the pen and swung open the heavy door.

"Give us a hand will you, Ron?" MacDonell said.

"I'm a field officer."

MacDonell stepped in the pen and told Lupe to grasp the animal by the muzzle.

"Hold him here," MacDonell said. "Extend the neck a little. Hold his jaw tight."

MacDonell examined the wire. It was a coat hanger and it was twisted around the dog's neck.

"It's been here a long time, Lupe," MacDonell said.

"Long time," Lupe repeated.

MacDonell turned to Reyes. "Lay him down, Ron."

The whites of the dog's eyes bulged and it quivered.

"He stinks!" Reyes whined.

"It'll wash off," MacDonell replied. He pointed. "Hold his legs, there and there."

"Couldn't you give him something?"

"We could, if the city would buy it."

"Why don't you put him down now?" Reyes asked.

"His owner has seventy-two hours, Ron."

"What you gonna do when he bites me?"

Send your brain to the lab, MacDonell thought.

The work was swift. With the cutters MacDonell snapped the wire in two places and gently, gently removed it from the granulating tissue that had overgrown the wire. The dog exhaled and blew saliva. Lupe held tight. Once the wire had been removed, Reyes let go and the animal struggled to get up.

"*Tiene un amigo.* You've made a friend for life," MacDonell said, smiling. MacDonell's Spanish was poor, but Lupe understood. MacDonell stepped to the wall sink to wash his hands.

"Question, Doc?" Reyes asked.

"Sure."

"You know them six pits that come in yesterday?"

"Yup," MacDonell answered as he scrubbed.

"What's gonna happen to them?"

MacDonell looked at him. "They're being held for evidence. The owner's being charged with dog fighting."

"I know, but I hear he's croaked."

"Dead?"

"Back of his head got blowed off last night."

"Where'd you hear that?"

"Friend of mine," Reyes answered. "He wants to know, can he adopt them—or maybe buy them."

"You know better than that. They belong to the court."

MacDonell dried his hands and stepped back. "What's your friend's name?"

"Cap'n Bragg knows him, he's straight."

"What's his name?"

"I forget."

MacDonell shook his head. He was behind schedule. As he paced along the glass-walled corridor in the cat ward, he saw every cage filled. The bright colors matched the dog wards. Urethane paint, hand-troweled epoxy floors. Slick, efficient, easy to clean.

Through the bars of cages, kittens spilled onto the floor, then cried to get back to their mothers. A technician was trying to match kittens to queens. She crammed one in with a fat tom. He spit, dilated his pupils, and laid back his ears. By contrast, the scrawny queens tolerated them with half-closed eyes. For many they didn't have to match.

MacDonell stared through the glass. All this activity: climbing, fighting, crying, and nursing. It seemed so futile. In the yellow section, fifteen black plastic bags lay on the floor ready to be filled.

This was minimum wage work. When he found a person who could do this job, calculate the dose, restrain the animal, find the vein, and push the plunger—what could he promise? That was easy. He promised steady employment.

There was much more than destruction of life in this place. There was destruction of the spirit.

Over the speaker system an announcement blared and repeated, "301, pick up 333." He sprinted to the end of the hall, across the sun-splashed patio and into his office. Willie had Goodson on the phone.

"Sam. What's up?" he puffed.

"Anybody from the press talked to you yet?"

"About what?"

"About anything?"

"I've got standing orders, Sam. Everything goes through the department's PIO."

"Good. They know anything? About the killings, I mean?"

"I tried to explain some of it to Trimble. He wasn't interested."

"You got some pit bulls down there now, don't you?"

"We have a few."

"No, I mean, didn't you pick up a load from a crud named Martine Franco?"

"I can check." MacDonell didn't know who the animals in the prisoner's ward belonged to. "I've got six pits and a chow that we picked up on a dog fighting charge. Hang on." MacDonell punched hold and buzzed 336 in the kennel. Clemmons picked up the phone.

"Carol, what's the name of that dog fighter we took the pits from?" He could hear her ruffling a stack of cards.

"Says 'Marty Franco.' Why?" she replied.

"I'll explain later."

He pressed down the receiver and hit the hold button again. "The guy's name is Franco, all right. Marty Franco."

"Listen, Mac, for your ears only. Mister Franco was snuffed last night when he didn't pay off his crack man." Goodson spoke in confidential tones. "If anybody asks about them, let me know?"

"You have a lead on this thing?" MacDonell asked.

"Might be," Goodson replied.

"Well, I think your secret's already out. A few minutes ago, one of my officers mentioned that the owner got his brains blown out. I didn't think to ask the name."

Goodson was silent. Then he lowered his voice. "What's your officer's name?"

MacDonell's curiosity was piqued. "Reyes," he said. "Ron Reyes."

"Word travels fast, Mac. I told Galveston PD, when their snitch comes back to tell him some dogs are available."

"Is this the guy who supposedly went to Colombia with the dog buyer?" MacDonell asked.

"That's right. Right now our dog buyer could be on his way back to town." Goodson made a clicking sound with his tongue. "Tell you what, Doc. We're going to come around and talk to your man."

"I'll have him sitting in my office whenever you say."

"Quietly, Doc. Quietly. In the meantime keep your ears open. Anybody who knows the dogs are available might be tied into this thing."

MacDonell hung up the phone as Clemmons appeared at the glass door. She hesitated, but he waved her on in.

"Did you see those Franco dogs?" she asked.

He looked at her. "No. Why?"

"The five pits are absolute gangsters. A couple are over seventy-five pounds apiece. The small one is over fifty, and it's a rattlesnake. It tried to nail Lupe right through the bars about ten minutes ago. Never made a sound."

"Did Reyes talk to you about them?" he asked.

"Why?"

"Ron told me he has a friend who wants to buy them."

She smiled. "Fat chance."

Late in the afternoon Willie stuck her head in the door. "Doctor Trimble's secretary is on your line," she said, then added, "oh, by the way, did ya'll know, your cactus is blooming?"

MacDonell gave her a puzzled look and picked up the phone. He stretched his neck to observe the clay pot by the door. There was a splash of color. Then a chilly voice cut in. "There's a reporter here from the Chronicle, doing a feature. Something about animal bites. He's asked for clearance to talk to you. He says you may have some statistics he can use."

MacDonell put his feet up on the desk. "Not interested," he said.

"I thought you loved talking to the press."

"You thought wrong."

"Chance to get your picture in the paper."

"What's the matter with you people. Dr. Trimble told me not speak to the press. He made it pretty clear."

"Dr. Trimble's out of town."

"Then you handle it, you're the information expert."

MacDonell sat looking at the instrument. Lights flashed on all eight lines.

Willie buzzed in. "Dr. Mac, there's a lady on my line say she wanna talk about animal attacks. Sound like she got a case of the heat frustrations."

"Tell her I'm up to my duff in alligators."

"It could be true," she said and rang off.

CHAPTER TWENTY-FIVE

*M*acDonell wanted to get home early, but the office remained in turmoil. Phones jangled and a TV channel tried to interview Willie Fish. A junior PIO clerk probed Clemmons for a quote and she hung up on him. Frantic reports of a horse with an erection and a swarm of bees in an attic accounted for some of the calls. A detective came over from 61 Riesner and borrowed MacDonell's office. He questioned Reyes for two hours while the business of animal control whirled around them.

MacDonell sat outside his office, across from Willie's desk, and entertained himself taking phone complaints. Lonnie Kenner called several times trying to negotiate the quarantine of councilman Dockery's dog. Initially, there was a firm denial that Dockery even owned a dog. After Annabel Mooney's affidavit was presented to Kenner, the denial took a new form. Kenner claimed that his boss's dog was in compliance with all of the city's ordinances. Faced with MacDonell's computer records, Kenner called to ask for "professional courtesy."

"I'm being about as courteous as I can be, Mr. Kenner. First you said he didn't own a dog. Then you said this dog he didn't own, didn't do the biting. Then you told my captain this non-biting dog was vaccinated and licensed." MacDonell gave a deep sigh. "You could save us all a lot of time if you'd trot out the dog or show us the vaccination certificate. I'm trying to enforce a state law here, and I would think a city councilman could appreciate that. Ordinary citizens get one chance, then we slap them with a $600 citation for failure to surrender, and let the courts handle it."

Kenner promised to produce a dog the next day. MacDonell stared, in a moment of disbelief, at the small yellow blossom on his cactus. "Not *a* dog, *the* dog, Mr. Kenner."

He locked up his office and was past the big Airport when his radio blared. "Double Oh-3, what's the ETA to your next destination?" It was Gallegos in the dispatcher's office.

Identifying himself, MacDonell listened to a crisp request for him to call the director's office, *asap*! To hell with that, he thought. He moved on up the Eastex and across the San Jac bridge.

When he got home, Jeannie was holding back tears. "I let her out this morning," she whispered. "I didn't pay much attention after that. Oh, Duncan, Lil is dead."

MacDonell looked out through the patio glass and across the pool to the narrow garden next to the fence. Lil lay in her favorite spot, a comfortable hummock between two rose bushes, her chin resting on her forelegs. MacDonell sat on a kitchen chair and stared at her.

"Some lady called…twice…" Jeannie said between sniffles. "She said the health director wants to talk to you as soon as you're available."

MacDonell looked up at her as she hovered near his shoulder. He searched his pockets for a Kleenex. She put her arms around his shoulders and leaned her cheek against the top of his head. Her face was cool. He encircled her waist with a hairy arm.

"The phone's been ringing off the hook. Somebody from the Chronicle. Carol called, too. She said something about Bragg needing your permission to get a warrant to dig up a backyard. I wrote it all down."

MacDonell didn't answer.

"I'm sorry," she said.

Something caught MacDonell's eye near the old dog. "What's that," he asked, pointing to something fluttering in the rose bed near the dog's foot.

Jeannie blinked away her tears and looked.

"It's one of those cardboard tabs that pops out when you put a new film pack in a Polaroid," she replied. "I must have dropped it out in the yard the other day when I took those pictures of her. She was chewing on it…before she…lay down. You don't think that it caused her…?"

"Nah." he said.

Exhausted, MacDonell rubbed his head and stared at Lil. Something bothered him about the Polaroid tab—but for now his old hunting partner was gone. Five minutes later he was still sitting there. Finally, with great reluctance, he pulled himself up, trudged to the garage, and got a shovel.

"Aren't you going to change your clothes?" Jeannie asked in a quiet voice.

"I'm too tired. Call Carol back, will you. Tell her I said, 'permission granted.'"

It was dark and he was only half-finished with his digging when Jeannie came out into the garden. "That woman from Dr. Trimble's office is on the phone again. She's a little frosty. I told her I'd see if you were available."

"Tell her…" he gave out a heavy sigh. "Tell her I'll call him right back."

"I'm really sorry about this," she said.

"It's not your fault," he said. "I knew it was coming. I was afraid I was going to have to do it myself. Carol put down seventy-five this morning…but it's not the same." MacDonell stretched his back. "Did you call her back?"

"Yes. She said something about a witness, a maid."

"You want to go out again tonight?" he asked.

"If you think it will do any good," she replied.

Digging in the cool earth made MacDonell ache in his bones. Each spadeful was more difficult than the last. His thoughts went back to Germany, 1975, where he'd been asked to put the wing commander's dachshund to sleep. The old man who'd been shot down over Vietnam, and who now commanded three squadrons of brand new,F-15s, had shed some tears. A newly-promoted one star general, he was getting up in age and was not expected to make a second star. MacDonell recalled how he had wanted to put his arm around the man's shoulder, but rank and protocol seemed to discourage it.

MacDonell made sure the grave was deep. When he was done, he laid Lil gently into the ground. Covering her with dirt was the hardest part. After he pressed the earth down, he leaned for a long moment on the shovel, his whiskery chin dropping to his chest. He could see Jeannie watching from the kitchen.

It was only a dog, he thought, but he knew better. In her younger days, she had bitten him. Just a nip; it was his own fault. He'd been trimming her toenails and clipped one too close. He was more worried about her than he was about his own injury. By far most of the blood had been his. For days the dog had been contrite to the point of dishonor. When he finished the job he put the shovel back and went to the bathroom and washed his face with cold water.

"Want to pick up a rosebush this weekend?" he asked, when he returned to the kitchen.

She was making sandwiches. "That'll be fine," she said.

She reminded him again about the phone call. He muttered something unintelligible, got a cold beer, and went to the study. He put his feet up on his desk and punched out the Trimble's office number.

Whoever answered the phone was not helpful. "He left half an hour ago," she said.

"I'll call him at home."

"I'm afraid I can't release his home number," she squeaked.

"You're the one who's been calling my wife, aren't you?"

There was no reply and MacDonell broke the connection. Reaching in his pocket, he pulled out a small scrap of paper and punched in another number. The phone was picked up on the sixth ring.

"Hello, Sterling, this is Duncan. I understand you've been trying to reach me."

There was a crackling silence before Trimble spoke. "Dr. MacDonell? Oh yes, Dr. MacDonell. Doctor, your organization is taking up a lot of my valuable time, lately."

"What's the problem?" MacDonell asked in a tired whisper.

"To begin with, councilmember Dockery has been calling me all day."

MacDonell smiled. "He has?"

"He says your people have been harassing him."

Wonderful, he thought. "My captain has been conducting a bite investigation that involves the councilman." MacDonell affected his most relaxed manner. "He's following the letter of the law, as far as I can tell."

"Who's this Dr. Clemmons?"

"I asked if you wanted to meet her when you came out to visit us."

"Isn't there something you can do?"

"Rabies is endemic in Texas, Doctor. The dog was identified in a bite report. Mr. Dockery can't seem to provide evidence of vaccination. We suspect he's knocked the dog in the head and buried it in his backyard. The victim's mother wants it tested." MacDonell sipped his beer.

"He told me he doesn't even own the dog."

"Are you telling me he killed someone else's dog?"

Trimble was quiet for a second. "He said it was a stray. He said he rescued it and was merely feeding it."

"They all say that, Doctor."

"Still, it seems…"

"What would you do?"

"I think I'd try to remember whom I worked for."

"I'm very clear on that point, Dr. Trimble. I work for the victim—plain and simple." There was a long silence. MacDonell took another sip of beer "Anything else?" he asked.

"Yes, yes there is. I have a little proposition for you," Trimble replied. "One I'm sure you won't refuse."

Cute, MacDonell thought. "I'll consider anything you recommend, sir."

"I've been told you have several sporting dogs in your kennel, and I think I've found just the place for them."

"*Sporting* dogs?"

"Well, I believe they're called American terriers."

MacDonell took a swallow of beer.

"Robin Paine called me, and he's willing to take them off your hands to see if he can socialize them. He says if he can, they could be put to some useful purpose."

"You've been calling me at home about this?"

"Mr. Paine's worried. He says you might order them killed before he can rescue them."

"He said that, did he?"

Trimble continued. "He said they'd make loyal pets and courageous watch dogs."

MacDonell took another big swallow of beer and set the bottle down. "Did Mr. Paine mention which animals he was referring to?"

"Yes, he was quite specific. He said they belonged to a Mr. Franco, and that the man had recently passed away. He said since the owner wouldn't be able to reclaim his dogs, he feared you'd destroy them without a second thought."

"Passed away?"

"That's what he said."

There was a long silence.

MacDonell cleared his throat. "I'm getting tired of this, Doctor, so listen carefully. Those animals are part of a police investigation. After that's over, the next-of-kin have first rights to the animals."

MacDonell didn't hear anything. He hoped Trimble was listening.

"Another thing. Dr. Clemmons tells me the dogs are dangerous. This woman has thirteen years' experience as a practicing veterinarian and she knows what the hell she's talking about. If she says they're dangerous, then by God they're dangerous. And while were on the subject, I'd like to know what your problem is with veterinarians? That little pissant Paine needs to learn that tranquilizing a dog is no substitute for genetics, and you need to learn that I know what the hell I'm doing." He took a deep breath. The air going in seemed to be sweet and fresh. "And by damn, right now I'm running animal control in this city." MacDonell felt a wonderful exhilaration.

Trimble gathered himself. "Dr. MacDonell, my personal experience with Robin Paine is that he's quite knowledgeable about animals."

"Well, if that's true then his knowledge should include the fact that the *sport* those dogs engage in is considered a felony in forty-six states."

"Whatever," Trimble said.

Whatever? MacDonell pondered the density of the man. "Look, Doctor," he said, his voice rising. "I've worked with physicians for more than twenty-five years, and I've run into a few egomaniacs, but you sir, take the cake. I *cannot* release those animals. And even if I could, I wouldn't."

"And if I ordered you to do it?" Trimble said, trying to match MacDonell's rage.

"Put it in writing!"

"I may decide to do just that."

This was the ultimate challenge. MacDonell swallowed hard. "Then, I guess we'll have to get a judgment from the courts."

MacDonell could hear Trimble breathing.

"Yes, of course," he said, his voice taking on a more sophisticated tone. "I'm sorry to have bothered you and your wife at home today, Dr. MacDonell." He hesitated. "Duncan, I suggest you call my secretary next week and make an appointment. We need to talk."

"What about?" MacDonell heard the garage door going up.

"Your continued employment."

"Fine!" he said. He hoped it wasn't the beer talking.

CHAPTER TWENTY-SIX

*M*acDonell dreaded another night with little hope of success. On the way in he talked about Dockery's dilemma.

"What will happen to him?" Jeannie asked.

"It's just a couple tiny little class C misdemeanors, sweetheart. Problem is, it's been four days. Even as cold as it is the dog's brain will be jelly. The test will be unreadable and the girl will have to take the treatment."

"Can he cover it up?"

"Mooney's popular, especially with the press. If I know Carol, it'll leak out."

"Then Trimble will blame you."

"For what, doing my job?"

By 11:00 p.m., they had taken up a position on Austin Street, facing Webster. Traffic was one way and MacDonell snapped every truck or van that went by. He could see a burning barrel about two blocks ahead. The men who trekked back and forth were going about the business of survival in twos and threes.

Jeannie talked about the grandchildren and the potential for a summer vacation. MacDonell sat in silence. He had forced Lil from his mind and now was trying to decide whether or not to tell Jeannie about his confrontation with Trimble.

At 1:00 a.m. he handed the scanner over to Jeannie and leaned his head on the headrest. At 1:30, two men in shabby military field jackets came up Webster from the Vietnamese markets. They stopped across the street from the car. It appeared they were killing time. Then, after poking under the porch of an old house, they retrieved a burlap bag. Sharing the load, they clumped west on Webster. MacDonell watched until they disappeared into the gloom.

"Aluminum cans," he commented to Jeannie.

She turned her head so she could look at him. "Do you really think we're going to find anything out here?" she asked.

"We have to," he said, taking back the scanner. He lay back against the seat and stretched his legs.

"You seem preoccupied," she said.

"It's got to be one of these guard dog people," he said. "They're the only types who would do this. I mean regular attacks, and all with the same results. We've had their dogs escape before, you know."

"Then you don't think it's intentional?"

"That's harder to believe."

"Then you think it's Larsen?"

"I'm not positive."

"And you're going to dart one?"

"I'm going to try."

"What if it's two?" she asked.

"Sam may be closing in on it from the other end. He thinks he found one of the bidders. I already told you, Frank Bragg could be involved. He's worked with Larsen over the years. One of my officers may even know who the bidders are. A detective questioned him in my office this afternoon for more than two hours, then took him downtown."

Again, it was silent.

"I talked to Trimble," he said.

"You told me."

He could tell she didn't want to push him. He looked down Webster at the hunched-up men warming by the drums. Headlights turned onto Webster. He pointed and pulled the trigger. Nothing.

"We argued."

"What about?"

"I think it was about whether or not I want to retire."

Jeannie stared at her husband.

He looked at her, then closed his eyes. "I've waited two years to have a meaningful conversation with the dumb bastard…"

"Can you change his mind?"

"I don't know if I want to."

Jeannie turned to look out at the night. MacDonell opened his eyes and glanced at her, wondering how he had been so fortunate. She looked like an Italian cameo, burnished, but never aged. She seemed to have a glow, a patina gained from all the past challenges they had faced together. She was neither marred nor marked by time or temper. He twisted in his seat, trying to get the stiffness out of his back and shoulders. He felt like the grout around the toilet, shrinking, crumbling and falling apart.

"I can imagine Trimble pegs these sad derelicts just one notch above the animals we pick up," he said.

"What does he think of you?" Jeannie asked.

"From what I've seen, he thinks horse doctors should keep their mouth shut, play politics, love animals, and bend over for the humane societies. He certainly doesn't expect a public health officer."

"That's it? Love animals?"

"He expects you to make a big show of it."

"And you refuse?"

"I don't make a show of it, I guess," he said. He stared for a moment at the dash. "His idea of a veterinarian is James Herriot, or…" he laughed, "…or Robin Paine."

"What's Paine got to do with anything?" Jeannie asked. "I don't see how he fits into the picture."

Robin Paine? MacDonell didn't respond to Jeannie's question at first. He recalled the pictures he had seen in Paine's office. Polaroids…and the cardboard film tab Lil had carried around the backyard. In the photos taken at the site on highway 290, the piece of cardboard among the victim's possessions was a Polaroid film tab. Surely a wino didn't own a Polaroid. Another thought popped into his head. Bragg had taken the office camera out to record the 4H kids' pigs.

"Anything's possible." MacDonell sat up straight and thought about it for a second.

"What?" Jeannie asked.

"Well, for one thing Robin knew Franco was dead."

"Who's Franco?" she asked.

"He's a dog fighter the sheriff seized some pit bulls from a couple of days ago. We've got custody of them right now. Mr. Franco got blown away the next night by his coke dealer."

MacDonell looked at his wife. The pinkish lights from the streets illuminated her soft features.

"Son-of-a-…that's it!" he exclaimed. "That butt-head Trimble told me Paine wanted them. Paine told Trimble the dog's owner had kicked the bucket."

MacDonell slapped his forehead with the palm of his hand. "What a jerk I am! The little rat patrols around in this area at night. He has access to big nasty dogs that attack without vocalizing, and he has a Polaroid camera, and…"

"And what?" Jeannie stared at her tired husband.

"And he needs money to run his stupid park." MacDonell was kicking himself as the full horror of what it all meant sank home.

"You think he's the one who's training killer attack dogs and using these people as decoys?" Jeannie asked.

MacDonell was quiet. For a long time he sat looking out the window, not saying anything. He'd had her put tags on the van in pure desperation and maybe a little spite. He was a veterinarian, not a psychologist. He wasn't sure of the difference between a psychopath and a sociopath, but he knew Paine was a bigot. But could he be that evil? It was a good question. A lot of people exploit animals and still call themselves animal lovers.

"Let me ask you something else," Jeannie asked. "Do you think he's going to come driving by here tonight, with a television camera on his tail?"

MacDonell took in a lungful of air and let it out in a long measured breath. What were the chances of Paine coming down this particular street with dogs in his van? Millions of people, thousands of homeless, a six-hundred square mile city? And besides, he asked himself, was Paine really capable of handling dogs, or just drugging them?

"I don't know," he said. "He was down here a few nights ago."

"But, Duncan, he had Channel 12 along for the ride."

"I know. That's what doesn't make sense."

"You can't do this spy stuff forever," she said, and leaned back against the seat again.

It was silent on Webster. Straight down Austin Street, the gleaming towers of Houston, the space city, rose up behind the elevated highway. Million of stars had been captured and imprisoned in thin glass boxes. A layer of mist glowed in the reflected light. Below the elevated, blurred men warmed themselves over bonfires built at the very feet of the stars. The spectacle was electric, ultramodern, and darkly primitive.

Another hour passed.

On the right, down toward the Vietnamese markets, two street lights were burned out. A cluster of heavy oaks smothered the narrow passage of the street. The red and yellow running lights of an occasional big rig sliced south on the elevated. The lights would flash through the inky branches of the oak like fire-flies on strafing runs. MacDonell looked away from the sparkling skyline and stared down Webster. After tonight he might not have another chance. At 3:00 a.m. he fell asleep, then jerked awake.

"This is a waste of time," he whispered. "Let's go."

Jeannie closed the lid of the cooler and started to collect the Dr. Pepper cans and sandwich bags.

"I don't know why you humor me like this," he said.

He laid the UV light on the dash, aiming it up Austin, and absent-mindedly squeezed the trigger. The machine clicked and the readout displayed 000,010,115. He turned it off and pulled it again. It clicked and read 000,010,115 a second time. He leaned over and showed the number to Jeannie. Then he pointed to the computer in the door pocket on her side.

She opened the computer, turned it on and let it engage the hard drive. "That number's not on your list, Duncan."

"What?" he said. "It has to be."

"See for yourself." she said, handing him the computer.

True enough, it was an unassigned number. He cleared the scanner again, then, with the heel of his hand, slapped the instrument and pointed it dead ahead. Click! 000,010,115. Reaching into the backseat he zipped the canvas bag open and searched for the brown envelope. Pulling it out, he shook the contents. The remaining tags were inside. Spilling them out onto his lap he counted and compared them to his list. Puzzled, he looked around the seat and fished between his legs to see if any had escaped. He pulled his briefcase up and searched through it. There were pencils, some cough drops, and a yellow highlighter. No more tags. He counted the tags he had out, counted the tags in his lap. Added them together. It didn't come out right.

"Turn on the key so I can roll down the window, Honey."

The electric window on his side hummed into the door. He poked the scanner out the window and pointed it up Austin Street. 000,010,115 was again displayed on the read-out.

MacDonell put on his Stetson, got out of the car, and walked to the middle of the street. He pulled his coat around his middle. Traffic was nonexistent. Standing on the center line, he studied the parked cars directly ahead of him, eight of them. They formed a single line on the left side. In the poor light, nothing appeared amiss. The only thing: one of the cars, a 4-wheel drive, was parked facing the wrong direction. Other than that nothing was out of place. The street was deserted except under the elevated, where three men huddled next to a flaming drum. MacDonell walked to the Honda and got in.

"What do you think?" Jeannie asked.

"Danged if I know," he said, but as he said it one terrible answer turned over in his mind. "There is one other possibility," he whispered, half to himself. "Oh Lord."

"What?" Jeannie asked.

He stared down the street at the line of cars. Then he looked down at the computer screen and his long list of numbered tags. The cursor blinked a steady rhythm.

"I think I know who's parked down there," he said. He tapped his forehead with two fingers. "Talk about walking among us undetected!" MacDonell recalled the questioning of the two derelicts on the night Alexander Pitkin had been torn apart. The words came back…

"Out…Out…That's all I heard, man."

MacDonell squinted up the street. OUT! It was the command given at the end of an attack sequence by a Schutzhund trainer, *or* a military dog handler. A *military* dog handler.

"Look," MacDonell cried.

One of the homeless men—one who had been warming himself at the burning drum—was coming down Austin. As the solitary figure moved across Gray and came closer, a door of the 4-wheeler in the next block opened. The dome light came on for a few seconds. Even in the dim light MacDonell could see that the door was bright red. A long shadowy figure dropped down below the door.

"Jeannie!" MacDonell said. "It's J.D!"

The animal slunk under the door, circled the vehicle, and moved to the center of the street. At the shoulder, it exceeded thirty-six inches and moved with the grace of a shadow. In a moment the thing started its single-minded trot toward the man-prey. It was a world record gray wolf, or something just as bad.

"Start the car!" MacDonell shouted. "Hit the horn!"

Jeannie keyed the ignition and twisted the headlight stalk. When the lights flipped up, the animal stopped and turned to look back. The retinal reflections were green fire. It turned away and looked back at its prey. The homeless man was standing stock still, frozen in place.

"My lord, look at the size of it!" Jeannie said as she started the car. MacDonell reached over and squeezed the small black controller on her key chain to set off the car alarm. In response, the animal turned again, lifted its head, and howled, long and terrible.

Neither of them heard a command, but the animal did. It turned back to the Bronco with a wolfen lope and disappeared.

The warble of the small siren deafened them both. MacDonell began tossing his papers, tags, and equipment into the back seat. His hat went in the back, too. With scrambling fingers he searched between his feet for the tranquilizer gun. He found one barrel and the hand piece.

"Pull up beside that Bronco, quick!"

Jeannie put the little car in drive and accelerated toward the intersection, but the other car had come alive. The headlights and a bar of spotlights across the top flooded on and the Bronco came right at them. Jeannie stomped on her brakes and put her arm up to shield her eyes. The Honda squatted in front; MacDonell's head thudded against the padded dash. Skidding to its left in front of them, the Bronco tilted forward and streaked down Webster, rocking violently from side to side.

Jeannie wheeled right and in a few seconds she was closing the distance. The blood red Bronco leaned to its left as it took a hard right at the Eastex ramp. It scraped the guardrail in a shower of bright yellow sparks and screeched down the ramp, rushing out onto the southbound lane of US-59. Jeannie took the corner with greater care and dropped back a little. The Bronco moved to the center lane and lunged forward, steadily south and west. Both vehicles slipped under the Elgin overpass, as one. Where 59 and 288 split, the Bronco went under and stayed on 59. In spite of the needle on Jeannie's speedometer reading eighty-five miles an hour, the Bronco was edging away.

MacDonell worked his portable police radio: "Dispatcher this is Double Oh-3!" He paused. There was no response.

"HPD dispatcher...HPD DISPATCHER...Come on, man!"

Static.

"Damn it." MacDonell threw the radio on the back seat.

He struggled to find four darts. He drew three cc's into a syringe and filled the front chamber of the first dart. He capped the hub with an inch and a half needle. Then he checked to make sure that the tiny rubber sleeve was covering the perforations in the needle's shaft. He laid it on the floor and felt for the second. The guard rails flashed past. The Bronco changed lanes, Jeannie changed lanes, rocking the chassis. MacDonell filled the second syringe. It was like riding a quarter horse and giving it an enema at the same time. He put down the second dart and filled two more. Rice University exit came up and blurred past on the right. The car alarm was still yapping at a high pitch.

"How did you know it was her?" Jeannie yelled.

"Had to be," he yelled back. "She and Connie used her Bronco to plant the tags. There's got to be a tag stuck in her dash. That's what tripped the scanner. It must have slipped out of the envelope while they were driving around."

"Yes, but J.D.? I just can't believe it. How could she be doing this to these old men?"

"Well-trained animals could mean a lot of money, and you said her mother's pretty sick."

"Still, to train them using people? It's horrible."

"To us. But remember, she doesn't have much use for street people."

Jeannie nodded.

"She made some other little slips, too. I just let them go, I guess."

"Like what?"

"Saying she was retired. She's not retired, she got booted. And that pup of hers," he yelled. "It's a Jack Russell Terrier. It's not eligible for AKC obedience titles."

"Huh?"

"Nothing. Step on it."

MacDonell charged the rear chambers of all four darts with air and fastened a red tail to each. He threaded two darts into the first tube, one behind the other. Two tubes, four darts. Next, he charged the blue plastic hand piece for one shot. At five milligrams of keta-mine and one milligram of xylazine per pound, he realized that he would need all four darts, rapid-fire. And all four had better find their mark. The animal, he estimated, must weigh over a hundred and fifty pounds. He would have to carry the air pump and the tub-ing if he wanted to get off a second shot.

As the highway straightened out, the Bronco's red tail lights shot under three underpasses, zip…zip, zip, like a· ruby laser. Jeannie hit ninety, the car alarm screaming, and not a cop in sight. Still the Bronco was edging farther away. MacDonell saw brake lights. "She might try to ditch you at the Edloe exit," he yelled.

Sure enough, Longley was taking a hard right onto the feeder. The Bronco streaked past the Holiday Inn, through the Buffalo Speedway intersection, and past the mirrored United Savings building. Jeannie followed, but at a respectable seventy miles per hour. As they passed the Greenway Plaza high-rises, the brake lights on the Bronco flashed on again and then tilted, vertical. A flash of sparks boiled up from the overturned Bronco. Jeannie braked, fishtailed, and skidded to a stop. She was in front of the Summit, Houston's glass-fronted coliseum.

The double row of flags swayed lazily, and the big sign announced the earlier evening game. Rockets vs Timberwolves, the sign said.

In front of them, at Timmons Street, the Bronco lay on its side. Longley had hit a curb while trying to make the corner. The bolt-on top had sheared and lay like a broken clam in a pansy bed that filled the divider. Smoke or steam was drifting from the engine compartment. Jeannie eased up to the Bronco. It looked like a discarded toy, high wheels spinning lazily.

The non-human passenger scrambled up and over the sprung passenger door. It hesitated on top of the wreckage before it dropped without a sound to the street. Without a backward look, it loped off across Timmons toward the Summit arena.

MacDonell was out of the car almost before Jeannie could get it stopped.

"Keep trying that police radio!" he yelled. "And see how badly J.D.'s hurt!"

Lugging both barrels, the tubing, and the foot pump, MacDonell ran about fifty feet. At this angle he closed on the wolf. He dropped to one knee. Extending his arms to lock his elbows, he fired at the rhythmically-striding animal. Though he allowed for a little Kentucky windage, the shot was off. He had led the animal just a touch, trying for a shoulder shot. Both darts hit as one, in the rump. The wolf tucked under its hindquarters and sprinted.

MacDonell threw down the first barrel and took the second one from between his teeth. He attached it and stomped on the foot pump. With the animal's heavy coat, he couldn't be sure if it had been a clean, penetrating shot. He knew the site of injection had an effect on induction time, and a shoulder shot got the quickest results. He ducked his head, detached the tubes, and discarded the excess baggage. When he looked up the wolf had disappeared down the service entrance, just below the ramp up to the front plaza.

MacDonell jogged over to the Bronco. Jeannie had Longley on her back. The young woman was dazed and incoherent.

"You raise anybody on that radio?" MacDonell shouted.

"I used your old one and got Sergeant Gallegos." She had Longley's head on a flat cushion and had made sure her airway was clear. "He's getting an ambulance and calling HPD."

"Tell 'em to wake up Sam Goodson. He's done it to me plenty. I'm going after that...whatever it is." MacDonell pelted back across Timmons Street.

"Don't you have something better than that dart-shooter?" Jeannie called after him. He didn't hear her.

The steep ramp led down to the open parking area that serviced the concessions at the Summit. It was dark and 'For Service Vehicles Only.' By the time MacDonell got across the street and halfway down the ramp, he was already out of breath. His lungs were tight and starting to ache. The air going in stung and he tasted blood in his mouth. He hurried along, alternately walking and jogging. What if I run right into it? he thought.

The opening to the service area was dark and ominous. A red tailed dart lay in the middle of the drive. He picked it up; the needle was missing.

The animal came out of the far left side of the service area as he started in at the middle. He stopped for a second shot, but it turned the corner and cut back in behind some bushes and a big satellite dish. He trotted to where the animal had made the turn. As he got there, he saw a gray blur slinking out the far side. He charged in behind several parked service trucks, arriving at the opposite side in time to catch a glimpse of the departing animal. The long guard hairs made it glow in the street lamps as it cantered east on Norfolk. It headed straight between the Summit and the main parking garage. It was still carrying a dart in its right hip. Too far away for a second shot now, and the first two hadn't slowed it down a bit.

MacDonell calculated the chance of the creature running into some-one at 4:00 in the morning. It was slim, but he knew clean-up crews and watchmen pulled these shifts. He labored as he jogged up Norfolk Street and he thought he heard Jeannie's car alarm go silent. His side ached and his lungs were burning. He passed the long wall of glass doors. A voice from off to his right was yelling.

"It went that way, man! It was one big mother!"

MacDonell turned to look. It was a janitor in blue coveralls. He held the glass door open with his knee and pointed toward the parking garage at the end of the street.

MacDonell shifted the short-barreled dart gun to his left hand and waved with his right. "Uuhh!" He pounded on down the walk. The little green sign at the end of the street said 'Edloe.'

When he got to the entrance of the parking garage, he stopped and leaned against the wall. His breath was coming hard. Now the taste in his mouth was like copper or rusted iron. He tried to spit but his mouth was too dry. He looked back—headlights! No, flashers. It wasn't a cop or an ambulance. Good God, it was Jeannie. Stay back, he thought, stay back! MacDonell sagged, and then struggled around the corner.

The tunnel was lit with matching strings of bright orange lights, like flares. It also had a slight downward curve to the left. MacDonell plod-ded on, gasping and holding his side. There was minor relief in running downhill. As he rounded the curve, it flared out even more. For a moment he lost his balance and reached for the wall to steady himself. He stopped. His breath was coming in searing gasps.

As the tunnel spread before him, it revealed a honeycomb of possi-bilities. He stood still, listening. Microscopic flares popped behind his eyes. His scalp tingled. He moved forward looking hard into the shad-ows. Stopping, he listened again. Close by he heard a click, click, click…? It could be the toenails of a wolf or wolf/dog hybrid. Again he heard it but at a distance. Click, click…click…. click…? He tried to match the sound with a direction.

MacDonell moved several feet ahead and stood under a small overhead light. From here he could see in three directions. A pipe railing on his right marked the edge of a lower-level ramp. It was bright on the ramp, but the heavy concrete columns cast deep shadows on the greasy concrete.

Exhausted, he lowered himself to one knee and tried to suck up some oxygen. He shifted the dart gun to his right hand, wet his lips, and tried to spit. Neither mechanism was working well. As he bent his head, he felt he might vomit. Click, Click, Click, CLICK, CLICK! The animal was off to his left and coming closer. He turned, tightened his grip on the silly plastic handle, and squinted into the darkness. It had to be getting closer. He considered the possibility the pressure might have leaked out of the gun.

CLICK, CLICK? Both the sound and the sensation of a deadly juxtaposition came to him all at once. The enormous animal was there, ahead, tensing itself. MacDonell raised the dart gun.

The animal rushed forward and leapt. With some forgotten instinct, MacDonell dropped backward on the greasy floor, launching the double dose of darts at the chest of the massive beast. They hissed beneath the animal's body and sailed off into the dark. The giant wolf/dog/thing cleared him, and he could hear the air go out of its lungs when it thudded with a heavy 'whump' into the pipe rail. It turned, skidding and scratching back to an upright position.

MacDonell scrambled to his feet and backed away, holding the plastic grip at a feeble en garde position. The elegant creature lowered its body and curled its lips, revealing beautiful white canine teeth. It took two quick steps forward. It was stalking him now. Closing for the kill. It emitted a deep, wet rumble from its chest.

MacDonell stumbled and found himself up against the front of a car. Getting under the car flashed through his mind. No, the car was way too low and he was much too fat. He scrambled backward onto the hood of the small sports car, a refrigerator-white Corvette convertible.

The sound of screeching tires and running feet failed to register in MacDonell's brain. He was preparing to jam the plastic grip of the dart gun in the animal's mouth. Give them your left arm, the classes always taught. You'll need your right to fill out the report. In spite of the fact that in a moment he would be torn apart, MacDonell half-swallowed a laugh at the old saw. He switched the dart gun to his left hand. His wedding ring glinted in the dim light. He pushed himself higher on the hood of the car.

As if in a dream, MacDonell stared at the brute as it came for him. Its freezing blue-white eyes fixed on his. His mind raced past all that—the teeth, the horns, the wounds, the scars—past all the dangers he'd ever faced. Frothing bulls had pinned him in hot dusty squeeze chutes, bug-eyed stallions had knocked him galley west in the snow, lead-legged water buffalo dragged him through Thai jungle muck; all the animals he'd ever helped and the few he'd lost. Stupid, he thought. Stupid, stupid, to go out like this—and Jeannie, what would she do? Jeannie? Jeannie! The vast canine surged forward and jumped for his throat.

Flames spurted and blinding white flashes preceded echoing explosions. Afterward, MacDonell would always remember how, in that instant, the living carnivore checked its leap in mid-air and changed direction. One .38 cal. hollow point slug had entered the animal's skull under the left eye. The thing was already dead before the second bullet hit just below the left ear and shattered the first cervical vertebra. It crashed against MacDonell's chest, knocking him backward through the soft top of the Corvette. He smelled the beast's sour breath and felt something warm spray across his face. Frantic, MacDonell struggled to free himself from the torn fabric and the gear shift lever, but the giant attacker was already sliding down the hood and into a heap on the oily concrete. Twin rivulets of red followed it, streaking the stark white automobile.

Sucking hard to catch his breath, MacDonell looked away from the dead beast to where Jeannie was standing a few steps from the Honda, still braced in shooting position.

She approached the dead animal keeping the pistol trained on it. She lowered the Rossi and put it back in her shoulder bag.

"It isn't breathing," she said.

"Where'd you hit it?" he asked, staggering a bit.

"In the head, I think."

Jeannie stepped back to the Honda, keyed the trunk, and slipped her bag and the gun inside. Going around the car, she opened the passenger-side door, grasped a handle, and tilted the seat back. Somehow, she had managed to get Longley out of the street and into the front seat. In a grandmotherly fashion, she took hold of the young woman's shoulders and gently laid her against the headrest and fastened the seat belt.

"Hybrid," MacDonell said, looking back at the great canine. "She said all her animals were unconventional. She wasn't kidding."

Longley nodded. Tears started to flow. She reached up and touched the tears with her fingers. "Where's Bobby?" she said.

Epilogue

$\mathcal{S}$aturday MacDonell slept late. In the afternoon he took a leisurely drive to one of the nurseries on the 494 Spur and bought a rose bush.

On Channel 12's noon news Rhonda Ryder noted that Dr. Duncan MacDonell, the city veterinarian, had allegedly shot and killed a Liberty County woman's pet dog. While details were sketchy, it was tragically the second such shooting by the health department in the past month and, oddly, this one took place in the basement parking garage of the Summit, at around 4:00 a.m. More information would be available on the 5:00 o'clock news. According to Robin Paine, animal activist and dog training expert, the shooting was unnecessary.

✱✱✱

Sunday, MacDonell considered taking Jeannie to church. Instead, he opted to go with her to Carter's Country and fire fifty rounds at a silhouette. It was the sixth time in the past two years that her score was better than his.

✱✱✱

On Monday, MacDonell traveled with Sam Goodson to J.D. Longley's small ranchette buried deep in Liberty County. Eldon Grimes of the Houston Chronicle was invited by MacDonell to ride along. In an ancient barn, heavily remodeled and reinforced with salvaged iron pipe and hog wire, six adult wolf/dog hybrids were found. Two were pregnant. Within a month, and with the permission of Liberty County authorities, all the animals were humanely euthanized. Humane agencies protested, but to no avail.

***

By the end of the week, Jane Diane 'J.D.' Longley was tentatively identified as the winning bidder for the dubious privilege of selling trained security dogs to a private company in Cartagena, Colombia. The legality of that transaction was being investigated. The following Monday, HPD released a statement implicating three other individuals in the bidding: Mr. Erskin Fall (deceased), Mr. Stanley Rantelle, and Mr. Robin Paine. An unnamed fourth man from Katy, Texas was being sought for questioning. A further charge against Ms. Longley (importing an illegal wolf/dog hybrid into the state) was being studied by the Texas Attorney General's office. Ms. Longley was being examined by police psychiatrists prior to an expected indictment by the Harris County Grand Jury on four counts of capital murder. Galveston was also interested in talking to her about one case of aggravated homicide.

Friday afternoon, Goodson and MacDonell met for coffee in a sidewalk breakfast bar across from the Harris County Courthouse.

"There's no doubt in my mind that your girl was 'blooding' those monstrosities," Goodson explained. "My boys found an album. It had grisly Polaroids of every corpse, and a corresponding picture of each dog that did the deed. It's really sick."

"That's it?"

"What else do you want?"

"I'm not arguing with you, Sam. But I think she had other motivations as well. Jeannie located her mother up in Kansas, near McConnell Air

Force Base. I called up there last night. The woman lives in a nursing home. She's had several strokes, and kind of floats in and out of lucidity."

Goodson scowled and fished a gnat out of his coffee.

MacDonell continued. "I talked with her nurse most of the time and from what I could piece together, it seems the old lady used to run a puppy mill out on the Kansas prairie. One winter she picked up some drifter who was down on his luck. He was supposed to work in exchange for his keep, but after awhile the guy more-or-less muscled his way in and became like a stepfather." MacDonell tasted his coffee and made a face.

Goodson handed over the sugar dispenser.

MacDonell added a second spoonful and stirred. "The nurse told me she couldn't be sure how long he was there, but one day while Janie and her mom were in town this fellow's big stud dog got loose. She wasr't sure whether it was a wolf or they were breeding it to a wolf. Anyway, the two animals got loose and attacked Janie's older brother, Bobby. The little boy was almost ten at the time, Janie was five or six. The nurse said something about the boy not being able to hear the dogs coming up on him. He was torn up pretty badly and bled to death before they could get him in to the hospital."

"And this drifter?"

"Supposedly, he hightailed it down here to Texas."

Goodson looked deep into his coffee cup. "Whatever you say, but I don't have any problem taking this to the DA. We've got more than enough for an indictment."

MacDonell wrapped both hands around his cup, took a sip, and watched the picketers in front of the Family Law Center.

"You got another idea?" Goodson asked.

"No. No, I just wanted to tell you that Jeannie's going to talk to a psychiatrist and maybe get another opinion."

"She won't get her off."

"I don't think that's her intention."

＊

During the entire week not a word was forthcoming from the health department. The director's public information office exchanged calls with MacDonell, but no departmental press statement was issued. Both newspapers ran splashy reports of the five deaths. The Chronicle's first headline blazed, 'CITY VET SOLVES KILLINGS.'

After multiple delays, MacDonell's meeting with Dr. Trimble was permanently canceled. The director took several trips out of town. Then it was leaked around that Trimble was being courted by a health agency in Washington, D. C. Subsequently, he resigned to take another 'position.' His PIO chief moved to an interesting position with the Solid Waste Department. Three weeks later, B. F. Dockery announced his retirement from the Houston city council to, as he put it, 'pursue opportunities in the private sector.'

When MacDonell got home one afternoon in early April he had a letter waiting. It was from United States Automobile Underwriters, questioning a claim for damage to a third party's car in a parking garage. He would need to furnish a detailed explanation.

END

About the Author

Dr. Armstrong retired from public service after twenty years in the U.S. Air Force Veterinary Corps and another ten years with the Health Department of the city of Houston, Texas. He lives in Kingwood Texas with his wife, Nita, and their little dog, Charlie.

8